BORN
WITH A
TOOTH

ALSO BY JOSEPH BOYDEN

The Orenda
Through Black Spruce
Three Day Road

BORN WITH A TOOTH

JOSEPH BOYDEN

For Amanda, my flying girl

HAMISH HAMILTON
an imprint of Penguin Canada

Published by the Penguin Group
Penguin Group (Canada), 90 Eglinton Avenue East, Suite 700, Toronto, Ontario, Canada M4P 2Y3

Penguin Group (USA) Inc., 375 Hudson Street, New York, New York 10014, U.S.A.
Penguin Books Ltd, 80 Strand, London WC2R 0RL, England
Penguin Ireland, 25 St Stephen's Green, Dublin 2, Ireland (a division of Penguin Books Ltd)
Penguin Group (Australia), 707 Collins Street, Melbourne, Victoria 3008, Australia
(a division of Pearson Australia Group Pty Ltd)
Penguin Books India Pvt Ltd, 11 Community Centre, Panchsheel Park, New Delhi – 110 017, India
Penguin Group (NZ), 67 Apollo Drive, Rosedale, Auckland 0632, New Zealand
(a division of Pearson New Zealand Ltd)
Penguin Books (South Africa) (Pty) Ltd, 24 Sturdee Avenue, Rosebank, Johannesburg 2196, South Africa

Penguin Books Ltd, Registered Offices: 80 Strand, London WC2R 0RL, England

First published by Cormorant Books Inc., 2008
Published in this edition, 2013

3 4 5 6 7 8 9 10 (RRD)

Copyright © Joseph Boyden, 2008

The following stories have been previously published: "Born With A Tooth" in *Black Warrior Review* and *Potpourri*; "Shawanagan Bingo Queen" in *Cimarron Review* and *Blue Penny Quarterly*; "Painted Tongue" in *The Panhandler*.

LIBRARY AND ARCHIVES CANADA CATALOGUING IN PUBLICATION

Boyden, Joseph, 1966–, author
Born with a tooth / Joseph Boyden.

Originally published: Toronto : Cormorant Books, 2001.
ISBN 978-0-14-318801-8 (pbk.)

1. Indians of North America—Ontario, Northern—Fiction. I. Title.

PS8553.O9358B6 2013   C813'.6   C2013-903591-5

Visit the Penguin Canada website at **www.penguin.ca**

Special and corporate bulk purchase rates available; please see
www.penguin.ca/corporatesales or call 1-800-810-3104, ext. 2477.

ALWAYS LEARNING   PEARSON

CONTENTS

EAST
Labour

BORN WITH
A TOOTH

My wolf hung at the trading post for two weeks until that new teacher up from Toronto bought him. My long-legged Timber with half a left ear. A local trapper snared and sold my wolf to Trading Post Charlie, who skinned him and pinned him on the wall next to the faded MasterCard sign. He was worth more than $250.

The teacher's been here less than a month, sent to us by the Education Authority at Christmastime so the rez kids can learn the Queen's English. They gave him a little house and a parka, and I think he's lonely like me and has got a lot to watch and learn. He knows nothing about a snowmobile or guns or the bush or the insult and danger of looking in the eyes. I can tell by watching him. Maybe I can teach him. He's got a thin face and he's tall and awkward. My face is round, and I can drive a snowmobile as good as Lucky Lachance.

The one and only Lucky Lachance is my uncle, gone for four days of every week. He knows something's wrong because lately he comes back from work saying, "Just because your name's Sue Born With A Tooth doesn't mean you have to stay on this reservation the rest of your life, Jesus fuck." He works for the Ontario Northland railway on the Polar Bear Express. His

3

train runs from Cochrane to Moosonee, mostly taking tourists in summer and supplies in winter across Northern Ontario and up to our stomping ground on the bottom tip of James Bay. The tourists call it the wilderness, but Lucky Lachance calls it the asshole of Hudson Bay. He's French Canadian and he's got a dirty mouth. His sister is my mother, and I think my father's most probably dead. My father came carrying my name with him from somewhere out west. He brought my name to this place of Blueboys and Whiskeyjacks and Wapachees and Netmakers and even in this place my name stands out. Eighteen years ago my mother sewed my father his first suit, and seventeen years ago he got her pregnant with me. All I know is he was full-blood Cree and belonged to the Bear Clan. In grade four I learned that the name for French and Indian mixed is Metis. I always thought that around here that made me nothing special times two.

Lucky says I'm looking into my fucking womanhood, and if I want to see the world he'll get me a free train ticket to Cochrane. He says it's time to stop moping around. "If you're not in school, it's time to work," he says. But I don't want to leave Moose Factory. I can't imagine another place where in summer you have to canoe or take a motorboat or a water taxi to the mainland and in winter they plough a road across the ice so cars can come back and forth. My mother wants me to learn how to sew.

Trading Post Charlie might have wondered why I was around the store so often the two weeks the wolf was there. I didn't buy anything. Charlie's fifty and is comfortable around me and pointed out all the pictures of his grandkids under the glass countertop once, but I could see his wife was jealous, me coming every day to drink free coffee and smoke her husband's cigarettes. She figured my visits out, though. Charlie's wife sold my wolf to the teacher yesterday.

For fourteen days I just showed up in the morning, knocking snow off my boots and letting a steam of cold air in through the door. I tried to learn how to drink Charlie's coffee and tried to make Charlie tell me everything he knew about the wolf. I think Charlie probably did know it was the wolf I came for, but he wouldn't look me in the eye, or anyone else for that matter. He's OjiCree and too polite. He doesn't talk much, just sells milk and bread and shotgun shells to the locals, pelts and Indian crafts to summer tourists.

But Charlie finally began to talk when he saw I wasn't going anywhere. "The trapper got the wolf in a snare. That blizzard come up off the bay, and the trapper figures it was two or three days the wolf choked slow before the lines could be checked again. The trapper said he ended the choke with a bullet in the wolf's brain." Later Charlie said, "It's the rare one that comes to the island and stays for long. Trapper'd seen the wolf's prints in the snow last winter. This winter too. He tracked him a while. Usually a pack comes across the ice for a night of following moose, but they never stay so close to humans long."

I imagined I could see the black wire mark when I ran my hand against his fur. He'd already started collecting dust.

My wolf was skinny but brave. He came to see me often that winter two years ago, disappeared before spring, then came back again the next freeze. I watched him and loved him.

I still can't sleep, my head wandering and thinking the wolf waits outside for me. There aren't too many reasons to go outside in the dark when it's minus forty and trees pop and crack in the cold. Tonight marks that night two winters ago.

I couldn't get comfortable in bed so I pulled my parka

and mukluks on and went outside. It was the cold that makes your fingers burn through mittens and the moisture in your nose freeze and your toes ache no matter how many pairs of socks you wear. I walked just to walk, south on our road, smelling the woodsmoke and watching sparks fly from neighbours' chimneys. I looked up at the black and tried to find Mars and Venus, the stars that don't twinkle. I was hoping to see the northern lights. I wanted to walk quiet like the ancestors because I could sense them behind rocks and perched in the scrub pines, watching me and judging me. But my feet crunched on the dry snow and echoed in my ears under my hat loud enough that I felt silly. If the ancestors had been around, I had scared them away.

When I got to the edge of Charles Island, I lit a smoke and looked out at the ice highway running across the bay to Moosonee's twinkling lights. That's when I first came across him. I heard his paws in the snow, so I took my toque off to hear him better. I walked home slowly and felt his eyes on my back, but it wasn't spooky, only like an old friend come back to visit. Even though my ears hurt, I kept my hat off because I knew he was there. He followed me home but didn't show his face till the next night. That's when I laid my trap. Lucky's friend had gutted a moose, and I stole some innards and put them in a snowbank in our backyard. That next night I waited by the window for him, waited until past two. Then he appeared like a ghost or a shadow, slinking, lean, sniffing and jittery. I watched him drag my present into the bush.

Charlie tells me his name is Michael and he's only been teaching for two years. Lucky calls him a city slicker cocksucker and asks me what this guy thinks he can teach anyone. I follow this teacher to the trading post and coffee shop and post office. He never knows it. I wait for school to let out and follow to see where he lives. He walks along with his parka hood up, dragging his boots and humming.

I start thinking I want him to notice me, so I get bolder, crossing the street when he does and walking by him, or taking a seat near him at Trapper's Restaurant and only ordering a coffee. When he looks at me, I look away. When he smiles at me, I walk away.

It was three months, close to the ice breakup that first winter, before my wolf finally trusted me enough to stay in sight when I came outside. All winter I'd watched from the living-room window after Mom and Lucky had gone to their beds. At first I tried luring him with pieces of chicken or whitefish. I'd sit on the back step with my hand outstretched, waiting. But he wouldn't leave the shadows. So I'd arrange the scraps in a circle and go inside to my window perch and watch him slink across the yard. He knew I was there but wouldn't look up. He grew fuller and less jumpy. The night he finally ate from my hand, I knew something was going special.

Michael comes up to me at the coffee shop today and asks if he can sit by me. I say, "Okay," so he sits directly across the table and asks questions.

"Why don't I see you at the high school?" he says. I just shrug. He'll learn soon enough. Most of the rez kids make it to grade nine. That's when the government says it's legal to leave school behind. And that's when a lot of us know it's right. He asks me what my name is, and I tell him I'm Sue Born With A Tooth. He stares at my eyes, and I want to ask him if he's trying to insult me, but that would be rude. He's got little whiskers and his skin is very white and the fur on his hanging parka hood frames his jaw nicely. He says my hair is long and black and pretty, and I tell him I have to go. I leave change on the table and walk outside.

"Can we have coffee again?" he asks, following me out.

"I guess," I say.

"When?" he asks. "Tomorrow?"

"I guess," I say.

On the night he first touched me, I had no meat to offer the wolf, just a bone and gristle. But he was lonely and I was too. It was the act of offering and the middle of a long night and each of us growing used to one another. I held the bone in my bare hand and felt the moisture on my fingers freeze to a throb. I walked to the middle of the yard. He was in the shadows but slowly walked up when I stretched out my hand. He padded slow and tense from his hiding place and raised the fur on his neck. It made him look bigger and mean, and he kept walking out as I stood slumped and relaxed but wanting to explode inside. He stopped a couple of metres from me. I thought that would be as close as he'd come, but I kept my stare focused on the snow by his feet. He walked closer, till his nose twitched by my hand. He flattened his ears back and I looked at the left one, ragged and bitten or shot half off. I felt his eyes on mine, so I looked too. Yellow eyes. Harvest moons. He smiled at me with his black lips and opened his mouth and the white teeth gently took the bone. He turned around and trotted slowly back to the edge of the bush, then turned his head to me before disappearing.

I often wondered where he went all day, whether he was safe or if his visits put him in danger. I wanted to ask Lucky about the hunters on the island. I wanted to know if they knew about my stray. No one ever talked about any wolf tracks near their door in the mornings after a new snowfall. But still, I worried for him.

My mother talks so little that there are people in Moose Factory who believe she doesn't know how to. She works with her sewing machine out of the house. She's very small and very smart. You can see it in her shiny black eyes. "*C'est dommage*. It is too bad there is so much of your father in you," she tells me. "Unable to sleep at night, always wanting to dance with the ghosts." I wonder how much she actually sees and how much she knows to sense. I've watched her sew for hours, and the day comes that I will stitch too, but for now I get everything I need from a few coins in Lucky's money jar.

Michael asks me out to drink coffee most days after his teaching and continues staring at my eyes. I want to tell him that I don't think I really like coffee after all and that we should go to his house and smoke cigarettes instead. Lucky saw us and teases me at home.

"Sue hangs out with the city fuck. The skinny cocksucker thinks he's going to get some French and Indian ass at the same time, eh? He thinks the Metis like to mate, eh?" His words make me run to my room. But Lucky always knocks gently and tells me he is sorry. He says, "Metis means that you are stuck in the middle, Sue."

Whenever he says that, I know he's going to finish his talk. He reminds me that Indians consider me a Frenchie, and whites look at me like I'm Indian. But I imagine I don't feel different from most of the rez kids. Maybe I'm lonelier. My best friend has a husband and a baby now, and another friend

9

moved to Thunder Bay. Tonight Lucky says he is not here enough to watch out for me and I should be careful with the city boys.

Michael has him somewhere in his house. I want to sit by Michael's stove and look at him. Michael talks a lot when we go out to the coffee shop. He tells me about Toronto, the woman mayor, the Canadian National Exhibition, the men who sleep on heating grates in the middle of winter underneath huge glass buildings. He tells me about his little brother and parents. Michael asks if he can come over to my house for dinner. He says he's writing a paper on the Aboriginals of Northern Ontario. But I can hear Lucky saying, "Do you want another potato, cocksucker?" so I say I'll go to Michael's house instead.

It's a small cottage on Ministik Road, outside the rez boundary, just a clapboard living room and a kitchen with dried flowers on the tiny table and a wood-burning stove. I help him carry wood in, and we leave our coats and boots by the stove. He cooks dinner and fumbles with the plates while setting the table. He talks a lot, asks a lot of questions about me and Moose Factory. I tell him my daddy was a full-blood Wolf Clan Cree. That he worked in the bush and was the son of a hunter. I lie and tell Michael my father was killed while hunting. I don't know why I say this. I look down at the floor, then at the walls. I don't see him.

After dinner we sit on the sofa and listen to music, drinking beer.

"You're not the most talkative person," Michael says. "Aren't there things you want to know about me?" He leans closer and takes my hand in his. It's sweaty.

"Do you have a girlfriend in Toronto?" I ask.

"No," he says. "There's a woman I like, but ..." and I stop his talk with a little kiss.

Lucky would be angry if he knew I was alone with Michael in his house. But Lucky's on the train tonight, somewhere near the Soo.

I want to tell this one about the other. About how close we were by the second winter. How he'd come up to me in the middle of the night almost as friendly as a dog and take gifts from my hand, then go back to the edge of the bush to eat. He wouldn't let me touch him, didn't want the smell of human on his fur. I want to tell him about that time when the ice was beginning to break up on the bay and even snow-mobilers weren't crossing anymore. It was late and I offered him a strip of venison. He walked up and ignored my hand. Instead he nuzzled me hard between my legs. He could smell my blood. I felt his hot breath and tongue against my jeans for just a moment.

Michael looks awkward pulling out the sofa bed. "If I had known I'd be living like this," he says, "I'd have shipped my futon up with me." He's holding onto me and unbuttoning my shirt. I want to know what a futon is, but I lie back and let him struggle with my jeans.

I can feel his tongue and his breath in the dark. He's come back to me, nipping and licking, tasting me. He slides up and I can feel the hair of his chest on my belly, on my breasts. He is hard against me and pushes inside for my first time, his shoulder across my neck. The white flash of pain is his smile and dark lips. He nudges my legs wider. I bite his ear and he yelps and I can feel him release inside of me.

Michael mumbles and half talks in his sleep, so I quietly get up and pull my clothes on. The stove's gone out and I can see my breath, so I squeak the stove door open and fill it with wood. I leave and walk down Ankerite Road, listening to my boots crunch in the snow and trees moan in the cold. Tonight it's so dark and empty I wonder if anything is alive.

The days are getting longer again. Michael and I don't go out for coffee much anymore. People in town started talking, asking why the teacher and a seventeen-year-old half-Indian girl were hanging out so much. Michael ran into Lucky and thought he was a big bearded lumberjack come to chop him down. Lucky says he didn't say a word to him. Just looked. When we do meet for coffee, this teacher doesn't look at my eyes anymore, just mumbles into his cup and watches out the window, then kisses my cheek and leaves. I wanted to tell him he was the first, but I can't now.

Sunny days leave the ice highway slushy and dangerous to cross. I only asked Michael about my wolf one time, a little while ago. I tried to sound casual and like I didn't care, but my voice came out squeaky and tense.

"That pelt, the damaged one?" he said. "I sent it out on the mail plane to my woman friend in Toronto. She loves northern stuff."

I try not to think of my wolf anymore, sent to hang in that woman's house.

Michael calls me today after the first freighter canoe race of the year, the one from Moose Factory to Moosonee celebrating the spring. He asks me to meet him at the usual place.

"I'm leaving, back to TO," he says as I stare out the window at the river and people on the water taxi dock. The trees will bud soon. He lights a smoke. "I thought I might want to renew my contract and stay through the summer. But I've got business to take care of back in the city." He smiles. A casual smile. "Besides, I hear the blackflies drive you crazy in spring. Don't worry, though. I'll write. Maybe you can come visit me sometime."

He always talks too much. I light a smoke and look him in the eyes. He looks back for a second, then looks down and plays with his cigarette pack. I stare at him till he gets up and leaves.

The last night he visited me a few months back, I knew my wolf could smell the evil in the air. He was jumpy and his yellow eyes looked dull. I was tired and didn't want to get out of my warm bed. But I knew he was there, looking up at my window from his shadows at the tree line. I knew he wanted to see me. There was no food to offer so I poured him a bowl of milk and went outside. He sneaked up to me, then looked over his shoulder. He sniffed at the saucer but let the milk freeze. I wondered what he had done all day, if he had caught a hare or run from his enemies. Half awake and not thinking, I reached out to scratch his torn ear. I lazily ran my fingers over his scruffy head and scratched his neck. Just as I realized what I was doing, he nipped at my hand and walked away, looking back over his shoulder at me until he disappeared into the dark. He had the smell on him.

I don't like coffee anymore, but I still go to the coffee shop and drink it. When Michael left, Lucky said that the city fuck was worried the blackflies might chew his cock off if he stayed any longer.

My stomach's getting puffy so I try not to smoke, but it's become a habit. It won't be long before Mom and Lucky notice. It won't be good. I'll have to tell them soon.

When it comes, the pain will be like that night with him, and worse. I will open my legs wide and scream and curse and howl. Then the midwife will back away, muttering prayers and crying. My baby's grey furry head will enter this world. He will bare his white teeth and gnaw through our cord. He will look at me and smile with black lips and yellow eyes. He will run off into the bush, and he will cross the ice highway.

SHAWANAGAN BINGO QUEEN

Springtime brings the blackflies. Clouds of biting gnats that dig into your ears and nose and scalp swarm to the reserve in the first warm days to feed on us and keep us indoors for the four or five weeks that they eat and mate and die. You might not be able to see their teeth or even their little bodies crawling in your hair, but when blackflies start sucking, you know it. I remember, when I was a small girl, I was playing out back by the edge of the bush and a chainsaw scream started up in my head and sent me wailing to my mother. I put my finger in my ear and pulled it away all bloody. My mother said, "Hush, Mary," and stuck the point of a rolled-up towel in and wiggled out three of the buggers. Then she took her bottle of rye and tipped my head sideways and poured some in. My first taste of whisky came running down my cheek, mixed with blood that I licked off the side of my face.

Sometimes I think I fell in love with my husband, Ollie, because no matter how bad the blackflies got in spring, he'd still go out and about, working on his old car or hunting in the bush. He didn't let a thing stop him. When we first married he'd get a bottle of American bourbon that had been smuggled from over the border and take me out in his little boat late at night to look at stars and get drunk and silly. He'd take his shirt off, even if it was early spring with a sheen of thin ice forming on the lake, and stand on the bow and say, "Look, Mary, that bright one there is the dog star. It's my lucky star. Me and him, that dog, we talk to one another." Then he'd howl out until his voice came bouncing back across the water, and I'd join in and yelp to his star and to the moon until we were both out of breath. We were young and crazy. When Ollie got killed, there was grumbling and rumours it wasn't an accident. Maybe it wasn't planned, some of the old ones said, but it wasn't no accident, either.

Then our band council brought the Bingo Palace to Shawanagan. The one road running out of the rez got paved, and Chief Roddy bought his Cadillac. The Bingo Palace changed a few things.

There are still blackflies in spring, and old Jacob the hunter still keeps our freezers full of deer meat in winter. What's changed now is we got a common focus on the rez, something to look forward to most weeknights. We got the *wasichu* driving in with their money, ready to spend it, sometimes driving all the way from Toronto. The Palace has given us a name.

Wasichu means white man. Grandmother never had the chance to teach me the Ojibwe word, so I borrowed from the Sioux. Don't mistake me for a Plains woman, though. I'm a proud Ojibwe. The Sioux, when they came this far east, were our enemy, and we only feared and respected the Iroquois more. My grandmother spoke fluent Ojibwe, but she's dead a long time ago. Before Ollie came along, I once learned some Indian from a South Dakota boy. He was Oglala Sioux and carried it proud like his barrel chest. Even though the words he taught me weren't my language, they were still Indian, and better than nothing, I figure. In return, I taught him to say the only Ojibwe I knew, other than swear words. *Ahnee Anishnaabe* means "Hello, Indian" in my language. One of these days I'll take a break from the Palace and learn some Ojibwe, something I can pass on to my two kids.

But what I can pass on to them now is my knowing bingo. I thought it was the stupidest game I ever heard of when word of the money started drifting in eleven years ago, with Yankee Indians in big new cars. Chief Roddy knew we were all down and out and there was no future for anyone collecting pogey and baby bonus cheques. Roddy was big enough to see that bingo might bring us some freedom.

You have to be a smooth talker to try to swing the elders in your favour, especially when you're selling something as foreign as gambling. In the end, it came down to the council elders, the old women, to decide. Roddy brought money backers in from an upstate New York rez, Iroquois with slick black hair in ponytails and three-piece suits and eagle feathers. They carried charts with red lightning zigzags on them and slide projectors under their arms.

The Iroquois dazzled our old women with talk of money for schools and autonomy. Well, we never got a school. Some built onto their houses, and many have newer cars. But you know there's still burnt-out war ponies with no windshields and most of the rez has rotted plywood and tarpaper roofs. The biggest difference when you look around is the Palace, on Centre Hill beside the rusting playground. The Palace is an old corrugated airplane hangar, insulated against winter and big enough to play a game of hockey inside, with room for spectators. There's no windows to look out onto Killdeer Lake. Just tables and chairs to sit 450 people, and a high stage for me to call numbers from, and eight TV monitors spaced along the walls to show what ball's being called.

It used to be that the inside was filled with card tables and folding chairs, so empty and drafty that it was ugly. I learned soon enough to judge how well we were doing by the changes inside. After the first two years the cheap furniture was gone, replaced by sturdy pine cut from the bush. But the real measure is the walls. Roddy commissioned local kids to draw murals and paint pictures. Big colourful stuff showing Manitou and Indian princesses, the Sun Catcher with her buckskin arms stretched up welcoming another day, the Circle of Protecting Buffalo. One boy drew his red and black impression of a Jesuit being tortured by Iroquois. Roddy thought it would upset the *wasichu* and made the boy alter it. Now, on the wall behind the stage, there's a drawing of a Jesuit priest and an Indian warrior standing on a cloud shaking hands. Even though Ollie would have hated it, the Bingo Palace has become a nice-looking place over the last eight years.

Everyone is here to celebrate our eighth anniversary this weekend — cottagers up for the summer, townies, Indians. It's even larger than the council expected, with the chance to win a $50,000 pot and tons of advertising in advance. The money we're offering tonight is unheard of around here. A bunch of people have already come up and asked if the flyers were a misprint. "Fifty thousand dollars!" Abe from North Bay says real loud in my ear. "Goddamn if I'd ever have to work another day in my life!"

This is the first chance Roddy's ever taken in terms of the house making it big or going bust. First the people have to come. The even bigger chance for us is whether or not somebody walks with the $50,000 pot, the final game of the night. I've never seen Roddy so nervous before. I must admit I've got my fingers crossed, toes too. If nobody walks with the jackpot, Roddy's plans for a full casino — blackjack, craps, roulette, you name it — can go into motion.

An Iroquois rez out by Beaverton's already got a building going up with the same plan in mind. The Ontario politicians tried to stop them, and it was *wasichu* courts that declared Native autonomy. Roddy's got that silver shovel in his closet and he's ready to dig the first hole. After a big fight, he got the council to put up $25,000 when our New York Iroquois partners offered to help finance the casino deal. The Iroquois want to see if we can draw the crowds. It's now down to the money to bring in the bulldozers. Roddy told me he wants me to be a casino manager.

You couldn't ask for a better day. The blackflies are gone for the season, so the clouds and little bit of rain's made the cottagers antsy to get out and about. We open the doors at three p.m. sharp and have a buffet of casseroles and macaroni and venison. Old Blanche Lafleur from the tavern claims that, when she walked from her place to the Palace, she counted five hundred head, not including the little ones yelling and darting among the grown-ups.

Saturday nights were never like this seven years ago when I first got a job working bingo after Ollie died. Word of our Palace hadn't spread yet when Roddy hired me on at the snack counter. I worked my way up to official stage caller pretty quick, faster than I ever imagined. It's quite a thing to sit above the crowd and pull balls from the air popper and hear the hush when you call. Tonight won't be much different. As six o'clock comes near it looks like every chair in the house is taken and people have got their sheets of cards spread in front of them and are arranging all their doodads and charms.

You've never seen such a strange sight — troll dolls with bright pink or green hair shooting up from their heads, pieces of lucky clothing or real child hair and baby teeth. And daubers, lots of coloured bingo daubers. Most serious players always have a handful lined up, although it takes a lot of plugging away to run a dauber's ink dry. The stylish ladies carry all their bingo gear in crocheted bags. A few even have authentic-looking wampum pouches, made from moose hide with beaded Indian scenes on them.

I notice that the teenagers form their own group along the far wall. They've got torn jeans and long hair and pretty designs on their T-shirts. They're mostly rez kids, Johnny Sandy, Veronica Tibogonosh, and Earl Thibadeau among them. A few years ago, a lot of the more troublesome ones, the tricksters in the group, used to show up and do things like call, "Bing —" and then "Oh-oh," a few seconds later, like they mistook winning a game. The older ones didn't like that, I tell you, white or Indian. Don't ever cross a player and her game. It's like spitting on someone's religion. The Indians never hushed up the trickster kids. It always seemed to be the old white ladies with thin lips making snake noises against their wrinkled fingers. Roddy finally chased the bad ones out. I don't know exactly what he did or said, and I'm not sure I want to know. But there isn't much trouble during the games anymore.

Tonight I notice a woman and her husband bring their little ones in to sit with them while they get ready to play. My floor runner, Albert, goes over, and it looks like he's telling them that children aren't allowed in during the games. You never saw people leave in such a huff. I've never seen the family in here before, and don't expect to again any time soon.

That's one of the disagreements my husband, Ollie, had with the band council so many years ago. Roddy tried to sell bingo as a business good for the whole community when Ollie started up his petition of names against it. Ollie knew there was no room for the rez kids in the Palace. In the final band vote, his big opposition speech ended with talking about our Rachel and Little Ollie. It made a stir with the older ones, but the Palace was like a black bear waking in spring, too hungry to stop.

Ollie didn't live long enough to see bingo run on the rez. He died when he fell out of a tree. He was way up, near the top of a big pine, sawing dead wood threatening to come down during the next thunderstorm. A cottager had offered him fifty bucks for the job. The cottager was an old man then, but seems much older now when I occasionally run into him at the trading post or in town. He still sends me a prayer card every year.

It's funny, you know. Even now I sometimes don't believe Ollie's gone. He was always falling out of trees or driving his snowmobile too late in spring and going through the thin ice or tearing the hull of his boat on a shoal at night. But he crawled back into our bed, wet and cold or scratched up, telling me another story. After all these years it still doesn't sink in that nobody saw Ollie fall out of the tree or gasping for breath for half an hour with a branch through his stomach like the coroner told me. Ollie's luck ran out. I think the rumours are just Ollie's spirit flying around on the wind at night, stirring up trouble and rattling the pine branches.

There wasn't much time for mourning with Little Ollie and Rachel at home. Little Ollie remembers a few things about his daddy but Rachel was only two when it happened. That bothers me a lot, the fact they'll never know him.

Roddy knew I never liked the idea of living off government money, that I hated the idea as much as Ollie did. After the funeral, Roddy offered me the job on the snack counter at the Palace. The thought of Ollie looking down from his star and shaking his head, disappointed that I sold myself out to something like bingo, bothered me. It always will. But it wasn't my fault that he left us early, and it seems to me that working is better than welfare. And I'm a hard worker. I moved up quick and ignored the grumbling from the others who worked the Palace till midnight and drank till dawn. Once I heard one of the townie kids call me Mary Goody Two-Moccasins. I bitched him out good.

The Palace chatters like a forest full of grosbeaks when I walk up and take my seat by the popper, on the stage a good four metres above the crowd. It's a bird's-eye view through the haze of smoke rising to the rafters. The noise stops with the croaking and fumbling of my mike, and you'd think a priest had walked in to say church or a judge to read the sentence. There are no empty seats. Even stragglers lean on walls or sit on the floor, arranging.

"Welcome to the Shawanagan Bingo Palace," I say. "As a lot of you know, Queen or King for the night wins ten dollars every time their ball number comes up in play this evening. Please refer to the lottery ticket you received with admission." I call out the number and wait for the winner. Old Barb from Magnetawan stands up and calls out, "I am Queen of the Shawanagan Bingo Palace!" Albert runs out and puts the red felt bandanna on her head. Old Barb looks very proud. People all around nod to her. It's a serious business. I make a note that her ball is B-6. All Barb has to do is call out, "Pay the Queen," whenever her number is announced in a game and Albert runs over and gives her ten bucks. It can add up.

I jump right into the Early Bird Special, with two games of straight bingo and two games of Full Card X. It gets the interest up and people loosened for the night. I call the balls even and a little slow, holding them in front of the camera attached to the monitors long enough that the older ones who can't hear too well have enough time to squint out the numbers. I notice a lot of regulars in the audience tonight. There's Barb smiling away in her red bandanna and the Burke's Falls Lions Club gang with their matching shirts. I notice that even the Judge came out tonight. I gave him up for dead a while ago. He's a retired lawyer from Toronto who moved up here alone. We call him "Judge" because he uses a dauber shaped like a gavel and pounds away all serious at his cards like he's ordering the court to silence. The Early Bird winners walk with or split a hundred dollars a game.

One hundred dollars seemed like a fortune to me back when Ollie and I married. He was never much for government handouts, even though there were plenty of days we needed cash. Ollie was a wagon-burner, for sure. He sniffed out trouble and rolled in it faster than a hunting dog. He liked to piss people off. I met him at fifteen and could see it in his eyes. He'd hitch-hiked into our rez from the Quebec interior and decided he liked the lake. So he stayed. But he could use a chainsaw and drive a logging truck, so he wasn't much of a burden. Old Jacob took Ollie under his wing and taught him about fishing and hunting. Jacob is a legend around here. He feeds most of the rez through the harder months. One winter Ollie and him bagged seventy deer and fed a lot of mouths through to spring.

Then Ollie got a crush on me. He claimed it was a vision he had after hiking to Moosejaw Mountain, which isn't so much a mountain as a heap of old quarry stone, and he got stuck there a couple days after his lunch bucket ran dry.

I'll never forget the day he walked back onto the reserve, shouting that he was a man now, that he'd had his first true vision — one of a large brown animal whispering my name in his ear as he lay naked and sweating on a rock.

I laughed at Ollie from my doorstep, so he left and I didn't see him again for two weeks. When he came back, his chest had swelled bigger. Ollie made sure to tell all my girlfriends that he had hitched the five hundred kilometres up to Moose Factory in pursuit of his vision, knowing it would get straight back to me. I'll tell you now I didn't like the idea of a moose popping up in Ollie's head whenever he thought of me. We ended up marrying a year later.

After a game of Four Corners and a game of Make a Kite, I call intermission. Tonight Jan What's-Her-Face comes and gabs in my ear like usual. She's a *wasichu* cottager who wears "Free Leonard Peltier" or "American Indian Movement" T-shirts. Jan tells me that last night she had a vision in her dreams. The vision told her the winning combination of balls I would call in the jackpot game, and she looks forward to seeing if her vision was worthy.

"I always get such a feeling of freedom when I drive onto your reservation," she says, and takes my arm in her hands. "Just imagine winning $50,000. That would be freedom too."

She's only a summer cottager. Her place up here isn't even winterized. I wonder what she'd think about freedom, stuck in the house when it's thirty below and the walkie-talkie tells you the road won't be cleared for days.

Between the two intermissions we play Block of Nine, Anywhere, Half Diamond and Full Diamond games. They're simple enough, but I see people's focus is on the cards. There's not much chit-chat while play's in progress. The winnings are too big. Albert runs and hands out $2,000 before I call intermission again.

Bingo calling's like any other job in that it can get boring after a while. I learned to pass my time on the stage every night watching faces and goofing around, calling numbers too fast and laughing inside at all the eyes looking up at me like panicked raccoons in car headlights. Or I'll call real slow for a long while, listening for just the right moment when people are chatting and not paying attention. That's when I call a few balls super-fast and listen for the angry wail of "Call again," or "Bad bingo." Ollie would have laughed at that.

But tonight there's no fooling around. Roddy paces the floor like an anxious bear, his black braided ponytail flopping almost to his bum.

Our Shawanagan Special tonight is the biggest ever. If you want to play, you have to buy special strips at $5 a pop, but the winner walks with a guaranteed $4,000. We have to sell eight hundred cards just to break even. Roddy decides to leave the cashier box open a couple of extra minutes despite cries of "Let's play," and "Get on." From where I sit, with all the scurrying about and money changing hands, we'll break even. But you're never positive until the accounting's done at the end of the night.

Roddy comes up to me before I start play again. "Remind the crowd about the jackpot game tonight, Mary," he says. As if they need to be reminded. I clear my throat and switch on the mike.

"Let me just tell you about tonight's jackpot game." Everyone goes real quiet and stares up at me. "The game is included with your admission price. You can buy extra cards at $25 a pop. Jackpot game is fill your card in forty calls or less and win $50,000. In forty-one calls, $40,000. In forty-two calls, $25,000. In forty-three calls, $15,000. In forty-four calls or more, $5,000." I see the glow in people's eyes. It's an addiction.

"The point isn't to win, it's to win big!" Roddy tells the Palace workers at our meetings. "You either lead, or you follow, or you get out of the way." It's a good scare tactic but doesn't leave much room to argue. I sometimes take a walk and look around the rez and wonder.

I was out walking with Little Ollie and Rachel when I heard about Ollie. Ernest, the band's police chief, roared up in a dust cloud. When he got out of his Bronco, he looked sad and red-eyed.

"I got bad news, Mary," he said. "Come here away from the little ones for a minute." I remember thanking him for telling me, and walking the kids down the dirt road to the pond Ollie always took them to.

"Daddy can't take you fishing here no more," I said. "Or to school or out in the bush." Their deer eyes looked up at me. Little Ollie figured it out fast and ran away on his skinny legs, his sneakers slapping up puffs of dust on the road. Rachel cried and wanted her brother to come back.

Little Ollie isn't so little anymore. He's eleven now and he blames Roddy but can't reason it out exactly why. I tell my boy that it was his father's time to go to *Gitchi-Manitou*, that he's up in the sky as a twinkling star now, looking down at us. The few rumours are just rumours. But my boy fights it. He's not named after his dad for nothing, I figure.

I start in the thirteenth game with one of my favourites, Telephone Pole, where you've got to fill in the right numbers to make the design on your card look like one. The next game, Picnic Table, goes along the same lines. "Buy extra jackpot cards soon," I remind everyone. "Jackpot is five games away." I glance at my watch. Tonight's going to be a late one for sure. The kids are long asleep.

My mother watches the kids on bingo nights. She tries to refuse my money, but I pay for her time anyways.

"We take care of our own," she says to me. "We've always taken care of our own. We're Ojibwe."

After Ollie died and I started working, Mom and me started fighting. One night I got out of work real late, and she got angry when I went to pick up the kids. "Ollie wouldn't want you working there," she said. That got me mad. "He thought bingo wasn't Indian. It's a white man's game."

I knew that already. It got me madder. "Indian?" I said. "Indian? We're Ojibwe and you don't even know our language." I tried to pass her to get the kids, but she stopped me and wrestled me to the ground by my hair. I began to cry and shouted, "Where were all the Indians when Ollie fell out of a tree?" She had me pinned beneath her, her cheeks shaking and her chest against mine.

"Where were all the Indians when Ollie fell out of a tree?" she asked. Our eyes got big at the same time. And then we started laughing at what I'd said until my sides were about to burst. We just lay beside one another on the floor and laughed. It felt good. We've been tight ever since.

I've asked Mom to come out and play bingo. "I'll find another sitter," I tell her. But she doesn't like the thought of a room packed with quiet, serious people and smoke.

"I could go to a sweat lodge if I want to see that," she always tells me. But I can see the question in her eyes, whether it doesn't bother me to be working for something Ollie hated.

I don't think it bothers me.

Really, I don't.

Roddy puts the word out that there are professional gamblers up from Toronto tonight.

"You just call those balls, Mary," he says. "You call 'em during the last game and pray hard. I don't want to see you call out the big one tonight."

As if I got a say. If somebody wins, Roddy loses the council money, not his backers'. That's the truth. If someone wins the big one and I get blamed, I'll just laugh and tell him, "Ollie came to me in a dream and said, 'Fuck you.'" I'll just walk.

"Next game is Crazy H," I say. My voice is muffled by chatter and smoke. We play mostly tried-and-true bingo strategies here. Roddy's travelled as far as Montreal and Vancouver to keep up on the business. He wants a slick operation, only the best.

The Bow Tie and Cloverleaf games slow things down some, but the Inside Square and Outside Square games go faster than I've ever seen. I've barely called twenty-five balls and both are won. There's so many cards out there tonight, house odds are way down.

When I call intermission before the big one, a line forms at the cashier box. The jackpot is actually three games in one. The best we can hope to fork out is $7,000. A grand for the first person to get One Line Anywhere, another grand for Four Corners and, if we're real lucky, only $5,000 for the jackpot.

Most are already in their chairs when I call them to play. Every other person has a smoke lit. I start the big one, and I call fair and slow, leaving each ball on the monitor for seven seconds before calling the next.

The One Line Anywhere goes to a young woman in just eight balls. She calls, "Bingo!" then squeaks like a chipmunk and begins giggling. Albert calls her numbers back to me. I wait a few seconds for effect before saying, "That's a good bingo."

The Judge calls, "Bingo," calmly after clearing his throat. He got Four Corners in twelve balls. Roddy's pulling his hair out over in the corner. I've never seen people win so early. After Albert calls the Judge's numbers and I verify, an old Indian lady I don't recognize calls "Bingo" as well. The Judge frowns. Albert calls her numbers back. She made a mistake. The Judge smiles again.

Twenty-eight calls till we clear the first one. Roddy oversold tonight. There's way too many cards out there. I call tons of B's and N's and O's. When an I or G comes up, people tense and search their cards hard. I call the thirty-second ball when I notice a woman eyeing the far monitor carefully. I call a G. She doesn't budge. She's only got one game sheet in front of her; obviously she's an amateur. But she's lucky tonight. It looks like all she needs is one or two I's to win, best I can see. That means there's got to be dozens of players on the edge of taking it. Ball number thirty-eight is an I. I call and close my eyes. Nothing. Another B on the next call. People moan loud. I reach in the popper for the fortieth ball. It doesn't feel right. I turn it over to reveal I-28. I can feel Roddy's eyes on me. A couple of people squeal loud but then a wave of sad shouts rises up. I see Roddy smiling.

The next two balls are an N and a G. Roddy's smiling bigger. The pot's down to $15,000 when I pull another G. People must be thinking the popper's rigged, so few I's have come up. Just as I'm about to pull the ball for $10,000, a shaky voice calls out, "Bingo," near the front door. She's a down-to-the-wire girl. She just won herself $15,000. Everybody turns and voices rise in grunts and swear words and anger. Albert runs to the unofficial winner.

I can see it's a young woman. She's thin and pretty. I like her long hair. Roddy walks over to help verify the numbers. I call out, "That's a good bingo." People clap and some cheer. The young woman doesn't even smile. But I smile when Roddy pulls out the cheque book. It's nice to see a winner. I get up and stretch and head down to congratulate her.

You've never seen a place empty faster than a bingo hall after the calling's done. There are a few of the woman's friends around, smoking and talking to one another. Roddy holds her arm. He's smiling but he's not happy.

"Congratulations!" I say.

She seems to know I mean it. "Thanks, ma'am."

"What you going to do with all that money?" I ask her.

"Fix my husband's Ski-Doo and get myself a new rifle, I figure. Put the rest away."

She's got almond eyes. She looks half Indian.

"Before you go making plans," Roddy jumps in, "what about considering a donation to the council? You know we took a thumping in the wallet tonight to get interest up in a new casino. I'm not asking for all of it, miss, maybe $5,000. Think of it as an investment with guaranteed return. The new casino would consider you a very special guest. Always."

I don't believe Roddy's nerve. "Roddy!" I say.

He shoots me a stare. "Follow or get out of the way," he says.

It's late. I've got to get to the kids.

As I near the door, the woman says, "Bingo's as much as I can stand. I'm just really not much of a gambler. I ... I can't imagine having luck like this again, and that's the truth."

I'm going to get out of the way, then.

I shut the Palace door behind me. There's no moon and the wind blows along the pine tops. I hear the wind's whisper. The stars are out bright. Finally to be in fresh air makes me laugh loud. I look up and say to the dog star, "*Aneen Anishnaabe.* Hello, Indian." It's the star I told Little Ollie is his dad.

YOU DON'T WANT TO KNOW
WHAT JENNY TWO BEARS DID

Summer barrelled up from the Great Lakes and rolled across Georgian Bay. Its heat killed the blackflies, and when the mosquito droves replaced them in the first warm nights, the weekenders arrived in swarms from Toronto and Oshawa and Hamilton and the northern States.

There was little Jenny could do about it. Weekenders meant business for the band along with the arrival of a handful of cute guys. Even a few old friends' faces among the white hordes that crawled like freshly dug grubs over the Turtle Stone Reserve. The arrival of the tourists meant a busy night at the big show on Canada Day, for the other bands, anyway. Weekenders meant a packed beach of excited and drooling teenagers, escaped from the confines of the parents' quaint summer cottages, grooving spastically. In the old days it had been Jenny's very own loud and alive all-Indian-girl band playing on the stages of small clubs, screaming out the Native blues. Now it was slick white boys from the city up there on the Mosquito Beach stage, strumming insolently on guitars and acting like rock stars. It was time to realize that Sisters of the Black Bear were no longer in vogue.

Maybe calling the weekenders grubs was a little harsh. But just today she had seen a sickly pale and blubbered woman in a sun hat trying to power a motorboat out of the marina, had watched in horror as she lost control and punched her bow into the hull of Jenny's little Streamliner.

Jenny tried hard to hold in her anger when she walked down to the office to register a complaint against Blubber Woman. When Mike, the supervising tribal cop on duty, filled out the report, he mentioned that he'd heard the council had chosen Sisters of the Black Bear to headline Mosquito Beach this year.

"Are you sure they picked us?" Jenny asked.

"Oh yeah," Mike answered. "Council said your new sound is great."

He congratulated her on her band's comeback. Her anger rubbed away now, Jenny skipped back to the marina, thinking how silly it was for her, a woman who'd be thirty-two this autumn, to be happy as a teenager. Her band had finally found a little of its old glory. Oh, they had lived through a real heyday in the mid-eighties, one year even being voted Best Female Band in the punk rock category by an underground Toronto newspaper, but that was then. Now the Sisters were set to headline the biggest bash of the year. Canada Day celebrations at the beach meant a crowd of hundreds, it meant vacationing club owners up from Toronto hungry for talent to be booked, and it meant revenge against all the bastards in the area who laughed at the notion of the band still slugging it out after all these years. Tina and Anne and Bertha were going to shit. This was the return of the old days. Jenny tried to ignore the thundercloud of worry gathering around her head. Exactly how she'd managed to get the big gig was her own dirty little secret.

"The council wants us to play Mosquito Beach?" Tina asked, slouching on her drum stool at practice that night. Jenny had called an emergency meeting, and the girls were a little pissed at having to show up a second time in as many weeks at their rehearsal space, the old and abandoned marine mechanics' shop butting up against the green water of the bay.

"I really don't think we're ready to play something as big as Mosquito Beach," Anne chimed in. "I haven't picked up my bass seriously in weeks. And I know for a fact Bertha hasn't touched her guitar in longer than that." Bertha nodded meekly, holding her guitar in her chubby fingers as if it were a wilted flower. "Let's call it off."

"That's not a possibility," Jenny said. The Sisters sat for a few minutes, looking at one another.

"Why the hell would the council choose us to play something as big as that anyways?" Anne asked after a little while. "It doesn't make sense. Fluff music is what's in. We're too hardcore for them. How'd they decide to pick us?"

Jenny wanted to tell the Sisters how she'd finagled it, but her burning face wouldn't let her.

Thirteen years was a long time for any band to keep going, with all its original members still hammering away at their respective instruments. Sure, there'd been a few sabbaticals when it was time for Tina or Anne or Bertha to scream out another kid. More than a few; they'd had thirteen "baby breaks," as the Sisters had taken to calling them, over the last 156 months. In good years, those three managed to have their babies within close proximity, so that the Sisters could take one extended break rather than a whole bunch of them. These sabbaticals gave Jenny a chance to concentrate on her clothes-making, to fill back orders for mukluks and parkas and stitched blankets for the trading post. And in turn, her sewing gave her an excuse for not becoming a baby oven. "You think I've got time for procreation when I've got orders coming out my butt for more beaded moccasins?" Jenny would say to Tina or Anne or Bertha when they teased her about her indifference to the little babbling droolers.

Sometimes there was heartfelt questioning on the part of Jenny's mother, who'd taken on the slight burden of managing the band over the years. "It might be good for you to have a baby," Ma would say over a cup of coffee at the Schmeeler Restaurant or in her own kitchen. "A child opens your eyes to the world's possibilities." Ma liked to talk in feel-good statements that fell apart quickly when you began to pick at their meaning.

Sometimes the desire to have a baby whined in Jenny's ears like a far-off outboard motor needing a good tune-up. But that was about it. Tina and Anne and Bertha, on the other hand, wore their babies on their sleeves like fat, brown little medals. Knocking out another one was for them as easy and by rote as Gretzky scoring a goal against the Toronto Maple Leafs. They treated it like some ridiculous hockey game: Tina 5 — Jenny 0; Anne 4 — Jenny 0; Bertha 4 — Jenny 0.

But one good thing came from their birthing rituals; when they returned to practice after sweating another one out, a whole flood of inspiration followed. The Sisters played like demons for the next couple of months. Jenny imagined that the four of them were psychically plugging into whoever the new mother happened to be, surfing her wave of pent-up and finally released estrogen. Some of the Sisters' best songs had been born, so to speak, during jam sessions interrupted by constant breastfeeding and diaper changing. It was a shame that so few people actually got to hear the music now, a shame that punk rock had become a dinosaur. The Turtle Stone Hall only had the guts to book Sisters of the Black Bear once a year — on New Year's Day, of all days, when bingo was the last thing on people's minds. Obviously, live music was too. The band had decided unanimously to pull a no-show this year if the hall came knocking lamely in late December. The band was Jenny's baby, and she wasn't going to have her child laughed at and scorned by a bunch of hung-over bingo players anymore.

Other than the annual New Year's gigs, the Sisters hadn't played live much in the last number of years. Last winter, after a particularly brutal blizzard that had shut down the rez and kept almost everyone indoors for three days, Tina had shown up at practice with a sheet of paper. "I worked something out," she announced, waving the paper. "In the last ten years we've played approximately forty-six hours in front of a live audience, including encores. That's about four and a half hours a year, maybe two gigs annually, on average." Jenny and Anne and Bertha stared back at Tina, speechless. "I was shut in the house with Joe and the kids," Tina said defensively. "I went a little stir-crazy."

"So what you're saying," Anne said, "is that, other than the annual bingo gig, we manage to play only once a year."

"Not exactly," Tina answered. "Back in '86 we played four shows in one year. But for the last five years or so, New Year's Day has been about it."

"So what are you saying?" Jenny asked. "You don't think we should bother anymore?" Nobody answered. "Is your silence telling me you all want to quit?" she asked, raking the others with her eyes.

"Maybe not quit," Bertha finally spoke quietly, looking tiny and round and meek. "But maybe we should try some new material or something. Punk's been gone for a long time. I mean, there aren't too many people around anymore who are into the two- and three-chord thing."

"She's right," Anne said. Tina nodded.

"Bertha means the three-*power*-chord thing," Jenny said angrily. "Isn't that what brought us together in the first place? The angry force of rebellion? A kind of music that allowed anyone to play it? We didn't just learn three chords, we mastered them! Don't forget the glory days."

"That doesn't mean we can't go in a new direction," Anne said.

"Yeah. Look at Nirvana or Hole or Green Day," Tina followed. "They've done something good without selling out."

"They're a bunch of glam rockers, a bunch of poseurs," Jenny mumbled.

"Maybe," Bertha whispered, "we're just too old for this." Jenny stared at Bertha holding her beat-up Stratocaster copy on her lap, fiddling with its volume knob. "I mean, we got families and jobs and stuff."

"I'll tell you what," Jenny said. "We stick with it through summer, and if nothing comes of it, if we don't get at least one really good bite by then, we can pack it up for good."

"We get to experiment with new material," Anne added.

"Definitely," Jenny said. "But no Anne Murray covers."

And so all that winter and into spring the girls prac-tised more regularly. They tried new material, Jenny actually enjoying the challenge of testing her vocal range. Where before she'd had to rely on throaty chants pierced by howls and screams, now she was actually singing, making words come out of her throat that an audience might be able to interpret. Bertha's guitar miraculously became rhythmical, to some degree, and she started experimenting with solos outside her holy trinity of chords. Tina sat back and stroked her drum kit with finesse, and Jenny could tell from her smile that playing the drums was a lot easier on her child-strained lower back than frantically beating them. And Anne — well, Anne was the real musician of the group. She played her bass with head down, her long black hair covering her face as she concentrated on crisp runs of deep notes, forging a steady and intricate rhythm that the band relied on. For months it was almost like the old days again, the Sisters eager to show for practice, creating new songs and fine-tuning, even slowing down considerably, their old ones.

But late spring brought a lag in energy. Everyone was busy preparing for the onslaught of the weekenders, and the old lackadaisical spirit returned. It might be Tina calling to say, "Julia's sick again and threw up on me, I can't make practice," or Bertha announcing that she couldn't come because her husband was complaining that he wasn't seeing enough of her.

With Canada Day and the big Mosquito Beach gig only two weeks away, the Sisters had been slacking off. Not only that, Jenny thought. Soon, very soon, she was going to have to tell the others her little secret. She remembered putting together a tape of the band's new stuff early last winter and titling it *Return of the Sisters of the Black Bear*. She'd given it to Ma to send out to different clubs in Northern Ontario, and even a couple of the old ones in Toronto that were still around. But the bingo season was raging and Ma was on a very long winning streak. She was too busy to send the tapes out, or had just plain forgotten, every time Jenny enquired.

When word spread about the council accepting musical applications for Canada Day at Mosquito Beach, Jenny felt the baby of an idea being born in her head. The Sisters were slacking again, they needed someone to give them a boost. But when she listened to their new tape, she realized that they were far from ready. The band sounded slow and scared of the new stuff. The only highlight was Anne's talented bass bopping along through each uninspired song. So Jenny had dug through her tape collection and finally pulled out an all-girl band from the late seventies, a band with the atrocious name Girls' Night Out. They were happy and fluffy and sang in harmony. They'd made a minor splash and were long forgotten. They were horrible but in a sweet, girly way. Without thinking, Jenny dubbed the tape onto a blank one, dropped it in an envelope and scrawled *Sisters of the Black Bear Get Happy* across it, and sent it off to the council.

There was no way they would choose it, Jenny had thought. But she was pretty sure the old men and women on council would snap their fingers, maybe even try and whistle along to the music, decide not to give the Sisters the gig but write a letter saying how nice their new music was and maybe next year, blah, blah, blah. The Sisters would be inspired anew to keep playing.

But the council loved it. Things had progressed too far for Jenny to reverse them. The girls were just going to have to face it and play their own music. They were going to have to find some of the guts they had had in the old days, when the Sisters were a band to be taken seriously.

All of them called the first years of the eighties the "old days." Punk rock had swept into Canada from overseas with the Sex Pistols, The Clash, the Stranglers, the Subhumans.

Seven Seconds and the Circle Jerks and the Dead Kennedys and dozens of others had poured into Canada from the south. Jenny still remembered the thrill of the four of them jumping into the car and making the drive down to Toronto to catch the blistering music and feel the intensity of angry youth expressing early-adult angst in little basement clubs.

The Canadian bands had begun making a stir in 1980. DOA and the Young Lions, the Day-Glo's and SNFU all made regular tour stops in Toronto, and even sometimes up in North Bay. "Oh, that Joey Shithead in DOA is so cute," Jenny remembered saying often.

One late night, during the long drive home to the rez after an especially intense show, Jenny said, joking, that the girls should start a hardcore band. They all laughed.

"What would we call ourselves?" Bertha asked.

"How about the Deerslayers?" Anne said. "Or maybe Red Power."

"Nah, I like the Scalp Sisters," Tina said.

"No," Bertha answered. "The Four Skins would be better."

They had decided that night what instrument each would play, and suddenly the jokes had become serious. Within a month each girl had bought her own used, crappy instrument and they were practising in Ma's basement under the name Sisters of the Black Bear. Ma liked the idea a lot, but thought the music wasn't very pretty.

"We're not about pretty, Ma. We're about making a statement on the condition of Canada's indigenous people and especially its indigenous women, and that's ugly. Therefore the music is too."

"But you're not ugly, Jenny," Ma said. She didn't get it, but she'd been helpful in getting the girls their first gig at the hall.

Shortly after that, the Sisters made Ma their official manager. She had lots of cousins all over Northern Ontario, and they helped her find gigs for the band. Ma was very polite-speaking to Toronto club owners she didn't know, and Jenny was sure this helped the band get booked there too.

Sisters of the Black Bear had lots to say, and the songs poured out in their first couple of years. By tapping into native anger they found a deep source of creativity, Jenny thought. After all, Leonard Peltier was rotting in jail for crimes he hadn't committed. Indians all over North America were living in abject poverty. Teen suicides were way higher in Native populations than in any others in North America.

It wasn't until the band released its first tape in early 1981 that the Toronto gig offers started pouring in. After much debate, the band titled the tape *Sisters of the Black Bear — Welcome to the Maul.* Jenny considered every song a minor classic: "Blowing Up the Bingo Hall," "Custer Wore Arrow Shirts," "The Government Gave Dad a Bottle of Whisky for Christmas and All I Got Was This Lousy Smallpox Blanket" and "Who Has the Red Face Now?" All got lots of air play on college radio stations. For a while the Sisters were playing Toronto so regularly that they considered moving there. It wasn't only Jenny who felt swallowed up after a couple of days in the big city, though, and in the end everyone was glad they hadn't moved. As quick as punk came in, it began sinking, replaced by cheesy "progressive rock" and synthesizer music. But by that time the band was a part of the Sisters' lives, and they continued practising together in the hopes that one day punk rock would be recognized again.

And here we are, Jenny thought, come full circle.

The band had their chance to make a statement again, in front of a really big crowd of kids and adults who needed a lesson. She felt stronger telling the Sisters what she'd done.

"You did what?" Anne asked, the night after the emergency meeting, back again at the rehearsal space.

"I gave the council a tape of somebody else's music."

Bertha gasped. Anne's and Tina's mouths dropped.

"Well, we'll just have to tell them to find another band," Anne said finally.

"I say we play and we play hard, just like we used to do," Bertha said suddenly. Everyone looked over to her, standing up now, strapping her guitar on and turning up the volume knob.

"Yeah!" Tina shouted. "We've got new stuff. We'll play that along with our best old songs. We'll kick ass."

Jenny hadn't seen those two so excited since the night of the show eleven years ago where the whole club had become a giant mosh pit. Tables and chairs were smashed that night; the audience bruised and battered themselves. The police eventually arrived and shut the show down. The band had never been happier.

"What do you say, Anne?" Jenny asked. "If this isn't punk guerrilla tactics, I don't know what is! This is the statement we've been wanting to make again all these years."

Tina, Anne and Jenny stood together, looking down at her. Anne eventually nodded, then smiled, picking up her bass.

"All right," she said. They were back in business.

"Old Jeremy on the council told me you girls turned a new leaf," Ma said to Jenny over their daily coffee a week before the gig. "He says you're actually making real music now. You didn't say nothing to me about this, Miss Two Bears." Few could pronounce a name like Jenny Tobobondung, never mind remember it, so back in the old days the girls had replaced their Ojibwe names with shorter, more memorable monikers: Tina One Bear, Jenny Two Bears, Anne Three Bears, and Bertha Four Bears. It had been a sign of solidarity.

"Well, Ma, the music is a little different now."

"You're not going to go smashing Bertha's guitar on stage for her again, are you?" she asked, looking worried over her cup, her grey frazzled hair sticking up out of her head. "I still remember that show in Toronto a long time ago, when Bertha tried to smash her guitar. But she was too small so you had to do it for her. You girls missed three shows trying to scrape up money to buy a new one."

"No, I won't smash anything, Ma," Jenny answered, sipping her coffee. "So what exactly did Jeremy say about our music?"

"He says it's real pretty, and you all harmonize real nice together now, and it reminds him of music again."

"It'll be a good show, Ma. A nice show. Don't worry." The Sisters' new material was plain bad — atonal and uninspired. Jenny didn't know what they were going to do.

"Wear something pretty for me," Ma said.

The days before the gig flew by too quickly for Jenny. The four of them spent every hour they could find in the practice space, but still they sounded bad. "Too much distraction!" Jenny found herself shouting one afternoon to the rest of the girls after Bertha's four-year-old rode his tricycle across Jenny's mike cord, catching his pedal in it and ripping the mike from her hands. Tina tried to turn the problem of having kids in the rehearsal space into a creative coup by getting them to sing along on certain songs. The idea sounded brilliant, but persuading any of the kids to contribute more than monkey sounds or farting noises proved impossible. Jenny was sick with worry, wondering how she'd ever managed to nail herself into this particular punk rock coffin.

Ma kept the Sisters filled in with early phone reports of crowd size out at the beach as they huddled at her house, trying to psych up for the show. The first band, a pop rock trio from Barrie who called themselves the Brews Brothers, were set to go on in a half hour, followed by a Gordon Lightfoot–inspired balladeer named Serious Henry, backed by his middle-aged band.

Ma's calls from the pay phone at the beach were beginning to grate on Jenny's nerves. "Jenny? It's your mother. My guess is that there's two hundred people here now. Did you fix your hair nice?" A half hour later the phone rang again. "Jenny? It's your mother again. I had little Frank run around and try to count heads. He says over three hundred weekenders are here, not including locals. What did you decide to wear?" When the phone rang once again, Jenny couldn't hear her mother very well over the din of the Brews Brothers and the screeching crowd. "Over five hundred," she heard her mother say. "Get down here quick."

Jenny walked into the living room where the others sat. Anne nervously smoked a cigarette and checked over the set list.

"Okay, we open with 'Thirty-Something Wasteland,' right?" Tina asked as she drummed her thighs with her sticks. "What comes after that?"

"Don't worry," Anne mumbled from a cloud of smoke. "You'll have a set list taped by your kit."

Jenny looked over to Bertha. She sat on a big chair, her feet not quite touching the floor, quiet and still as a small stone. "You okay, Bertha?" Bertha's nod back wasn't too convincing. "Well, Sisters, time to head to the beach," Jenny said, trying to sound chipper, the words coming out shaky.

Jenny suddenly realized that, without anyone actually saying it out loud, all of the Sisters had chosen their original stage dress. As they stood up and headed towards the door, the band's classic look — black combat boots, black torn jeans and black T-shirts — somehow calmed her. They were ready to do battle. Sure, the black didn't exactly have the slimming effect that it had had ten years ago. But there was no getting around the fact that they looked intimidating, a stocky army of women on the warpath, despite all the procreation the other three had been involved in. A little blocky, maybe pudgy, but still intimidating. As Jenny walked down the steps towards the waiting van, she felt the tight tug of her jeans. She'd never had babies, so what was her excuse?

The Sisters stood in the shadows on the stairs leading up to the stage's side, Serious Henry crooning sadly above their heads. The crowd appeared monstrous from this angle, hundreds and hundreds of people stretching back along the beach, right to the water's edge two hundred metres away. The beer tent along the side was wall-to-wall weekenders and locals. Half the audience listened intently; the drone of talking and laughing and hooting rose from the other half, mingling with Henry's melancholy voice. When he stopped singing, though, the crowd erupted in claps and cheering. Henry tipped his cowboy hat to the audience and, through the roaring, mumbled, "Thank you. Thank you very much. Please stick around for Sisters of the Black Bear."

The Sisters nodded to Serious Henry as he exited the stage and walked down past them, tipping his hat again. Jenny watched the roadies running around the stage, pulling apart Henry's shiny equipment and lugging out the Sisters' battered and sad-looking gear.

Anne handed Jenny a mickey of rye, and Jenny tipped it up and took a big gulp. The horrible taste made her gag. It was fully dark now, and the event coordinator came up to brief them quickly. "You've got a full hour and a half to do your thing, ladies," he said. Jenny thought that if he had whiskers he'd look like a little white rat. "You got a real happy crowd out there. I was told it's the biggest Mosquito Beach turnout ever. You can go on any time now." He walked down the steps and hurried off.

"Give us the set lists," Tina said.

Anne's mouth dropped. "Oh my god. I left them at your mother's house."

Jenny felt her stomach sink to somewhere below the tight waist of her jeans. "It's okay," she said, before a panic attack could wash over her. "We basically know exactly what we're going to play. Just keep the communication lines open onstage. We'll be fine." The Sisters walked onstage, into the bright lights and small roar of the crowd.

Jenny felt as if she might be floating towards the microphone, the blood rushing in her ears, until she stumbled on a wire snaking across her path. She straightened up and muttered, "Good evening, folks," into the mike, but no sound echoed across the audience. The damn thing wasn't turned on. She fumbled along its shaft and hit the switch. The microphone squealed to life and Jenny tensed at the feedback. "We're Sisters of the Black Bear," she said, her voice booming shakily across the crowd, "from right here on Turtle Stone Rez. Welcome to the Maul."

There was a short silence. Jenny had been hoping that this would be enough cue for the Sisters to kick into their first song. She looked back and saw that Bertha wasn't ready yet, was still strapping on her guitar. The crowd grew silent. Jenny looked out through the lights and smiled meekly. "We thank you for coming," she muttered, feeling her face begin to burn. None of the Sisters had ever been in front of so giant a crowd. She could feel a thousand eyes staring at her. She looked back again. Bertha gave her the nod and started strumming into the first song. The rest of the band joined in, so slow it seemed they were playing under water. Jenny leaned towards the mike, closed her eyes to the glare and opened her mouth to sing. Nothing came. She'd completely blanked on the lyrics. She felt the band tense up behind her.

They kept playing the song heroically. She stepped back from the microphone as casually as she could, turned around and looked at them helplessly. Anne had her head down, hiding behind her veil of hair, her fingers picking out the notes. Bertha stared at her with a doe's eyes, unsure whether to keep playing or not. Tina glared from behind her drum kit, not caring, from the sound of it, if she was even keeping time. Jenny shrugged and made an apologetic face to them. The song whined down and petered out.

Jenny stepped back to the mike and half whispered, "We call that one 'Thirty-Something Wasteland' … uh … we try to make our music match our feelings on the issue." A few people laughed. A fat man close to the front of the crowd shouted loudly and drunkenly, "That sucked!" He got more laughs from the crowd.

Jenny reddened. She made his face out through the bright stage lights. He was a true grub. "This next one's called 'Scalp The Fat Drunk.'" The crowd hooted, which made her feel a little better. Anne nudged her. She still had her hair covering her face.

"Don't sweat it, Jenny," she whispered. "Let's do 'Smoke Signals.' You're real good at that one."

The crowd was restless, talking and laughing quietly. The tone reminded Jenny of a wake. "This is where we start for real," she said into the mike. "This one's called 'Smoke Signals,' and it's dedicated to all the politicians blowing smoke up our collective asses."

The same heckler shouted, pointing up to the stage, "You could blow a lot of smoke up those girls' big collective asses, eh?" Jenny stared down at him. He'd taken his shirt off and wrapped it around his head. His hairy belly jiggled as he laughed with his sunburnt friends. The band kicked into the song. It was supposed to have a tribal rhythm, a beating of the war drum, but Tina was so nervous that she was sounding like an epileptic having a seizure. Jenny leaned to the mike again and began singing scratchily. It was hard to find the beat with the ringing in her ears. *There's smoke signals in the sky*, she quacked, her voice shooting back at her from her monitor, *There's little reason asking why*. This new song was pathetic. All of them were. *It's big industry polluting the sky / Leaving another child left to cry....*

Jenny was grateful when the song finally ended. A smattering of applause. The audience refused to make eye contact with the band.

"Now Glenn Miller had a big band," the fat grub up front shouted to his buddies, making sure to shout loudly enough for

Jenny and everyone else to hear too, "but I guess you'd call these chicks a *really* big band." Nervous twitters from people around him. "Hey, what's your band's name? The Bear Sisters?" Jenny noticed that his few remaining friends were polite enough to turn away from her to laugh.

Jenny walked over to Anne. The crowd didn't seem to know what to do with itself. "Do the instrumental," Jenny said to her. "'Powwow Highway.' It might get the crowd dancing." Anne nodded her hair-covered face, then walked to Tina, then Bertha. They kicked into the song as Jenny walked back to the front of the stage, dangling her microphone so that it nearly touched the ground. She tapped her foot to the music and stared down at the fat man. He stared back at her, smiling, centre stage and six or seven metres dead ahead. The crowd had cleared a small space around him, and he danced theatrically, sticking his tongue out at Jenny and rubbing his belly.

Jenny smiled back and began to swing her mike in a slow circle, like a stripper with a feather boa. A couple of guys hooted. The band picked up the pace. They actually sounded tight, hitting the right chords hard, surfing along the fast tempo. Jenny swung the microphone faster. The fat man gestured to himself with both hands, mouthing, "Oh, baby," to her. Jenny was whirling the mike on the end of its cord, picking up speed, as the song reached its crescendo. When the man reached down and squeezed his crotch in mock seduction, Jenny let the mike fly; it sailed like a silver arrow aimed true towards the man. He was still grinning when it hit him square in the forehead with an amplified and hollow BONG.

Jenny pulled the microphone back in, hand over hand, the screeching of feedback a nice touch, she thought, to the end of the song. She placed the mike back in its grip and stared down at the man. He was sitting on his ass like a fat child, rubbing his forehead. Jenny was halfway to the stage stairs when the clapping started. Just the smack of maybe ten hands together at first. It quickly multiplied so that, by the time she reached the stairs there were hundreds and hundreds of hands clapping, voices rising in shouts and whistles, a beach packed with admirers demanding more. Jenny looked back to the Sisters. They were still standing in place, dumbly staring out at the sea of noise.

There was nothing else to do; Jenny ran back to the mike and shouted, "This one's called 'Burning Down the Bingo Hall.' Hit it, Sisters." Jenny growled into the mike as they kicked in fast and hard behind her. *The Bingo Hall's burning / The Bingo Hall is burning / The Bingo Hall is popping balls and it's burning hot tonight.*

Within a minute a mosh pit had formed, swallowing up the fat man, forty or fifty crazed and happy cottage kids jumping in a circle around him like movie Indians, pumping their fists in the air and howling along. More and more people joined in. Jenny grabbed the mike off the stand and paced the stage, spitting out her words, the words a tribal roar now, flying above the guitar and bass and drums. She spotted Ma on the right, back a ways from the melee and leaning against a birch tree. Wiry grey hair bobbing, Ma tapped her foot fast as she could to the music, grinning big.

SOUTH
Ruin

PAINTED
TONGUE

Painted Tongue cocked his ear to a loon calling from the lake, and it was like a dream, the sound dancing across the big water, the water pulling the sun into it. He laughed to himself.

I must not talk like Grandfather. Repeat one hundred times. I drink, therefore I am. Repeat. Write it one hundred times on the blackboard, then sit in the corner facing away from the class.

He laughed to himself again, then took a swig from his mickey of vodka. There was nothing left, so he sucked on the brown bag that held the bottle. He rocked on his boulder and sucked on the bag and hummed a song that his mother used to sing to him at Cedar Point.

Gnooshenyig go tobogganing. Your grandchildren go tobogganing. *Nooshenyig* go tobogganing. My grandchildren go tobogganing.

The words knotted around themselves before they left his tongue, so he flattened the letters with his damaged mouth and turned them into a hum that increased in tone until the sound echoed back across the water towards the loon. Painted Tongue hummed louder to remember his mother's song until the story in the song came back to him, the story of children sledding and falling through the weak ice of a river, the song of warning to children who acted foolishly with friends who didn't listen to the warnings of their mothers. He was drunk. He had a righteous buzz and wanted a drink. He wanted a drink so bad it made him shake, but the humming helped stop the shakes for a little while at least.

The boulder that he sat on was his boulder.

Let someone try to take it away, goddammit. I will cut your throat from ear to ear and count coup upon you, motherfucker.

This was his boulder on the lake, removed from the confusion of downtown, the rock heavy and squat and thick with a little natural chair cut into it at such an angle that he didn't have to see the ugliness of people, just the water and the sun dancing upon the water. This was Painted Tongue's rock, and he'd defended his turf against stinking hobo invaders. He'd counted many coup against them with rocks and broken bottles and his fists, and now this was his rock. Painted Tongue stopped his humming as a jogger in very white sneakers ran by behind him along the railroad tracks, the jogger turning his head away from this man who defended his rock, this man with long straight black hair and the crooked nose of a warrior.

You are a coward! Painted Tongue wanted to shout. The way you turn your eyes from me as you cross my rock. Don't run near here anymore.

When the man had run away, Painted Tongue cocked his ear again, this time to the clang and chug of a train leaving the train yard far to his left. The five thirty p.m. Go Train express to Oshawa. A warrior didn't need a clock to tell him what time it was. All he needed was to listen and watch the things around him.

When the sun was gone he would make his way back downtown to hustle change with his cup. His bottle was long empty and his lips were dry, and soon it would be time for dry lips to move downtown. Everything travelled in a circle. The sun, the moon, joggers, the world. Today already Painted Tongue had been hustling change at the corner of Dundas Street and Bay. He'd made enough by mid-afternoon to buy the mickey of vodka. He'd walked down Bay and underneath the moan and echo of the expressway, across the train tracks and to the crown of his boulder, far enough away from the electricity and noise of downtown, to where he could imagine for a time that he was back at home, back in the bush. And very soon he'd do his route again. Life hadn't always been this way, but memories of the rez dropped as fast as the sinking sun.

Oh my brothers and sisters, Painted Tongue hummed to himself. The old ways die in the face of the new. They have taken our land, broken every promise, raised the price on a pint of booze and a case of beer, made it near impossible to afford a pack of smokes. Repeat one hundred times. Write it out on the blackboard five hundred times, then sit in the corner facing away from the class and throw up between your legs.

The lake had nearly swallowed the sun now. Maybe tonight Painted Tongue would finally find Kyle Root. Kyle was the only friend he had from Cedar Point who'd made it to the city and stayed. And besides, Kyle owed him money. Kyle was a painter, an artist who could afford anything he wanted now and who lived in a loft in the warehouse district with pretty white women and pine furniture and a kitchen made of steel. Kyle wore suit jackets with his jeans, his hair combed back and neat in a ponytail held by a silver Haida thunderbird. He'd first made it big with a series of portraits of Painted Tongue:

Painted Tongue standing in a field with his bow raised to the sun, Painted Tongue leaping from a tall building and transforming into an eagle, Painted Tongue surfing a river with arms outstretched on the bow tip of a fancy canoe. Kyle was his best friend. He and Kyle used to run through summer back at the Point when they were five and six and seven, always with no shirts on, swinging lacrosse sticks and whipping pebbles at each other. They'd had a game. They'd sneak up on stray reservation dogs and smack the dogs' asses hard as they could with their lacrosse sticks. The winner was the one whose dog howled loudest. They'd always argued about which dog was uglier. Kyle used to read to Painted Tongue about their cousins, the Sioux, how they counted coup on their enemies, how they got close enough to touch them in battle. To count coup on one's enemy made the warrior a great man. Painted Tongue's stomach suddenly cramped hard, making him shiver with a closed mouth. It was time to make the circle.

He stood up slowly on the dome of his rock, humming a song to the departing sun, and got bad headspins. He stumbled and fell head-first, imagining for a moment that he was flying until the bright pain of his nose crunching on smaller rocks made him think he was swimming deep, deep under water.

Painted Tongue awoke in the hospital, surrounded by bright lights and men in green doctor's pants and nurses in white. He tried to leave quietly, but they wouldn't let him. He grew angry and hummed his war song whenever a doctor or nurse approached his cot. I will count coup upon you, skinny brown doctor man, he hummed. I am not even afraid to wrestle your fat white nurse who calls me heathen. Painted Tongue still had a righteous buzz and the pills they gave him made it roar. He hummed louder and louder, increasing the burn of the new stitches on his nose that they had given him while he was unconscious.

You can do the paperwork if you want to call the psych ward, Painted Tongue heard one doctor say to the other as he hummed and rocked on his bed and stared them down. As he was about to leave again, a doctor who was older than the others appeared from the hall, asking, What's the problem here?

He sat on the end of Painted Tongue's bed and spoke. He was the first man in a long time who didn't speak down to him, but spoke, without staring into Painted Tongue's eyes, directly to him. You're lucky a jogger found you and called the police, the doctor said. He was white but his nose looked very much like Painted Tongue's normally did. Have you considered leaving the city and going back to your home? Why don't you stay at the Harvest House on King Street if you don't want to go home? Painted Tongue listened politely. You get drunk and hurt yourself again, and I'll make sure you get institution-alized, the doctor said before letting Painted Tongue go. He knew the doctor meant it.

All last spring, summer and winter and again into this spring, Painted Tongue had held onto the chain-link fence and watched the construction workers swarming inside a big pit below him near the waterfront. He'd hum, There are four or five good workers among you. The rest are lazy shits who don't know how to work the foremen, and the foremen don't know how to work a crew. He hummed this until the hum had become a song that he'd moan every day as the construction in the pit reached street level then grew higher with the seasons. Now the building was almost finished.

He'd watched these men from the very beginning, these sunburnt, windburnt workies straying too close to his turf by the railway tracks, these men gouging a huge empty lot until it was a pit, then framing and pouring concrete all last summer, creating a foundation for something too big, it seemed, for the earth's back to bear. Almost every day for this whole last year, Painted Tongue had taken his walk around the site's perimeter, along the sidewalk that circled it like a huge track, stepping slowly so that a footfall was timed to hit the sidewalk every two seconds. I am a well-tuned clock, Painted Tongue hummed. Left foot, stop, one-two. Right foot, stop, one-two. He'd take a long and measured stride, stop and count, then stride again, stop and count. He walked slowly, exactly, to measure the distance around the site. He walked this way to try to slow down the people rushing all around him. Everybody always seemed in a hurry. Every day he walked the same route in his manner, the crowds on the sidewalk parting like a river around a boat's hull. He ignored the odd looks and laughing and catcalls of Whisky Joe or crazy drunk or fruitcake. The people in this city were not capable of understanding.

It took Painted Tongue ninety minutes to walk the site's perimeter. He'd never witnessed so big a job, so huge a building being born from men and cement mixers and steel girders and cranes. Every day over the last few seasons the walls of the building had grown higher, as if they were being pulled by magic from the tired skin of the earth. Painted Tongue liked to stop after his walk and watch the men work; he recognized the good ones from the lazy at a distance. He was keeper of the secret of their daily progress. Now they were almost finished. The good and the lazy were almost finished.

Today Painted Tongue stood in his usual place at the site,

the start and end of his daily walk around the construction, his hands above his head and holding onto the chain-link fence. His nose throbbed from last night's fall. He brought one hand down to his nose as he stared up at the workies scrambling around on the building, the workies straining and shouting and jackhammering the last of the domed roof into place. A large white bandage over Painted Tongue's nose concealed the zigzag of six stitches running the bridge. The pain pills had made him feel almost weightless, like a crow's wing, but now they were all gone. Last night's fall had been a good thing, he thought. It had loosened up some memories in his head.

That this huge building was round as a medicine wheel was no surprise to him. Nothing in the world existed without a reason. He stared up at the white dome roof, curved like an egg, curved like something he could still not quite figure. The big sign on the other side said in blue letters as tall as a person that this was a stadium, a dome for men to play in and for spectators to cheer. For the last two months Painted Tongue had felt an ugly fear, a wolf spider, creeping up his back. All fear made no sense, and this was no different. Painted Tongue was afraid of the day the men would finish construction, of the day they would pack up their tools and leave this new thing completed. Maybe it was the falling and the pills that were now helping him to recognize just what it was the men were building. His gut tightened in awe and fear.

Painted Tongue began his slow, long strides around the structure. His nose throbbed with each step. The pills were all gone. He glanced over to the site once in a while, then looked back quickly to the ground in front of him, trying to capture the essence of this stadium in the corner of his eye. His mother had once taught him a little trick. If you are trying to remember something, she said, and it is on the tip of your tongue, do not try to force the memory out, for very little good comes from force. Think of other things. Forget what you are trying to remember, and that memory will soon get lonely and come back to you.

Painted Tongue reached the first big curve and again peered quickly towards the dome. Nothing. He went back to the day he'd made a little boy, a small blond boy, cry. It was downtown near the entrance to First Canadian Place where Painted Tongue often sat on a piece of cardboard collecting change. He watched the boy walk along the crowded sidewalk towards him, clutching his pretty mother's hand. The boy stared at Painted Tongue, at his face and then at his paper cup containing a few coins. As they got nearer, the boy pulled on his mom's arm, trying to get her attention, trying to get her to look at the Indian crouching on the sidewalk surrounded by all the white men in business suits and the ladies who wore pretty dresses with sneakers. Painted Tongue spent his life watching. He knew from the boy's eyes all these thoughts he was thinking. The mother ignored the child's tugs.

As the two passed, the little boy held his nose. Painted Tongue screwed up his face and pursed his lips in an O, then blew hard through his mouth. He made his face mimic the Iroquois mask, the Wind Spirit, he'd once seen at the Native Canadian Centre at Spadina and Bloor. The boy's eyes widened at the sight of the man with long black hair and a warrior's crooked nose and pockmarked skin. The boy wailed in fear and Painted Tongue felt the surge along his spine. The mix of sadness and victory made him want a gulp of vodka.

He saw his own eyes in the boy's. When Painted Tongue had been one year old he'd gotten thrush. He wouldn't stop crying. He remembered even now with his pill-fuzzy head as he walked his slow walk around the site, his mother holding him, whispering, *Gdaakwos na? Kaagiijtooge na?* Are you sick? Do you have an earache? And finally, quietly angry, *Aabiish ogaabinji-bayin?* Where do you come from?

His mother told him stories later of bringing him to the reservation doctor who gave him a needle, then to the band's old medicine woman who told his mother to take him into the sweat lodge and hold him tight against her bare chest.

It wasn't until his tongue turned white that anyone figured out why he was sick. He got better and received his nickname.

Although the thrush had nothing to do with it, Painted Tongue remembered developing a lisp when he first learned to talk. The children teased him so much that he began talking less and less. By the time he left Cedar Point at eighteen, he didn't talk at all. His mother said he'd forgotten how. She was the only one who still called him by his birth name. Now, eight years later he still couldn't talk, and everyone who knew of him assumed he was dumb. Painted Tongue liked it that way.

As he neared the end of his slow walk, Painted Tongue began to grow angry that he had no booze and no money, and that whatever this goddamn building was would not show itself to him. I will blow you up, motherfucker stadium, with a thousand kilos of dynamite, he hummed. I will count coup on you, ugly concrete piece of shit. Why would anyone construct a building with a hotel and restaurants and stores and a baseball field in it? If a man desired, he could go inside and never have to come out again. It was crazy. This was a crazy fucking world.

At least the stadium was the same size. Painted Tongue walked up slowly to where he'd started his walk, staring down an ugly woman in tight shorts until she backed away from his place along the fence, the one that offered the best view of the stadium. Back off ugly woman from this warrior on pills, he hummed. I have no booze and I am not afraid to kick a woman's ass in such a state. At least the pills gave him an appetite. He couldn't remember the last time he'd eaten. A hot dog would be good about now. Cree Agnes from Penetanguishene would give him a hot dog. She was a good woman. And she knew Kyle. Kyle was a friend, and Kyle would have some money that he rightfully owed. But Painted Tongue needed to think of polite ways to ask him for it. Walking up Sherbourne, he thought of polite ways to ask for what was owed him. A hot dog would taste good about now, he hummed to himself.

It had been many weeks since he'd seen Kyle. Kyle had given up looking for Painted Tongue to take him out for a meal or coffee or drink a long time ago. Kyle had walked far from working construction with Painted Tongue, the first job the two had found years before when they'd driven together in the old Dodge war pony from Cedar Point to Toronto. Work was easy to find back then. Painted Tongue was as good as any goddamn man with a hammer and a level. He was never afraid to do roofing or construction way up high on a building, either. Balance and bravery were in his blood.

But Kyle had hated construction work from the beginning. It callused his fingers and left his hands too sore at night to hold a paintbrush. Most lunch breaks he'd go to whatever tavern was closest to drink beer and talk to Painted Tongue. Painted Tongue remembered those days with good feelings. Those afternoons when he first started drinking were warmer with a belly full of beer, his eyes focused only on the nails to be pounded or joists to be cut and fit or the shingles to be pulled and replaced. He and Kyle had been thrown off many jobs for being drunk, but there had always been more jobs waiting.

Then Kyle got a fancy job in a gallery selling others' art and, after a while, his own. Now he was Big Chief in the city, and he'd given up the booze. Painted Tongue was left to find his own jobs, and the jobs got harder to find. Not many foremen wanted to hire a man who didn't talk. Kyle moved in with a pretty gallery woman, and Painted Tongue, after some decision-making, left walls and a roof on the first warm spring day two years ago to live more simply. He enjoyed living like the grandfathers, his days spent searching out food and drink, protecting himself from enemies and sitting quietly, listening to his few friends talk to him on park benches, or lying in the grass still left between the concrete buildings. He waited in winter until the heating grates of apartment buildings couldn't keep him warm anymore to search out a bed in the hostels or, if he was lucky, a reinforced cardboard box and blankets in a quiet thicket of pine in High Park. A warrior walked the earth on strong legs or else he perished. Kyle knew that too. Although he'd taken a different path, Painted Tongue was sure Kyle respected him highly for his abilities as a warrior on the streets. Kyle knew what others couldn't see. Painted Tongue had found the circle to walk, and along the route of that circle he found everything he needed to live.

When Painted Tongue arrived at the Native Centre, Agnes was busy with customers, so he wandered the gallery and admired the paintings and wood carvings and jewellery. He stopped suddenly at a large painting of a turtle, each section of its curved shell coloured green or red or black. Its nose was hooked. Small squiggled people and pine trees grew from its back. The artist had titled the painting "Earth Mother Turtle."

Painted Tongue recognized Kyle's signature, curved and sharp like a knife on the bottom right-hand side. Agnes stayed busy with the customers for a long time, so Painted Tongue went outside to hunt for food.

Four nights later, Painted Tongue sat by a small grove of trees and a pond in High Park. He stared up at the stars and three-quarter, late-spring moon that shone through the city's lights. Ducks by the pond honked out warnings whenever a raccoon or cat, or some bigger, shadowed animal that he guessed was a dog or fox, prowled close to the small flocks huddled by the water's edge with their beaks buried in their wing feathers. As soon as the ducks settled down and grew quiet, the same or some other predator would make a leap from nearby bushes and send the flocks quacking and hissing, beating wings to the safety of the middle of the pond. It made Painted Tongue so nervous that he wrapped his arms around his chest and moaned out loud.

He heard the sudden, angry shouts of a small group of people through the trees by a hill to his left. He guessed they were about fifty metres away. He could see a good deal in the moon's light, but the men shouting were somewhere in the shadows of the trees. Their voices were sharp and mean, three of them, maybe four. Then some other man screamed, Leave me alone! In his fear he almost sounded like a woman. Painted Tongue got up on his haunches, rocking slowly and humming quietly, Where are the police? They sleep in their cruisers while men are beaten in High Park.

They were hitting the man with the high voice. Painted Tongue held on to himself tighter. The man was wailing now, and his pain filtered through the trees with the thud of boots and open hands on flesh followed by screams. Painted Tongue searched hard for his warrior song but it wouldn't come. This man needs help, he hummed. They are hurting him bad.

This was an empty part of the huge park. There was no one around but Painted Tongue and the men hidden in the trees. He could hear the honks of cars far off on Lakeshore Boulevard hundreds of metres over one hill and another. Finally it got quiet again. After a little silence, Painted Tongue stood in a crouch. He wanted to look in the trees. The voices erupted again.

Motherfuckers! the wounded man screamed.

He's running. Grab the bitch!

A naked man came dashing from the trees towards Painted Tongue with three men close behind him. He was streaked red in the moonlight and ran hard, but with a limp. Painted Tongue dropped quickly into the shadow of a bush without the man's seeing him and held himself rigid as the other men swooped by.

They quickly caught up to the wounded one and tackled him. They took turns kicking his head and groin and stomach with their boots. Two had shaved heads and the other wore his hair long like Painted Tongue. They chanted, Dirty faggot, cocksucking faggot, through their clenched teeth. Painted Tongue tried again, but his warrior song would not come. The long-haired one pulled out a knife.

Don't. Please don't, the man on the ground said, curled up and holding himself. He was close enough to Painted Tongue that Painted Tongue could taste the copper tang of fear in his own mouth. The long-haired one dropped down on his knees with both hands held above his head.

Do it, one of the standing men hissed.

Stick him. Fuck him, the other said.

Die, bitch, the long-hair said after a few seconds, then swung down hard. The bleeding man howled. Painted Tongue shivered as the three men ran into the darkness.

Painted Tongue stood up after a long while. He slowly walked up to the body on the ground, bent over him and peered down. The man blinked at Painted Tongue and Painted Tongue jumped back quickly. The man's chest was gurgling and his lips opened just a little. Then his chest stopped moving. Painted Tongue's legs told him to run away as fast as he could, but instead he hummed a death chant for the man slowly and quietly. Your last moments were spent in fear, he hummed, but now you are peaceful and sink into the waters of sleep. Your last moments were spent in fear and I could not help you, but now all is peaceful as you slip into sleep.

Painted Tongue thought he could see his own face for a second, reflected in the man's open eyes, but knew that wasn't possible. He realized as he ran back towards downtown that the man's last sight had been of an Indian standing over him and humming, looking down like a death angel, an Indian with a hook nose and black hair almost long enough that it tickled the man's face.

Two hours later, Painted Tongue made his way into a bar at Queen Street and Richmond and took a seat in one of the dark corners. He couldn't sit quietly, so he got up and went into the bathroom and washed his hands and face, then went back to his chair. He wanted a drink. He wanted to get fucked-up drunk. He'd seen two other men die in two years on the street, but both had been old rubbies whose bodies just gave up and quit on them. Those two had prayed every day for death to come and take them. This was different. There was no honour or peace in this man's death. Painted Tongue sat in his chair, rocking, and hummed, Bad trouble, there is bad trouble and I've seen it. He hummed it over and over again. Repeat one hundred times. Write it on the blackboard one thousand times. The old men and younger boys and girls who were crowded around the bar ignored Painted Tongue. They did not understand. When one of them got up to use the washroom, Painted Tongue weighed the odds of being able to grab her unattended drink. He went silent and watched until the people around him forgot he was there. He spotted a full bottle of Labatt's 50 on a table near him and, when nobody was looking, he grabbed it and drank it down in two gulps.

That's it, that's all, rubby, a big man said, grabbing Painted Tongue by the back of the neck and dragging him out the door. He heard people laughing as the big man gave him a final push, Painted Tongue's elbow whacking hard against the door frame. I will cut your throat a wide smile with a bottle neck, Painted Tongue moaned as he made his way down the sidewalk. I will count coup on you, smelly bouncer, and take your woman for my own. I will teach your children that you are worthless shit.

He walked to Kensington Market cradling his bruised elbow and found an alley that didn't stink so badly of fish. No one bothered you in the alleys here where crates of rotting meat and vegetables were left out for the garbagemen to pick up late at night. Painted Tongue held his hurt elbow as he sat in the alley and thought hard. Other than the beer, he hadn't had a drink since morning. His body shook and shivered. He wanted a gulp of vodka to take the copper taste out of his mouth. To calm himself he thought about when he was a child and he would sit with his mother on the rock jetty facing Christian Island. She liked to tell him stories of his father and the Ojibwe.

He hummed himself the story of his father, and his mother's words came pouring back in the alley. His father had been hired with other men at the Cedar Point Rez to build bridges in the bay, roads running up into the sky that linked the big islands to the mainland. The government thought that Indians had good balance high up in the air above the water, so building bridges was fine work for them. And the Indians were good at their job, Painted Tongue's mother told Painted Tongue as they sat on the jetty facing Christian Island and its lighthouse. The Indians scampered around on thin beams way up in the sky and the men didn't use safety lines because safety lines were for women. At Manitoulin Island Painted Tongue's father fell from a bridge and drowned when a big wind blew up off the bay. The Iroquois wind spirit — the blowing spirit — did it, Painted Tongue's mother told him, because the Iroquois and Ojibwe were old enemies. The Ojibwe made friends with the Jesuits long ago, and the Iroquois tortured and killed the black robes because they considered the black robes devils. But trouble between the two tribes had always been, from the time the earth was born.

That night he tried hard in the alley to remember his mother's story of how the earth came to be. He recalled her saying that before there was such a thing as land, a giant turtle rose up out of the water. Eventually, rocks and trees and animals and finally *Nmishoomsag*, the Grandfathers, sprouted from the turtle's back. Painted Tongue remembers the look in his mother's eyes, her stare out towards Christian Island. She believed the stories she told, and this made Painted Tongue want to believe them too.

It was the middle of the night now, and it would be impossible to find Kyle. But Kyle always knew what was going on.

He always had the right answers. Even though he walked a different circle than Painted Tongue did, they'd both had the vision of the turtle. Kyle's was in paint and Painted Tongue's was in concrete. Although Painted Tongue hadn't talked in years, hadn't actually spoken in words for many years, he felt he wanted to talk again. He wanted to tell Kyle about the man getting killed in front of his eyes. He wanted to tell Kyle about the huge building growing out of the ground, the way it resembled a giant turtle with its roof nearly in place. Strange things were happening all around Painted Tongue, and they were frightening. All of these events were omens warning him that something big and awful was coming. A new turtle had risen on the waterfront, a new world had been born in front of his own eyes over the last year, and Painted Tongue needed to know its significance. Big men were hurting smaller ones; three killed one and another had smashed Painted Tongue's elbow. He needed Kyle to sit down with him and talk it out. He needed a drink bad.

He felt calmer just before the morning broke. He walked from the alley and began the trek to the lake and his boulder, walking quickly and quietly underneath the expressway. There were men who lived in cardboard boxes and old refrigerators there, men who didn't want others like them in their territory. They stashed bricks and pipes and sharp shards from bottles. They'd chased Painted Tongue many times before, whooping and hollering, shouting, Cut up the wagon-burner.

Painted Tongue made it safely to the water and shimmied up his boulder, then turned east to watch the rising sun. Just as the sun's rays crawled then shot over the grain elevators and shipyards, dense, low clouds scuttled up on the horizon from the lake. It wouldn't be much of a sunrise today. He loved feeling the sun's warmth crawling across the water and rocks, the heat settling on his face. He lay back with his arms outstretched, let his hair fall down the boulder's side, shivered in the dawn, then curled up to sleep for a few hours.

His stomach woke him. This day is the colour of a pigeon, he hummed, and the forecast calls for pigeon shit. His stomach was empty and burning and made him feel sick. He crawled from the boulder, dropped his pants and squatted. The evil poured from him in a stinking rush.

He was hungry and he needed food in his belly. Then he could hustle change and get a mickey in the afternoon. He walked slowly up to Spadina and Bloor, stopping occasionally to catch his breath. He'd considered walking his circle around the stadium. It would give him a chance to sort out the troubles of last night, maybe offer him a clear direction to take, but now saw that the construction workers had put up a large fence on the lake side of the stadium. They were already busy levelling the ground for parking spaces.

It wasn't a good thing to go without a drink for long. His luck had been bad lately. He wanted the man who'd been killed in front of him last night to have disappeared like a bad dream this morning. All of this was bad. No more walks around the construction. They'd broken his circle. No good could come from it.

When he walked into the hallway of the Native Centre, he saw Agnes sitting in a chair reading a newspaper. He recognized the man's face taking up most of the front page. Above the picture the words "Hate Crime" were written.

Ahnee Anishnaabe, she spoke, looking up to him. Hello, Indian. *Aanish ezhwebiziiyan?* What is the matter with you?

You've hurt your nose. Painted Tongue leaned on the wall. You look sick, she continued. You need food. I'll get you a hot dog.

They walked to a cart on Bloor, then cut up a side street to a little park. Agnes spoke to Painted Tongue slowly between bites of her food. He kept trying to sneak glimpses at her newspaper, but she'd folded it and left it sitting on the bench beside her. Your old friend Kyle is doing good, she said. The McMichael Gallery has been asking about him. He's got another girlfriend again, and they moved to the Beaches together.

Painted Tongue noticed that Agnes didn't say anything about Kyle asking after him. The smell of the cooked meat made his stomach feel worse.

The government's starting some new work programs up north, Agnes continued. It isn't my business, but maybe you should go back to Cedar Point for a while. You can rest there, maybe find some work.

Painted Tongue nodded his head slowly to be polite. Agnes stopped talking for a long while. Finally, she said, You can come over to my place and clean yourself up. I'll do some laundry for you. You can have a hot shower. Painted Tongue nodded a thank you. Again she went silent and they listened to squirrels and the traffic on Bloor.

When it was time for Agnes to head back to work, she gave Painted Tongue ten dollars. He knew that she knew he'd buy booze with the money, and her eyes told him she didn't like it but was doing it anyway. He held onto her newspaper as she was leaving. Agnes looked down to him, then handed it over.

Painted Tongue sat by himself and read the words. The man was a jogger. He was a lawyer. He was a gay. The newspaper was calling it a hate crime, a crime against a minority.

Painted Tongue hated when people called him a minority. It made him feel small. The police were looking for leads and witnesses. He wanted to leave the bench now. He wanted to go find a field to lie in and watch the clouds. He wanted to find Kyle and take him to a field away from the noise and traffic and all the people living. He'd seen the minority murdered. His circle had been broken. Painted Tongue would find Kyle and surprise him by talking to him.

Painted Tongue walked to the liquor store with his back a little straighter. I will get a bottle and pray for the spirit in that bottle to release itself and talk to me, he hummed. The best spirits are in vodka because vodka is distilled from potatoes and potatoes are the fruit of the earth and live under the ground with other spirits of the earth, he hummed, walking into the liquor store. But the man at the counter wouldn't let him come inside, so Painted Tongue had to give him his money first and point to the row of shiny vodka bottles. The man handed him a bottle in a bag along with the change, and Painted Tongue left for the Beaches in search of Kyle Root.

A small crowd had gathered on Queen Street near the Beaches. Painted Tongue watched from a distance as a man on a box in a shabby black suit screamed at the people gathered around him. The Lord told me last night, the man shouted, looking at the crowd with fiery eyes, that there is no place in sweet heaven for those of you who sin. There is no room in the sky for those of you who gamble, who drink, who find false love in a married woman's arms. The Lord will purge the wicked from the earth. He will cast out the cheaters, the homosexuals, the unbelievers. He spoke to me in a dream last night, and told me to pass the word.

Painted Tongue left the crowd quickly. He'd heard those

words before. Now the man in the black suit had forced him to remember.

A new world is coming, boys, Mr. Grainger, the white teacher, used to shout out the window of the rez school when he caught Painted Tongue and Kyle behaving badly during recess, chasing girls with garter snakes or taking the air out of their enemies' bicycle tires. A new world is coming, and this one will erupt in flames. There is no room for your heathen beliefs in God's heaven, boys! he'd shout louder from his window, his face red and shaking when Painted Tongue and Kyle laughed at him. The innocent will perish because of the wicked, and the wicked will gnash their teeth in hellfire. Hellfire will burn your heathen ways from your bodies and minds! Think about that next time you act heinously against Janine or Tom. The Lord is watching!

Kyle would talk to Painted Tongue about the cuckoo teacher after school. Even the students he gave A's to thought he was mad. Even though they agreed the teacher was a crazy old bastard while they sat out at the dock puffing cigarettes stolen from their parents, Crazy Old Grainger still scared Painted Tongue horribly, the way his face turned red and shook when he screamed about burning death, the spittle flying from his mouth. Kyle thought it was good that Grainger always separated him and Painted Tongue from the rest to scream at, but Painted Tongue, in some small way, started believing that he was worse than the rest. Sometimes even now he'd wake up sweating, the ghost of Grainger's face come to remind him of the Second Coming of the Lord.

Kyle was nowhere to be found. Painted Tongue walked west on Bloor with the setting sun, stopping in doorways of shops to take a swig of vodka. The nothing smell calmed his stomach, gave him courage enough to wander along Bloor. He could tell by the crowds that it was Friday night, the streets busy with students finished with school and people who liked nights late in the spring. Painted Tongue walked by the bars and stores with his mickey snug in his belt. There were a few good gulps left. He'd make it through to midnight when people were everywhere and easy with their spare change.

I will count coup on this man-made turtle, Painted Tongue hummed as he walked. I will count coup on the god with the white beard who wants me to burn in hell. I will find a thousand kilos of dynamite and blow you up, motherfucker. Kyle will help me and call it art. I will seek revenge for the gay who was stabbed in the park. Repeat two hundred times. Write it on the blackboard two thousand times then you can drink the rest of your vodka.

When Kyle was found, Painted Tongue would get him to take him to the police and Kyle would draw a glorious picture of what Painted Tongue had seen in the park. The men would be caught, and Kyle would sell the picture for thousands of dollars and give the money to Painted Tongue so that he could buy enough explosives.

At Bloor and Clinton, Painted Tongue spotted a man from behind that he thought must be Kyle, a man walking with his arm around a woman with blonde hair. He ran towards them as they climbed into a car, the man holding the door for the woman, then shutting it and walking around to the driver's seat. Painted Tongue tried to shout his friend's name, but only a hot wind came out. The car pulled into traffic just as Painted Tongue reached the passenger side. He pounded on the window and the woman looked up at him through the glass and wailed. Painted Tongue strained to look in the window as he ran beside the car, trying to see Kyle's face. The car veered sharply away and sped up until Painted Tongue was left gasping by the curb.

It could not have been Kyle. If it was Kyle, he did not see his old friend Painted Tongue. He walked back along Bloor.

His nose was itchy, the stitches drying into his skin. He sneaked into a bar with a loud band and went into the washroom. He stared into the mirror and picked at the stitch knots, six of them in a crooked line that ran the bridge of his nose. One by one, he found a good enough hold to yank five of them out. I will not go back to do battle with that fat nurse, he repeated over and over again in his hum. The threads burned as they exited. The skin on his nose mostly held together, but beads of blood popped up and ran in little lines to his mouth. The last stitch held stubbornly, so Painted Tongue took a gulp of vodka and walked outside.

He found an empty paper coffee cup. He squatted by the bar's entrance and held it out in front of him for coins. When the loud band took a break, the people poured outside and stood talking around him. A group of boys in baseball caps gathered near and talked loudly about Painted Tongue. The one with bright eyes looked down at him.

Are you an Algonquin? he asked. Painted Tongue looked away. Are you Cree? the boy continued. Painted Tongue pretended not to notice him. The boy's friends stopped talking and looked down at Painted Tongue.

Do you want a beer? another asked.

Of course he does, another said, and they all laughed.

Are you Iroquois? the one with bright eyes asked. Painted Tongue stood up angrily. His head was spinning, and now off the sidewalk he felt unprotected. He pulled his bottle from his belt and drained the rest.

I will count coup on you, baseball cap motherfucker, Painted Tongue hummed. The tones of his war chant came to him. I will take a knife and cut your scalp from your skull for calling me Iroquois. I will rip your ears from your head and eat them in front of you. He let his hand drop, dangling the bottle. The boys backed away a little.

Lookit that! He's got attitude, one of them shouted as they formed a circle on the sidewalk around him.

Painted Tongue began to pace slowly around the inside of the circle. He felt a warrior's control suddenly, all eyes upon him, watching closely his every move. When Painted Tongue walked by one of the boys, he'd stare at the boy's eyes until he recognized the wolf spider of fear in them. He walked carefully, slowly by their feet, watching their faces pass his. The boys widened the ring. Painted Tongue concentrated on his own feet moving. He picked up the pace. He could hear the pound of the drum in his head. The boys began clapping in time. Check it out, one said. He's on the warpath.

Painted Tongue reached out and touched each boy as he passed. He counted coup upon every single one in the group and watched the look of shame and disgust on their faces as they shrank away from his outstretched hand. He was happy. He was a warrior. He moved faster, bent far forward, lifting his knees high. He closed his eyes and danced the circle. It was effortless, like a strong wind picking him up and carrying him. He saw red behind his eyelids, then yellow and blue. In his mind it was he and Kyle running fast, chasing their shadows on a bright day in the tall grass, their shadows stretching in front of them and trying to get away.

They ran across the field that turned into a hill that got steeper and steeper. Kyle caught his own shadow and Painted

Tongue could see Kyle's body now, his thin brown back, his red shorts, his skinny legs pumping. Kyle was always the faster one. The circle of boys sped up their clapping in time with Painted Tongue. The hill grew steeper and the grass thinned out to smooth grey stone. Kyle was getting away. He was near the top where the hill curved round. Painted Tongue's chest heaved with the effort of catching up. He looked behind him for a second and could see the field far below. He was so high up it made his head spin. Painted Tongue reached the top and it was the stadium, a colourless turtle shell he was running upon. Kyle was gone.

Just when Painted Tongue knew he could dance no longer, he felt one of the boy's boots catch his foot. Painted Tongue was happy for it. His dance was over. He stumbled over the boot and the momentum carried him forward with arms outstretched, one hand still clutching the empty bottle. He really was flying into the air now, off the stadium roof, off the turtle's back. I am flying, he tried to hum. Oh shit, I am flying high.

His hands hit the pavement first and the bottle shattered. The long broken neck of it pointed up to him like a skinning knife. He wanted to keep flying but the earth was pulling him down, wanted to say that the circle had not been completed yet but there wasn't enough time.

BEARWALKER

I don't know whose story this is. All I know is that my oldest friend — the one I first rode bicycles around Annunciation House Reserve with; the one who, too shy to ask Pam Tozer for a date at the age of twelve, got me to ask for him; the one I shared my first beer with — is after me with a big Buck knife. His name is Dink and the Nishnabe-Aski Police Force told me to take this serious. They're blaming him for one stabbing already on reserve. As much as I don't want to believe he stuck Antoine Hookimaw through the lung and the liver, there's no denying Dink snapped not long after his trip to the Big Smoke, the megacity of Toronto. He has since disappeared into the bush. The doctors say Antoine is going to die.

The trouble started shortly after Dink and my little sister, Gloria, his girl, returned from Toronto. Their plan had been to live there and become, over time, city people. People of the Smog, my father calls them. But they ran out of cash after a couple of months and took their time returning home. I could see how easy it would be to run out of money there. I was told once that a bottle of beer at some nightclubs can cost you five or six dollars. Five or six dollars! Can you imagine? To tell you the truth, I can imagine that. There are desperadoes up on those dry reserves on James Bay who'll pay a hundred dollars for a mickey of vodka. When Dink came back from the city, he was so broke that people claimed he was sniffing glue and gasoline, and that accounted for his behaviour. He'd changed from a quiet kid, the best tracker on reserve, to a crazed bastard who beat up Gloria. Worse even than that, Dink made no secret of it that while down south he'd learned from a dark Ojibwe shaman on Manitoulin how to shape-shift.

I've had the ability to talk from the age of seven months. Full sentences in both English and Cree. I'd often, and still do, mix them up in the same sentence and not even realize it. My mother told me when I was still a young *geegesh* that I was on this earth to be the one to tell the *tipachimoowin*, the stories. This is because my mother is polite and could never get me to shut up. But her little announcement stuck with me, her saying to me, "Xavier Bird, I thought your father was a talker. But you! You I cannot make stop your foolish talk." She actually said this, "foolish talk." In Cree it's *pukwuntowuyumewin*. Maybe I remember my mother's words too fondly sometimes, more fondly than the reality. But it was her telling me that I was the talker, the storyteller, that made the biggest impression on me.

It was Antoine Hookimaw who explained to me that the next logical step for the right storyteller is to become a shaman, a healer. "It is one thing to talk to entertain, Xavier," he told me. "But it is a more powerful *menewawin*, a more powerful gift, to talk in order to teach. If you become a good teacher, you are on your way to healing some of the things that have gone wrong." It was old Antoine who was trying to show me that way. And it was Dink, my best friend, who stabbed Antoine and wants to do the same thing to me. I'm only twenty-six. Far too young for *nipoowin*. Who ever wants to die, anyway?

When Dink and Gloria came back from that trip, they were driving an orange Pinto with a big red heart painted on the driver's door, a diamond on the passenger side, a black spade on the back hatch, right below the fishbowl window, and a large black club like an ominous clover on the hood. Thinking about it now, I guess he was trying to send all of us a message. He'd gone into that big world with nothing and come back having gambled, gambled with the *omosomuk*, the grandfathers, and won some of their secrets. Dink even went so far as to strut around the reserve and crow about his new specialized talent. Of course nobody believed it, and of course we called him on it.

The day he got back, the moment he arrived in town, he was bragging. Even before I had a chance to see my little sister, Jeremy and Christine and Elijah and me were cornered by Dink. He brought with him a case of beer and this helped take the edge off his new-found ability to inflate himself. We sat at Christine's table and before the first beer was drunk Dink blurted out, "I've learned the art of bearwalking." We all just looked at him for a while, then went back to drinking our beers.

"You're a bearwalker?" Jeremy finally asked. Jeremy is 380 pounds, and when he breathes he sounds bearlike.

Dink nodded.

Jeremy wiped the corner of his mouth. "Well, turn yourself into a cow, because I'm starving." That started the fun rolling for a little while. Dink hated to be teased.

I asked Dink to turn into a crow. Christine asked him to turn into an elephant because she'd never seen one in real life. Elijah asked Dink to turn into a beluga whale because the sight of a beluga always made Elijah happy and giggly like a schoolgirl. With each request Dink just shook his head and looked at us like you look at little children who are stupid.

"OK," I finally said. "Something simple. How about a bear? After all, doesn't that Ojibwe guy, Oliver Sandy, down on Manitoulin claim he's a bear man?"

At the mention of this, Dink bristled, and I thought to myself, huh! Maybe he's going to turn into a porcupine. But he didn't.

"Don't ever speak the name or mention the likeness of Oliver Sandy in joking, or even at all, Xavier Bird. He has more power than you could ever imagine, more power in his foot than some *storyteller*," he spat the word out, "some storyteller with big dreams of becoming a healer." And with that, he stomped out of Christine's. Oh, we got a good laugh out of that. You don't grow up around here making big claims and not being able to live up to them. Annunciation House is a rough reserve. And after all, the four of us had helped raise Dink.

Dink's real name was Francis, but he grew up with the nickname Toad Boy and, when he was older, Toad Man. Poor Francis was born ugly enough to be given many ugly nicknames. One time a girl he was trying to pick up in Cochrane said, "Get away from me, you dink," and his new name was born. When Dink was a child, the white schoolteachers thought he was slow, maybe a little retarded. His drooling didn't help. Most of the other kids pelted him with dog shit, soft and stinking in summer, hard as the hardest rock in winter. So Elijah and Jeremy and Christine and me took him under our wing in grade six. He was such a pathetic little sight. We taught him best we could how to walk like a warrior, to never take an insult but to strike back blow for blow, even if it meant he was lying unconscious in the schoolyard with the nuns hovering over him tsk-tsking like a gaggle of grouse hens. It was the only way to survive. Slowly Francis toughened and drooled a little less often.

He moves slowly, as if he is under water or always walking in a strong headwind, and maybe this is why he is so good in the bush. My mother used to say that *Gitchi-Manitou* never once created a person without giving him or her some special talent, and Francis' is knowing the ways of the bush. He can sneak up on a moose or caribou and practically touch its ass before that animal even knows he's around. One of the craziest sights I ever saw was way up north in the bush, hunting one winter. I watched as Francis ran through a herd of caribou like he was one of them, the caribou ignoring him the way you ignore a bothersome friend.

Dink can live in the bush for days, slowly, quietly picking his way through the thickest brush, eating edible plants and berries as he walks, spotting animals even before the elder hunters are sure what's around. He has the gift in a dying culture. Once that gift would have been worth everything but now it's worth a few hundred dollars a week to Yankee hunters up from Michigan or Minnesota. Dink isn't an ugly kid in the bush, he is the man.

It's hard to travel anywhere within three hundred kilometres of Annunciation House and not find someone related through blood or marriage. But Dink was double cursed. He came from a dead family line. He was the last man named Killomonsett that anyone knew of. His father drowned seven months before Dink's birth. His mother died during it. He had no brothers, sisters, uncles, aunts, cousins. In the rough country of Northern Ontario where family is granted one of life's few comforts, Dink was alone, raised by nuns. The belief around the reserve was that when Dink's mother saw what she'd brought into the world she couldn't live with it, and any other living relatives died of the shame of him.

My family, we're big and noisy. I've got seven older sisters and six older brothers. When I came out, everyone figured I was the last for sure. My mother was in her mid-forties by then and, as far as I've ever been able to tell, I was an accident. But really, who isn't in this world? My mother was forty-nine when she found out she was *kekiskawusoo*, pregnant, once again. "Thirty-three years of pregnancy!" she shouted at my father when she found out. "You're cut off, you!" One month to the day shy of fifty, my mother had Gloria. She celebrated a half-century of life with yet one more child attached to her breast. "I can't even have a cold beer to celebrate," she growled at my father. But my mother loves Gloria. She's always been the special one in my mother's, in my family's, eyes.

Two of my brothers, Michael and Raymond, are sitting with me at our parents' kitchen table the day after my teasing Dink, the day Gloria promised to come by to visit us. We're drinking coffee and chatting with our *otawemaw* and *okawemaw*, our parents, inseparable after fifteen children, like two wings to the same goose. None of us three brothers says out loud that we're here to see Gloria, but when we arrived at our house and saw one another, we all knew we were here to see her. Gloria is the baby, the spoiled one.

We sit with our old father and speak of the spring goose hunt. "The *niskuk* didn't come in big numbers this year," my father says. "I wonder what happened to them down south over the winter. Maybe they decided they like Florida better than here, eh?"

"They're being overhunted by the *wemestikushu* down south," Raymond says. "And then their government turns around and says we are the people overhunting!" Raymond is the political one.

"If only they knew what bad shots we are, they wouldn't say that again," Michael says. My dad and me, we laugh. We're a lot alike.

"I don't want to hear no swearing," my mother shouts from the back porch. My father points at his ears and mouths, "She's going deaf," then says with a little volume, "If we laugh, she thinks it's about something dirty." We all nod and sip our coffee knowingly, as if it's a medical fact that the more babies one has, the worse the hearing gets.

"I'm glad Gloria's decided to come home," Michael speaks up. "Cities are no good for you."

"Wouldn't you feel lost wandering around in crowds of people like that?" I ask. "You'd always feel like you were" — I pause for the word to come — "surrounded ... by a bunch of white people."

"That's never a good situation for an Indian," Michael says.

"We're already surrounded by them," Raymond speaks up. "Just look at the laws we are forced to abide by. Turn on the TV and look at all the white faces spewing out white ideas."

"We're surrounded by them?" my father asks, looking puzzled. "The only ones I know of are those teachers there at the school. There can't be more than eight or nine of them." Father stops and thinks for a moment. "But one of them doesn't really count because he learned how to speak Cree better than most of you."

Raymond gets up for more coffee. He knows his arguments are like clouds to Dad's sunshine mind.

The sound of a car on the dirt road outside has us all straining to look out the window. But it's only Bert Trapper in his rattle cab, dropping off the neighbour, Old Lady Koostachin. The dirt kicked up by his tires hangs in the air. The shiny green leaves of the trees are covered by the grey dust of the road.

"We need some rain soon," my father says. "No rain all summer means a hard winter."

"Looks like the road needs to get oiled again," Michael says. "The dust is enough to choke me good."

We hear another car pull up in the afternoon silence. I hear low talking and what might be quiet crying. The car door slams.

"It's Gloria," Raymond says, standing up and walking to the front door. He opens it and in comes Gloria, with sunglasses on, looking a little chubbier than when she left, like she's been able to find enough goose down in Toronto. I think the weight looks good on her. She's always been such a skinny kid.

We all say our hellos and I point to the sunglasses she's still wearing in the cool darkness of the house. "Did you become some kind of movie star when you were down there?" I ask. She just smiles.

"Tell us about the south," my father says to her, my mother in from the porch now and hugging her, cooing over her.

"It's scary down there," Gloria says quietly. "Too many people. Everywhere you go, people."

"I was down there before," Raymond says. "When we did that march and protest over unceded lands."

"Here, take those off," Mother says. "I need to see your eyes to talk to you right."

She reaches up to remove Gloria's sunglasses, but Gloria reacts quick as a rabbit, stepping back and reaching up to hold her sunglasses in place. "What's this all about?" Mother asks, reaching up again to Gloria, this time Mother the quicker one, snatching them away.

We all stare at Gloria, none of us talking. Her right eye is puffed almost shut, the area around it black, circled by lighter shades of green and yellow.

"What's this?" my father asks. "How did you hurt yourself?"

"I ... I ... it's a long story," Gloria says. "It doesn't hurt as bad as it looks."

"Did somebody hit you?" Michael asks, his voice full of disbelief. He is six foot three and maybe the strongest man on the reserve.

"Was it a city person?" I ask.

"It was Dink," Gloria says finally. My first reaction is to assume it was some sort of accident.

"He hit you?" Michael asks.

"He's not been himself lately," Gloria bursts out. I can't picture Dink hitting her. "He's sorry for doing it," she says. "I know it."

Michael and Raymond are already in action, walking towards the door. I run to join them. "You stay at my place for a while," I say to her before my brothers can.

"Please don't hurt him," Gloria says. "That's not going to make anything right."

We walk out into the afternoon sun, us three brothers, walking long strides down the dirt of the road, looking for Dink. I'm torn. I know I shouldn't be. He shouldn't have hit her. But I'm torn.

We get down to the trading post and people hanging about know something's up. The Bird brothers are obviously on the warpath. It's the body language. Dink's not gone into hiding.

We can see his car a hundred metres away, in the parking lot of the Northern Store. Raymond and Michael point to it at the same time. We get there and wait by his car for maybe five minutes before he appears from the store with a bag of groceries under his arm. He's close, maybe ten metres from us, before he even looks up. He doesn't look surprised. He doesn't try to run.

"Wachay," he says in greeting. "What's up?"

"You know what's up," Raymond says, walking to him.

"And you definitely know it has to do with Gloria," Michael says, following close and to the left. I circle around to the other side, shaking my head.

"What were you thinking? We treated you like family for years," I say to him. He seems resigned to what's coming. He places his groceries on the ground.

"If you're going to shape-shift, you'd better do it now," Raymond says, reaching out and grabbing Dink's arm. When I grab his other arm, it's cold. Not just scared cold, but cold as a fish or a bottle of beer from the fridge. We start swinging, doing what we have to do.

We leave him conscious but with swelled eyes that will blacken by nightfall and bruised ribs that won't let him sleep tonight so he can think about what he did. We could have been much worse, but I think my brothers felt the same bond beginning to break that I did.

As I walk back home, I think about how Francis was, how he didn't utter a word the whole time, how when his eyes were open, he just stared at the sky. As we left him he uttered some words I couldn't make out. They didn't sound English or Cree.

"Don't curse me with your bearwalker bullshit," Michael said, acting like he was going to go back and hit Dink some more.

"It's not bullshit" is all Dink had to say, lying on his back. We got out of there before the police showed up.

Long after I'd gotten back home, what I'd done was still bothering me, so I went out to my old friend Antoine Hookimaw. Antoine is known for hundreds of kilometres around as a healer, a medicine man. It was him who first noticed something special in me. When I was just a kid he went to my mother and said, "You know, there's something not right about your boy." My mother agreed. He offered her and my father his help in the form of taking me out in the bush, teaching me to watch and learn patience, to do sweat lodges and other old-school Indian things. He kept at it as I got older because I had the desire to learn. I became his student.

I walked down the railway tracks a couple of kilometres and into the bush to Antoine's house. I guess he's the closest thing I got to a *moshom*. Both my parents' fathers are dead a long time. Antoine Hookimaw. Antoine the Boss. He's not the boss of anyone but himself, that's just how his name translates from the Cree. Antoine once told me about how names were given to the Indians by Hudson's Bay Company traders when they first came around.

"Those traders, they couldn't pronounce any of our names," Antoine said. "Those traders, lots of Scottish, they treated us like we were *awasheeshuk* with dirty diapers, but they had a sense of humour, some of them. So when they asked my grandfather to give himself a name they could pronounce, he told them Hookimaw. Everyone on the reserve got a good laugh out of these Scottish calling the little Indian who brought them furs 'boss.'"

Antoine's at home, cooking bannock on his wood-stove and talking to himself. He's ancient-looking and smells of smoke and his eyebrows are bushy enough to nest whisky-jacks. Whenever I visit him, he tells me about last night's dreams as he boils us water for tea.

His parents and his wife and two of his sons who are dead now come talk to him all the time when he is sleeping. They tell him how their day was and scold him for not eating right or for his rare habit of going on a bender for a couple of days, drinking bottle after bottle of Cold Duck. Antoine's father retells stories of how he and Antoine's grandfather used to live in the bush for weeks at a time, trapping beaver and lynx and hare. His father talks to Antoine only in Cree and his sons talk to him only in English, so there are many times I have to explain expressions his sons have used the night before, the best I can translate them into Cree.

There was a time years ago when Antoine experienced a bad sickness. He doesn't talk about it much, only told me about it once. He got sick so that he didn't want to get out of bed. Kids came at night and threw pebbles at his window or scratched tree boughs across it so that he might be fooled into thinking it was a bear. Drunks would show up in the early hours and talk to one another outside his door. Antoine bolted his door by jamming knives into the crack between the door and frame. He didn't want kids or drunks seeing him when he was sick like that. He lay on his couch for a week, sipping only water and sleeping bad.

At the end of that week, the Lord came with two helpers. They were all dressed in black suits with white button shirts. The Lord sat by Antoine for a long time, holding his hand and talking to him in Cree about scripture. The Lord talked and Antoine listened while the helpers boiled tea and swept the place out and fixed a couple of broken chairs and taught themselves to make tamarack birds using one of his as a model.

"I want you to believe in me," the Lord told Antoine. "My name has been used to pit Indian against Indian, and I don't like that. You can help me make a difference here." Antoine thought about that for a long time, and finally nodded his head OK. "I'm going to give you a special gift," the Lord told Antoine. "I guess you could call it that. You can see into people, see what is bothering them. It might be physical sickness. It might be something in their thoughts. I want you to believe in me."

Antoine nodded. The Lord and his helpers left. Antoine felt better not long after that and got up. The knives were still in the exact place he'd left them.

That was a long time ago and, even though he never talks of that incident, Antoine's reputation as a medicine man has grown. He's one of the few people with the respect of both the Christian and the old-school Indians around here. As he hands me a blue tin mug of tea, I know he knows something is up with me. He's good at that. I used to try and mask what I felt in the past, acting happy and silly when I was sad, quiet when I had good news to share. He always knows, though.

"He's back, eh?" Antoine says, sitting down in his chair by the stove.

"Yeah," I answer. "Me and Raymond and Michael beat him up today, too."

"I know," Antoine says. I look at him. His powers are getting strong in his old age. "My nephew came by and told me," he says. "There's no such thing as a secret on this reserve. Only old news."

"He hit Gloria," I say. "I had no other choice but to do what

I did. Dink knows that." Antoine looks at me with that look on his face, the one that says, "You're still just a novice."

"He's not the same Dink you helped to raise," Antoine says. "He started out different from what you wanted him to be, a long time before his *papanoowin* down south." He stops talking for a while, gets up and refills his mug.

"What do I do?" I ask.

"You avoid him, Xavier Bird," Antoine says, giving me a rare look straight in the eyes.

"What? You believe in this bearwalker thing?" I ask.

"You can't see electricity, and you might not know much about why it works, but it's there. It lights up your house. And if you aren't careful with it, it can kill you."

Now I get up and refill my tea. It's my turn to wait for him to talk.

"Nature's full of things that aren't good or bad. They just are. Storms, sun, lightning, animals. There are a lot of forces that are neutral, but when they fall into certain hands they can become good or bad. It depends on how the user wants to use them. You can train a dog to be friendly or mean."

"But do you believe in this bearwalking?" I ask again.

"When I shot a bear for the first time, I cried when my father and me skinned it. When you remove a bear's fur, when you take its clothes off, it looks just like a man. The old people believed in a bear spirit that was related to us." I look at Antoine in frustration. He begins to talk of hockey after a while and I know it's impossible to get him to tell me any more.

When I'm walking back along the railway tracks, I think about what Antoine said. It's hard to picture Dink harming me. The world just doesn't work that way. There's a hierarchy to things, and Dink was born lower on the food chain than most of us.

I don't feel like going home so I go by Christine's house to see what the gang's up to.

"You beat up Dink good, eh?" Elijah says. "I can't believe he hit Gloria."

"We didn't raise him to do something like that," Jeremy says. Christine shakes her head at the thought of such a thing.

"What do you think came over him?" she asks. "All that talk about magic, and his car!"

"I think it looks cool," Jeremy speaks up. "Every time I see it, it makes me think we should get a casino on the reserve and get with the times."

"Hey!" Christine shouts. "That reminds me. Let's go to the arena tonight. Big bingo."

I'm not much for bingo, but everyone else seems excited so I go along. The arena's crowded. The concrete surface where the ice is in winter is filled with tables. At centre ice the calling booth sits up on a square stage. People cluster in little groups and talk, waiting for the night's entertainment to begin. We get ourselves a table back to the left of the visiting team's goalie crease. I didn't realize the bingo was such a big deal tonight. The jackpot's for five grand, which is a lot bigger than usual.

Christine's got a dauber in each of her hands. We've had to arrange two chairs for Jeremy to hold his immense weight, one for each cheek. He leans over his card, his breath loud and raspy. Elijah, on the other hand, can't keep still. He's the one who's like a mink, thin and long and always jittery. He flicks his daubers like drumsticks as the caller calls out the first game.

Shortly into the game, a familiar voice calls out, "Bingo," and me only needing an I and one O to win. I look across the smoky arena and see that it's none other than Dink himself, wearing dark sunglasses. He's got his hair all slicked back with some sort of grease, looking like an Indian Elvis impersonator. Christine lets out a loud squeak when she sees it's Dink who's won. When Elijah and Jeremy see who it is, they both say, "Holy Wah!" at the same time. The caller has his runner verify the card, and when it's called good bingo there's some polite applause that's quickly drowned out by the chatter of the gossip. To my surprise, Dink actually gets up and bows. I've never seen such a hairdo in real life before.

Dink wins the third, fifth and sixth game and people are really talking now. I can see some of the old Catholic women crossing themselves when they look in his direction. Nobody seems too surprised when, ten minutes into the big jackpot game of the evening, Dink calls bingo again, getting up to take his little bow. I work out quickly that he's won almost seven thousand dollars. There's grumbling from one half about some kind of cheating going on, and the other half mumbles about some strong, bad medicine on reserve. I write it off to luck and consequence. After all, didn't a similar thing happen to Barb Blueboy a couple years ago?

Regardless of what other people have decided, no one is talking to Dink. It's as if he gives off some bad but barely noticeable scent, like the smell of sickness coming on, that nobody wants to be around. He leaves by himself, climbing into that orange Pinto, his pockets bulging with hundreds.

The days pass and things quiet down. Last I heard, Dink's gone off to the bush. No one's seen him, and I know he can stay out there long as he wants before he decides to come in.

Gloria stays at my house because it's the quietest. She's climbed into some dark corner I've never seen her in before. She doesn't want to talk to anyone or see her friends. Mother says a wounded heart needs time alone. I'm worried there's more to it than that.

I spend some time out fishing with Antoine. We talk of plans for the summer now that it's upon us. Antoine's got it in his head that he wants to go down to Toronto, see a big city for the first time. "I'm not going to be around forever, Xavier," he says. "There's things I've seen in pictures or on a TV that I want to see in real life. I would like to go up on that tower they got down there, stand on its balcony and look out at the sky. Pretend I'm an eagle."

"You'd hate it down there," I tell him. "All the cars and people always rushing around."

"I don't want to live there, Xavier. I just want to see it for once."

A week after the bingo, Dink's back from the bush, tearing around in his Pinto, spending money like crazy. His hair's grown even higher on his head. Elijah, who's knowledgeable of such things, says the hairdo's called a pompadour, and the rumour around town is that Dink keeps it up like that with spit and hairspray. A man using hairspray! Who's ever heard of such a thing!

Something's happened to him while out in the bush. It's like he's grown bigger. Not physically, necessarily, although he does look stronger. It's like he's grown in self-esteem. You can see it in his walk. It used to be he'd slink around like a beat dog, but now he walks with his head high, talking to anyone who'll listen. And what he says! I've heard from a few people that he's laughing at what my brothers and I did to him, saying that the beating only served to release more power in him. He's bragging to people that he managed to shape-shift into a bull moose while out in the bush, that he crashed through the trees all night and rutted with a cow moose at dawn by a patch of muskeg. He's told others that he turned into a crow and flew over the reserve a few days ago. He told Zachary Goodwin about the sturgeon he was pulling out of the river at the time, and told Old Lady Koostachin next door that the hole in her roof's peak is getting bad. All she did was bless herself and walk away. Dink has her spooked now.

People have started talking again. They always do. The old ones in the community, led by Old Lady Koostachin, began claiming they could see the black wings of death silently flapping about Dink's head. Other elders claimed it was *Weesageechak*, the trickster himself, who'd taken his body over. How else to explain the talk, the hair, this new, proud Dink?

I began keeping an eye on him. Not spying, exactly, but keeping track of what he was up to. Part of Dink's talk was about getting Gloria back. She was his first love, he was telling people, and she'd be his last. Gloria was his soulmate, so he claimed. I wasn't going to let him get his hands on her again.

Dink followed a certain circular route every day, I soon found out. You could find him in the mornings at the trading post, talking. But people are avoiding him more and more. If no one was around, he'd wander through the magazine section, buying whatever caught his eye — hot rod magazines, ones on fishing, women's beauty magazines, crossword puzzle books. Whenever something new came in, he'd buy it. In the afternoon he was at the Northern Store, wandering the women's under-wear section, touching the silky things and smiling to himself or juggling cans of Klik in the food aisle for the little kids. He bought many things here, too. Canned goods, camping equip-ment, an expensive fishing rod and tackle, a big shiny Buck knife. Late in the afternoon he'd follow the railway tracks away from Antoine's and disappear into the bush. I could never find where he was camping out. All the time I was following him, I knew he knew I was doing it. Trying to hide from him would have been pointless. He's too good a hunter.

———

I was following the tracks to Antoine's a little while later. The sun was starting to lose its heat and the shadows were getting longer. To the left and behind me I could hear something walking lightly, maybe a dog or fox, from what I could figure. It followed for just a while, then I heard it move quicker till it was ahead, then gone. Not a minute later, Dink stepped out from the bush. He walked to the tracks and turned to face me. We both stopped and looked at one another.

"Why you following me, Xavier?" he called out.

"I'm thinking of making a documentary on shape-shifters," I answered. "Their territory, their habits." I could see Dink tense up at the mention. It really gets under his skin when we tease him. He's always been sensitive that way.

"Don't follow me anymore, Xavier," he shouts to me when he gains his calm.

"Not till you stop mentioning my sister's name and forget about her," I answer.

"I love her and she loves me," he shouts.

"She doesn't love you, Dink. In fact she hates what you've become, all your bullshit. You beat her up, you asshole." I'm beginning to get angry.

"I didn't want to hit her. I blacked out when I did it."

"You're using drinking for an excuse?"

"I wasn't drinking. I just black out sometimes and don't remember nothing when I wake up. It's part of what I'm becoming."

"Don't use your excuses with me, Francis," I say calmly. "Gloria's already made it clear that you're not part of her life. You don't exist anymore where she's concerned."

Dink clenches his fists and begins shaking. I'm a bit shocked by this sudden reaction, like a little earthquake is in his body, but I try not to let on.

"Nobody can tell me anymore what to do," he says with a shaking voice. "Nobody will tell me ever again what to do or how to act. If I want something, I will take it."

I begin walking towards him, shouting, "You will not have my sister!" over and over. Something, some anger has consumed me, set off by Dink's tone, by the depth of his hatred for me right now. He turns and walks quickly back into the bush, is sucked up into it, it seems. I try to follow him, but he's gone.

I turn back home. Dink's intensity has jolted me into realizing that Gloria's not safe. When I get home, I find her in the kitchen, reading a book.

"Hey," I say.

"Hey," she answers, looking up from her book and watching me sit down.

"I saw Dink just a while ago, and something's up with him. You need to let me know what's going on." She makes a move to get up, but I stop her with my voice. "I'm worried, Gloria. Dink's acting dangerous."

"What can I tell you, Xavier?" she says. "What can I tell you that everyone else on the reserve isn't already talking about?"

"Tell me what happened after you left Toronto." There's silence for a while, but Gloria finally speaks.

"We decided to stop on Manitoulin Island to visit some friends after we left Toronto. Dink hooks up with this Oliver Sandy guy who lives out in the bush and who everyone on the reserve is scared shitless of." Gloria stops talking and looks out the window into the yard. "It's not like I was invited out with them to do whatever they were doing. The first time I met Oliver Sandy, I was on my period and he knew it. He told me I was. Like I didn't know it already. He acts all weird and scared of me, keeps saying I'm too powerful for him in that state, that I'm messing with his equilibrium."

"Do you believe in that stuff?" I ask.

"All I know is that I saw some weird shit in the two months we were there. I saw less and less of Dink."

"Did he hit you other than the time I know about?" I ask. Gloria pauses for a minute before answering.

"Yeah," she finally says. "It started one night a few weeks into our stay. Dink came home real late and woke me up. He was all excited like a little kid. 'Gloria!' he says. 'Gloria! I done it! I begun changing into a bird tonight!' I just looked at him. 'I begun changing into a bird! I stared down at my hand and it turned scaly, then it grew claws and then my hand was gone and in its place was a bird's hand!' I just started laughing. I mean, what else are you gonna do? He's hanging out with this freak who lives in the bush and they disappear together for days at a time, then Dink comes home telling me he's changing into a goddamn bird. I laughed and asked him what kind of drugs he was doing, and that's when he hit me the first time. His eyes went real dark and he slapped me hard."

I look at Gloria as she stares out the kitchen window. I let her talk more without interrupting. She needs to let some of it out.

"It was the usual story after that. He tells me he's sorry and will never do it again, but the longer he hangs out with Sandy, the worse it gets." She pauses again. "It sounds weird and nobody will believe me and maybe it's only my imagination because I'm scared, but he started smelling ... off. At first I thought it was because he was hanging out in the woods running around like a heathen, but even after I told him no more coming in the bed till you bathe, he still smelled. It was skunky, kind of, but real faint. You can smell it on him easier when he's sweaty. What else can I tell you? He didn't hit me often, only when I made fun of his new bullshit. But he changed, Xavier. Something that was nice in him before grew gloomy. Bad, I guess."

The sun's set and Gloria looks tired. "I'm going to bed," she says.

I sit at the table for a long time, thinking about all of it. I want to go talk with Antoine, but the truth is, I'm a little nervous to go outside in the dark right now and run into Dink. I never thought I'd feel that. In the living room I watch TV for a while, and by the time the news is on, I'm half asleep.

There's a scream followed by something breaking. I snap awake and sit up in the chair. There's some kind of late-night movie on and a woman in it screams as a man chases her through a house. I settle back into my chair and then Gloria screams and I jump to my feet.

I run to her room and burst through the door. In the dark I make out two figures struggling on her bed. The window's wide open.

"Hey!" I shout and begin towards the bed. The figure jumps up in the dark and, before I can do or see much of anything, dives through the window. It all happens in a few seconds. I turn on Gloria's bedside lamp, and she's on her back in the bed, looking frightened.

"It's all right. He's gone," I tell her. "Was that Dink?"

She begins crying as I go to the window. "It was Dink," she says. "But he was covered in hair." I'm looking out the window for movement. "He was trying to pick me up and drag me through the window." A nasty-looking little mutt sits on the road, growling at me.

"I'll be right back," I say to Gloria and run outside. The mutt is still there, growling at me. I walk to the road to look for Dink. The little dog charges at me, howling. I pick up a stone and throw it hard, hitting the mutt in the ass. It yips and limps away quickly, crying. There's no sign of Dink, so I head back inside. "He's gone," I tell Gloria. I lie beside her on the bed. "Maybe he was wearing a pelt or something," I say to her. "Don't worry. I'll sleep in here tonight. He won't come back."

Gloria has quieted. "That fucking Francis," she mumbles. I pick up a clump of black hair from beside her and throw it on the floor. We both eventually fall into a light sleep.

I'm out looking for Dink early the next morning. It all has to stop. Things are getting out of control. He's not at the trading post or the Northern Store. Nobody's seen him. I head into the bush, looking for his camp. All I find are signs that he's been around. An old fire circle, flattened moss. He's obviously not staying in one place for long. I don't know if it's my nerves, but I feel like I'm being watched. Heading back to town, I keep my eyes on the trail behind me as much as I keep them ahead. On the road into town, Dink passes by slowly in his car. The smirk on his face enrages me. I run after him.

I find his car parked by the arena. A bunch of kids are playing baseball on the diamond there, and Dink crouches by a fence, watching them. I grab a baseball bat from one of the kids and march to Dink's car. "Don't," I shout, swinging the bat and smashing the driver's side window of his car, "mess," I shout, smashing half his front windshield, "with," and the other half is smashed in, "my," and the passenger window crumples. "Sister," and with a mighty swing I bust out his big curved back window.

Dink is up and walking towards me with a heavy limp, but slows when I grasp the bat with both hands and stand facing him like a batter waiting for a sure fastball.

"Why are you limping, Dink?" I ask. "Anything to do with jumping out my window last night?"

"Actually, it was the rock you threw at me," he says. I don't let him see the little shock I feel inside.

"Your car will be you," I say to him, "next time you step near my house." I see that he isn't going to make a go at me, so I drop the bat and walk away.

I'm halfway across the outfield when Dink begins shouting, "You can't do that to me, Xavier. You've gone too far. There are things you love too that I can destroy!" I keep walking and ignore him, knowing how Dink hates to be ignored.

I stay up for most of that night, listening for signs of Dink. It's as quiet as it always is. I fall asleep just before dawn.

Not far into the morning, the phone wakes me up. It's Jeremy. As usual he's with Elijah at Christine's house. "Get to the hospital quick," he says. My first thought is that Gloria's there, but I can hear her in the kitchen. "It's Antoine. He's been stabbed."

I rush to the hospital, which isn't much more than a nursing station. Inside, the staff won't let me see Antoine. "He's in emergency surgery," the nurse says. "We flew a surgeon in from Cochrane." I wait for hours, pacing back and forth, cursing Dink.

When the doctor finally emerges, he looks tired and glum. "Only time will tell," he says. "Antoine's strong for his age, but he's very old. He's got a punctured lung and a lacerated liver."

The Nishnabe-Aski police interview me and I tell them about Dink's behaviour, his threatening words, his breaking into my house, my smashing his car windows. He becomes their main suspect and the search is on. It doesn't surprise me that he is nowhere to be found. I sit in the hospital waiting room all night. The nurses have promised to let me see Antoine if his condition stabilizes by morning.

In the middle of the night, I sneak into his room. Antoine looks tiny in the big bed. He's got tubes sticking out of him and his breathing is shallow. His long white hair is smoothed back off his head and frames his face. I hold his hand for a while and whisper stories to him about going fishing and to the goose blinds. At one point, his hand squeezes mine. I'm not sure if it's him or just a muscle quiver.

There are two news trucks parked outside the hospital in the morning. One is from Timmins, but the other has driven all the way up from Toronto. I'm told by Christine that Old Lady Koostachin got on the phone after the stabbing and spoke of shape-shifters and murder. The news has spread like bushfire all the way to the big city way down south. "It's a human-interest slash crime story with some mystical Indian stuff thrown in," I hear a cameraman say in the hospital cafeteria.

By noon, four or five more camera crews have arrived. All

the big networks are represented, CBC National, CITY, CFTO. Reporters and TV crews swarm around the reserve, eating up the tidbits about bad magic, interviewing anyone they can.

One of the first is Old Lady Koostachin. She wears her best kerchief over her grey hair and stands proudly but nervously beside the reporter. Her English isn't that good so her granddaughter stands beside her and translates. The reporter's a pretty, serious blonde woman who comes off as talking down to Mrs. Koostachin.

"So the belief," the reporter says, "among your people, among your tribe, is that Francis Killomonsett is a bearwalker, somebody who can physically transform himself into an animal of his choosing?"

Old Lady Koostachin's granddaughter tries to translate as best she can, but it's obvious she's having trouble. Her grandmother speaks quickly, waving her hands. She goes on for a while and the interviewer begins looking nervous, but finally she stops her monologue. The interviewer moves her microphone to the granddaughter.

"Grandma says that Francis has been spying on her, that he turned into a crow and has been looking at her through a hole in her roof. Grandma says that this is the way the government forces elders to live — in conditions so bad that men disguised as crows can peek at defenceless old ladies whenever they want." The interviewer doesn't know what to make of that. She nods understandingly and moves on to others in the crowd.

By that afternoon, every Indian on the reserve is an expert on shape-shifting and all other things native. Paul Martin brushes his hair back with his hand and talks about how Dink comes from a long line of evil medicine men. When asked if he believes Dink is responsible for stabbing Antoine, Paul looks squarely at the camera and says, "Oh sure, eh. Everybody's known for a long time that Dink was heading for trouble."

Jeremy and Christine and Elijah get into things too. I'm talking with them in front of the hospital when a camera crew pulls up to us and asks for an interview. I walk into the shade of the hospital. Last thing I want right now is to be on TV in some big city. But the others are more than happy to accept. A reporter from Huntsville with hair not too different from Dink's new look interviews them with the hospital sign behind.

"This is Bill Blair reporting live from Annunciation House Reserve on the James Bay frontier. A story of legendary proportions seems to be unfolding here on this semi-isolated reservation two hundred kilometres of mostly dirt road north of the Trans-Canada Highway and Constance Lake. An elder here, reportedly a medicine man, was brutally stabbed early yesterday morning. The prime suspect is one Francis Killomonsett, a young drifter from this same reserve. And get this, folks; talk here is that he is a bearwalker. For those of you not schooled in Native lore, a bearwalker is what the indigenous inhabitants around here refer to as a shape-shifter, a man capable of physically transforming into an animal. I have with me here three acquaintances of Mr. Killomonsett: Jeremy Blueboy, Christine Okimah and Elijah Whiskeyjack. The first question I have to ask all of you is, how much of this shape-shifter talk is folklore, and how much is reality?" The interviewer puts the mike in front of the three of them. They look at one another, no one wanting to speak first. Finally, Christine leans forward to say something.

"Shit yeah, it's true." The interviewer looks at her, horrified. "Excuse my French. Yeah, Dink can turn into an animal if he wants. Just the other night he turned into a sasquatch and tried to kidnap our friend Xavier's sister, Gloria, from her bedroom."

"A sasquatch?" the interviewer repeats with disbelief.

"Yeah, you know, a Bigfoot. All hair and stinky and shit."

"And after that," Jeremy pipes in, "he turned himself into a mutt and Xavier threw a rock at him and hit him in the ass so hard he was limping the next day."

"And before that, he was a crow," Elijah adds, grabbing the microphone with his meaty fist. "And he spied on Old Lady Koostachin walking around naked in her house." The interviewer doesn't know what to say.

"Who is this Xavier who seems to be such a vital player in the unfolding drama?" he finally asks when Elijah gives him the microphone back.

"Xavier, he's our buddy," Jeremy says. "We all helped him raise Dink since he was just a little kid 'cause he's got no family."

"And Dink dates, or should I say was dating Xavier's sister Gloria," Christine says, "until he got all freaky on her and beat her up a few times. That's when Xavier and two of his brothers beat the shit out of Dink."

"And Dink stabbed Antoine in revenge," Elijah adds. "Because Antoine is Xavier's spirit teacher."

The interviewer gets a gleam in his eye suddenly. "So what we have here is a classic example of good versus evil playing itself out in front of us. You heard it here first," the announcer says, looking straight into the camera. "A battle of darkness versus light, man versus manimal. All of our prayers tonight go out to Antoine Hookimaw, medicine man, healer, struck down in cold blood by a shape-shifter. This is Bill Blair, reporting live from Annunciation House Reservation in the Ontario wilderness."

The camera and lights shut off and Bill Blair hands the mike to his assistant and asks the three where he can find me.

"Well, if you look right there, you could ask him yourself, eh," Christine says, pointing to me. Bill Blair looks to me and I shake my head no. He calls to his cameraman to start rolling and grabs his mike back. Lights flash onto me and I dart quick as I can through the hospital doors. I turn to see the crew following me in and the police stopping them, the camera on me. I can just see my picture on the news tonight, looking scared, a caption under it reading, "Xavier Rabbit."

Over the next couple of days I expect things to die down, but the craziness only increases. There's a carnival atmosphere on the reserve, little kids running around and jumping up and down in front of the cameras, long-haired and dirty-faced. Some of the warrior types are taking potshots at any poor crow or reservation mutt that comes into sight. There must be enough film shot of the reserve to make a documentary about it by now. But still no Dink.

As it turns out, Gloria and I are close seconds to Dink in terms of people wanting interviews. Bill Blair has hit on the angle, and since Antoine, the good side in the epic struggle, is still unconscious, we've taken his place. We hide out at my home with the curtains drawn, sneaking around after dark to visit friends.

Gloria is getting antsy for other reasons as well. Whenever she peeks out the curtains to see who's around and spots a dog or bird, she's worried it's him.

While we're eating dinner, a big housefly lands on the table between Gloria and me. It walks around like it owns the place and, if we didn't know better, acts like it's studying us.

"Do you think Dink could turn into a fly or a bug if he wanted to?" she asks.

"I don't know," I say, shaking my fork at the fly. It doesn't move.

"Say that fly's Dink," Gloria says. "Do you think he's seeing us like a fly does right now? I mean, does he see a whole bunch of me like in a kaleidoscope, like flies do, or does he see just one of me, big as a mountain, looking down at him?"

"I don't know," I answer. "Do you think he sees this napkin?" I flick my napkin and squash the fly into a gooey blob of black and yellow on the table. "Do you think that would sting if it was Dink?" I ask. We both look at each other and laugh.

The manhunt for Dink has grown from a few tribal cops scouring the bush to a detail of OPP with dogs and a command post just off reserve. Since Dink is possibly on Crown land, the OPP say they have to be involved. Media coverage seems to make them nervous and official. All of us who know Dink laugh at the idea of the Provincial Police being able to find him, even with dogs. Dink is a master. If the dogs pick up his scent, they won't be able to stay on it for long, considering all the muskeg and rivers Dink knows about.

What's more dangerous for Dink than dogs is the limelight. We all know he must be going crazy out there, watching the lights and cameras and the reporters who want him. Not wanting to blow all those chances to boast in front of the cameras is what the smart ones are betting will lure him in.

It takes the police a couple of days of interviewing witnesses and of having officers coming in from the bush exhausted and bitten half to death by blackflies before they recognize the trap at their disposal. Dink is starving out there, not for food but for the attention he's always wanted. Be patient enough, the cops come to realize, and the fox won't be able to resist any longer. He'll be drawn in by the media he's responsible for bringing here in the first place.

Dink surprises me by coming in sooner than I predicted. It's sunset, four nights after Antoine's stabbing, and Antoine is still in intensive care and not able to talk. His heartbeat's so weak that they can't even fly him out. But I make sure to be by his bedside whenever they let me, trying to nurse him back with my stories.

Dink appears with the sun setting behind his shoulder, highlighting his pompadour and the swarm of bugs that have taken to it like a halo around him. He walks straight up to the band office and is circled so quick by camera crews and interviewers that the police have trouble getting to him.

"I want to talk," he shouts, and the OPP start moving in on him, pushing through the crowd like hungry wolves. The Nishnabe-Aski see what's going on, see that the OPP are trying to undermine their power in front of the spotlight. The tribal sergeant shouts out, "OPP, you are commanded to stand down on Cree territory," but is ignored. Indians start grumbling immediately, getting tussled out of the way by beefy white cops. Dink stands in the middle of the pushing crowd like a raccoon in headlights, blinded and staring. He regains his composure and tries to speak. The cops rush in and grab him roughly, throwing him onto the ground on his stomach. Kneeling on his back, they handcuff him.

"This isn't a press conference," the OPP sergeant shouts, as much for the ears of the TV crews as for Dink's. The police have no choice but to drag him through the pack of cameras and lights and angry Indians.

"Let me talk," Dink shouts as he is forced along to a waiting police cruiser. "This is all for me!" When he shouts that, I don't think there's an Indian on reserve who doesn't feel sorry for sad little Dink at that moment.

The cops drag him right past me. He sees me and tries to say something to me. I reach a hand to him but he's stuffed head-first into the cruiser. They slam the door and the Dink I knew when I was young, the scared little kid always being picked on and beat up, is staring out the window at me.

"Change," I mouth to him through the closed window. He just stares back at me with pleading eyes. "Change," I whisper again. The cruiser takes off, spitting gravel at me.

It doesn't take long for things to get back to normal. Dink not doing something dramatic like turning into a mad bear or rabid wolf was a letdown for the newspeople. When they saw the story was going to be wrecked by a slow court system with no understanding of pacing, they packed up their gear and got off reserve. The OPP took Dink down south to a medium-security holding facility to await trial.

Slowly, Antoine started feeling better. They took him out of intensive care and put him in a normal room. I visited him every day and told him stories, slowly bringing him back to health. It was a proud moment for me when he admitted that my stories had helped him regain consciousness. "I just couldn't lie there no more, listening to you go on with the same stories over and over again. I could either die to escape it, or wake up so I could tell you to be quiet. I chose waking up."

After a while, Antoine was able to sit up. We talked about all the crazy events of the summer. One day, Antoine said, "You know, I don't blame Francis for what he did to me. There was a lot of pressure on him. He was always the underdog and all he wanted was some recognition. He just got involved with the wrong kind. That can happen."

I nodded. "I can't picture him doing too well in a cell," I said. "He's a bush man. Being locked up will kill him." It was Antoine's turn to nod.

"I'll speak at his trial," Antoine said. "Tell the courts what they want to hear. Tell them a story about evil *windigo* spirits entering Francis' body, and when I was trying to exorcise them it was them who stabbed me and not Francis. It'll work. I'll tell them I don't want no charges pressed."

I knew it would work, too.

But there wasn't a chance for a trial to happen. A month and a half after Dink's capture, he just disappeared from the prison. The police were baffled. There was another manhunt, but it couldn't turn up a single lead. The media got stirred again for a little while. The detention centre was asked a lot of questions but couldn't come up with any answers. Over time, Dink was forgotten, just like he had been all his life. But everyone around here knew what had happened to him, or thought they did. There was talk of a Cree Indian inmate who swore he saw Dink turn into a crow in a corner of the exercise yard and fly away. The guy had a shiny black feather that he said came from Dink to prove it.

Not much proof, some would say. But for the ones around here, it was plenty.

MEN DON'T ASK

Not long after she's finally made her decision to do it, Sylvina is visited by a dream, a memory of her childhood. It is the memory of walking in on her mother and a man who was not her father wrestling half-naked on the couch. Sylvina was only four, and ran up and slapped the man's bare ass hard, shouting, "Get off my mother! Don't hurt my mother!" The man rose up and walked towards Sylvina, his big thing bobbing, angry at her. He smacked her with such force that she hit the wall. Her mother rose up screaming at him, calling him "bastard" and commanding him to leave. Sylvina remembers being cradled by her mother, squeezed against her brown sagging breasts, fighting the panic of suffocation. She awakes with her face in the pillow, rolls over and takes a gulp of air.

She can't fall back asleep, so she lights a smoke. Her husband is not in bed with her, she sees. No surprise. She wonders what could have summoned up that memory from the deep lake in her head. Her father left before her fifth birthday, and she never saw him again. Back when she was four and five, it was hard not to feel that she somehow was to blame. Sylvina thinks back to her mother and the different men who shared her bed after Father left. She fights the urge to try and compare the number against her own. The fear of slowly reliving her mother's life here on Moose Factory, day after day, week after week, year after year, keeps her far from finding sleep again. It is what has driven her to make this awful decision.

The pilot has no idea, Sylvina knows. No idea of what she's about to leave behind for him. He flies planes up to Moosonee, and a helicopter back and forth across the river during freeze-up, delivering passengers and supplies from Moosonee on the mainland to Moose Factory Island.

Her island. Her reserve. This place she so desperately wants to escape. She likes the pilot because he's tall and has a nice ass and doesn't talk much, like all the other white pilots. The other white pilots who come up for a couple of months each year to make money and the local girls. There's more to him, she guesses. More than this tall, silent type he tries so hard to be. Yeah, he's trying. Sylvina sees the tiny cracks in his act, like little fissures in the black river ice separating Moose Factory from the rest of the world. But still, he might be her ticket. She needs something to cut this invisible snare that tightens around her neck just a little more each day.

A couple of times now when he's taken her out, personally flown her in the company chopper over to Moosonee for beers at the Osprey, he's asked if she thinks he's cute, if he pleases her in bed. Men don't ask. Not the men Sylvina has known. They don't need to. They might have a beer gut or pockmarked face or rotten teeth, but every single man she's ever known knew in his heart that he was the man, the one. All the men Sylvina has known are warriors, little northern Geronimos.

The pilot's different. Oh, he tries to show the world that he is the man. But there's that hesitation, like a motor with shot timing. If she's anything, Sylvina's a seer. A watcher. She's good at reading men. The pilot was a sweet boy once who knew he was sweet and used it to get women. Now he's reached the age where the sweetness is an act and he must find another gig or risk becoming a hustler flyboy in the five years that cushion him from middle age. One night at the Osprey, drinking, Sylvina suddenly thinks that maybe *she* is the gig he's looking for. His very own *Anishnaabe* woman, still slim, with pretty black hair, who looks ten years younger than her thirty-four, only tiny pale rivers on her lower belly giving away the secret of her two daughters. The one thing Sylvina knows for sure is that one day she will be her old mother, seeing the world through watery eyes. This knowledge frightens her. There must be something more than this out there in the pilot's world, something more than this little life of hers in Moose Factory, which flies by as she watches.

The river freezes hard and the pilot tells her it's time. The cars and trucks can drive across the river on an ice road, and this has taken away all of his business. It's a strange start to this winter, one only the oldest on the reserve can remember happening before. The air has turned cold but the skies refuse to give any snow. Other winters the snow is already a metre or more high, the old men on reserve tell one another. This is a bad sign. The moose get confused and don't come out of the bush. The hunting will be very bad. Many hungry mouths in the old days. Sylvina's mother listens to the old men, warns Sylvina of the omen. Sylvina just laughs.

The pilot wants to fly his little plane back to his home and help a friend out at his shop, doing mechanic work until the ice decides to break up and people up here need him again. He wants to leave now, tonight, but Sylvina can't go on such short notice. "Tomorrow, early," she tells him and kisses his mouth, slipping him her tongue so he can't speak back.

At home Sylvina plays with her two little girls. Theresa, who is eight, gets sullen and quiet when Sylvina pays too much attention to her two-year-old sister, Peneshish, so Sylvina is careful to chase Theresa more through the house, pretend not to see her crouching behind the coats in the closet when they play hide-and-seek. Both girls are happy for this surprise attention their mother gives them. Peneshish laughs and runs clumsily through the house, not grasping the game, just its essence.

Peneshish is Cree for "bird," a name Sylvina and her husband decided on one evening shortly after their daughter's birth. They both liked the idea very much of giving her something from the past, of grounding her in a better time. Sylvina married her husband too young. By the time she was eighteen she realized the immensity of her mistake. She didn't even love him. Years went by, were swallowed up by aimlessness. Her late teens and early twenties, gone. What everyone else claimed were the best years of their lives, Sylvina spent with him. So she got pregnant, had Theresa, figured the child would make up for some of it. Then cocaine came to the reserve. At least, the first coke Sylvina had ever seen. And that helped things for a while, especially since her husband became such a wiz when it came to getting the stuff way up here. They had both been doing a lot of it when Sylvina got pregnant the second time, cocaine cut so many times that her nose would run blood. When the doctor warned Sylvina that her baby would die or be born brain-damaged, she managed to quit it all by the end of the first trimester. Her man couldn't. Instead he began doing her share too. Peneshish came out fine, but small. Still, Sylvina worries all the time now because Peneshish won't talk, or can't. Sylvina's mother has taken to calling her *Akakaketoot Peneshish*, Quiet Bird. Sylvina often wonders if her daughter's still tongue is due to the drugs ingested through her cord or if her name beckons old spirits who tell her there's no rush in speaking too soon.

Sylvina makes the children moose-meat shepherd's pie and buys a chocolate cake from the Northern Store. The meal is her husband's favourite, but he doesn't show. Out drinking or working a deal. It's just as well. If he does make it home tonight, he'll be too far gone to try and fuck her. Sylvina doesn't want him inside her. She wants to start things fresh with the pilot. When the girls are in bed, she calls her mother and arranges for her to pick them up from school.

"Why can't you?" her mother asks.

"I can't," Sylvina says.

"Why not?" her mother asks.

"I just can't," Sylvina says.

The pilot flies her south, following the river. Up here is dazzling blue. Sylvina can see the curve of the world. The sky is so bright that she puts sunglasses on. The land below is brown and frozen to a rock's hardness. Still no snow. It has become too cold to snow. Sylvina looks down at the river. It looks like a black road, she thinks. Frozen solid. Half a metre thick already. She can see wide pressure cracks running along its surface. The ice makes her think of her daughters, of taking them skating on the bumpy river, skating and skating for kilometres.

It's no good to think of them, so Sylvina takes her mind away by flirting with the pilot, squeezing his thigh so his knee jumps, running her hand up the inside of his leg to settle him.

She leans over and sucks on his earlobe. He acts like it's too much of a disturbance, but she can see by the way he shifts his weight that he's uncomfortably excited.

"Didn't you say once that this plane could practically fly itself?" she asks, kneeling in the little space between her seat and his.

"Sylvina," he says as she rubs him through his jeans, replacing her hand with her mouth, blowing a rush of hot air through the blue denim. He grips the U of the plane's steering tighter as she unzips and releases him. She takes him into her mouth as they fly over the dams. He moans the dam's presence to her like a faint-hearted tour guide. He cries out somewhere up from South Porcupine and they begin the quick descent to the airfield. Sylvina wants to think of it as a new beginning, but can't.

His house is small and drab. A kitchen, a bedroom, bathroom and damp, cold basement that smells of mould. He lives here, he says, because it's smack dab in between the airport and his favourite strip of bars. The first night home he takes her to a few of them — the Black Steer, Charlie's Roadhouse, the Bulldog. He introduces Sylvina to his best friend, Drew, at the Black Steer. "She's beautiful," Drew says, knowing she's in earshot. "You got yourself a real little Pocahontas there." Both men laugh and Sylvina blushes a little, feeling good, even though the compliment was a stupid one. Drew buys them all a round of rye, straight up, chased by gulps of Export.

It's eleven p.m. at the Bulldog and other friends have joined their group of three. All of them are lit up now, everyone shouting around the little tables they've pulled together, swearing and laughing and pushing one another. The men all comment to the pilot how pretty Sylvina is.

"You got a good one, bro," one says. "Just don't let her have no babies. It'll make her dumpy-looking." All the men at the table find this very funny, but their pudgy wives and girlfriends push at the men's arms in anger or look down at their glasses of beer. Sylvina knows she is prettier than the other women here. "Exotic-looking," one woman says. Sylvina likes that.

"The Indian women around here are all fat. And bad complexions," one woman beside Sylvina says to her friend. Sylvina was introduced to this woman but has forgotten her name. The woman turns to her and says, "Hey, Sylvia, you must be from a different band than the ones around here. They're all dogs, but you're not!"

"Must be," Sylvina says, excusing herself to the bathroom downstairs in the smoky pub.

She gets a shiver sitting, peeing. The high of a couple of hours ago has turned to full-on drunkenness, and it's easier now to feel the cold of sadness creep in under the stall's half door. For a while there, Sylvina was able to forget the girls. Forgetting her man is no problem, but Sylvina suddenly knows as she pulls up her jeans that there isn't enough beer in South Porcupine to drown her two little ones.

Drew comes out of the men's bathroom just as Sylvina passes it on her way upstairs to the noise and smoke. "Hey!" he says fast, reaching out and pulling her towards him. "Where you off to so quick? Talk to me a minute." From behind he puts his arms tight around her, hugging her so that she can feel it pushing against her. He grinds his hips a little.

"You're drunk," Sylvina says, trying to wiggle away from him. "You must be drunk out of your mind to be trying this with your best friend's girl."

"Aw, he won't mind, Sylvina," Drew says. "Me and him

share lots of things. He already told me how good you are with your mouth."

"Let go of me," Sylvina says as he pushes harder against her, biting at her neck.

"You smell good," Drew moans, grabbing her breasts and squeezing hard. Sylvina twists her body and slaps her hand sharply, palm down, on Drew's crotch. He cries out like a kicked dog and sinks to his knees. Sylvina is shocked that the simple trick she saw once in a movie is so effective. She's smiling as she sits back down. The fat woman who finds Sylvina pretty is in the middle of a joke about a man who's the world's lousiest lover. Sylvina laughs at that one, and the woman seems especially pleased at the response.

"She's a good egg, that Sylvina," the woman says to the pilot. "I used to think all Indian women were the same!"

"We are," Sylvina says, feeling bold now. "We're all a bunch of drunken wagon-burners!" The crowd is taken off guard. A few of the men laugh. The women smile with tight lips and look elsewhere. "You know it's true!" Sylvina says. She doesn't know where to take this thing she has created. Use it like a punch in their faces or make it look like she is Queen of the Cree and friend of the white. She just lets her mouth go. "You know what Jesus said to us Crees?" Sylvina looks around at the faces. "Don't do anything till I get back." Some more of them look at Sylvina now and laugh. "You know the one about the Cree girl who's getting raped by the fat guy?" Everyone is looking at her. "Stop it, mister! Stop it! You're crushing my smokes!" The whole table laughs now. Sylvina feels herself slip into their corner, into their pockets. She's not dangerous. She's a good joker.

"You're a funny one," one of the men says. "Not a peep out of you all night, and it turns out you're a regular Jerry Lewis!"

Drew appears suddenly, red-faced and sad. "Where have you been?" the pilot shouts out. "Looks like you got caught in your zipper or something!" Everyone laughs. Sylvina laughs especially hard, aiming the force of her breath at Drew. He can't look at her.

Even though Sylvina's had so much to drink, her dreams that first night are vivid and startling, ones she remembers long after she wakes up in the early morning. She dreams of her husband sitting in a snowbank, his eyes bloodshot with rage. Dark figures behind him, arms raised. The snowbank is cocaine now, and her husband lies in it, face down. Sylvina lifts off the ground and away from him, and she is flying in the pilot's plane, over the reserve, all by herself. At first it's exhilarating to hold the steering, to work the throttle, but slowly the skies turn darker and the plane makes funny, menacing noises. Soon the plane is doing the opposite of what she wants it to do. She tries to steer it down towards the earth but it climbs higher. She tries to speed up but it slows down until it floats high in the air. Sylvina's stomach rises into her throat as the plane begins to fall slowly, then quickly towards the reserve. She wants to scream but, just as the plane's nose hits the ground, she's startled awake by the thump of the drunk pilot's arm on her chest as he turns over in sleep.

Sylvina can't fall back asleep now, and she thinks back to her friends on Moose Factory. She has left friends who can see each other in the dark. Friends who can sniff one another out in a blizzard. They have good ears and noses, her friends. Her husband has the best senses of all, and uses them for all the wrong reasons. Finding the drugs. He has lots of connections, suppliers stretching all the way south to Winnipeg and

Toronto and even America. He has the senses to look for and find Sylvina, if he wants. She wonders if he will. When she thinks of her husband, she can't help but think of the drugs too. She misses all that shit about as much as she's missing him. The idea of them appeals to her once in a while. But the reality is uglier.

Two weeks later and the town is feeling as small as Moose Factory. This is not what I left everything behind for, she tells herself. The pilot is beginning to complain that their drinking is cutting into his savings. He's working at the shop, coming home later each night. He doesn't even bother trying to hide the smell of rye on his breath.

Sylvina would begin going out herself, but has no money. The pilot promised her the world when they first met, but she didn't realize then that it was going to be this particular one. On the long days he's at work, Sylvina wakes late, then moves from room to room through the house. She sits in each one and pictures her daughters there, each with her own room. She laughs when she realizes that the pilot doesn't come into her little day-time fantasy.

"Mom?" Sylvina says into the phone.

"Where are you?" her mother asks. "The girls want to know."

"I'm ... I want to come home. Send me some money. I'll pay you back."

"Not only doesn't Peneshish talk, but Theresa's quit too since she realized you're gone."

Sylvina pauses for a while. "I want to come home."

Sylvina's mother takes a week wiring her the money. It's punishment for acting so foolishly, Sylvina knows. She's taken to sneaking small bills from the pilot's wallet or jacket pocket late at night. He has turned mean and quiet, as if the winter cold has slipped inside his bones and hurts him but he is too tough to speak of it.

"I think you should get a job," he says one night as they lie in bed. Neither has touched the other for days now, since the time the pilot casually mentioned that it would be fun to have Drew join them in bed. Sylvina laughed out loud when he said that, imagining chubby, weird Drew in bed with the two of them. Her laugh hurt the pilot's feelings more than she could have guessed. He's barely said anything to her in days. Until now.

"I'd get a job, but things between us don't seem to be working out too good." Sylvina pauses and takes a breath. "I decided to head back to Moose Factory." She looks over to him.

"Oh," he says. After a few minutes of silence he says, "When are you leaving?"

"In two days. On the train."

The pilot doesn't say anything else. Sylvina wonders what it was that she ever saw in him. Tomorrow night she will go out and celebrate her leaving.

This bar is too loud. The shouting miners looking for drunk and easy ass, the band up front sloppily playing heavy metal, screaming waitresses. Everything in this town is loud. The pilot still wasn't home tonight when Sylvina left. She wouldn't be surprised if she saw him here. She lets a cowboy buy her drinks and touch her hair. "You got pretty Indian hair," he says over and over as they toast each other with sweet concoctions poured into shot glasses. The lousy band plays a sped-up version of "American Woman."

Sylvina looks away from the band, straight at Drew sitting at a table alone. He looks like he's lost here with no one around him. His eyes widen in surprise when he meets Sylvina's glance. He raises his hand slowly, not sure, it seems, if he should greet her. Sylvina turns away quick, but it's too late. She knows he's seen her but she can't make herself look back at him.

"You be my little squaw tonight," the cowboy says, leaning to Sylvina's ear, "and I'll be your Genital Custer." She doesn't laugh. The joke makes the sweet booze in her stomach burn. "Sorry," he says when he sees the reaction. He buys her another shot. "Where you from, anyways?" he asks after a while.

"I'm American," she says suddenly. She's never even been to the States. He smiles, happy. These are the first words she's spoken directly to him tonight. He thinks he's that much closer to getting her home now, she knows.

"You from New York State? Michigan?"

She thinks of pretty turquoise and silver bracelets. "Arizona," she answers smoothly.

"Shit! You're far from home!" She is.

He buys her another beer. The cowboy smiles and talks of nothing. She can tell from the cocky way he talks, from his eyes, that he fully expects her to come home with him now that he's lavished her with booze. But Sylvina is in control. She gets off her barstool and slips.

"Easy there, little darlin'," he says. "Where you goin'?" Sylvina knows it's time to sneak out of the bar. She'll go find another, avoid the end-of-the-night scene when he says, "Let's go to my place," and she is forced to talk her way out gently or feign shock and anger.

"To the little girls' room," she answers. She'll find a quiet bar, have one last drink, then go to the pilot's and pack her few things. The cowboy's had her here for hours. She's drunk.

"Godspeed," the cowboy answers.

When she thinks he's not looking, she slips her jacket from the barstool. She walks slowly in the direction of the ladies' room, trying to keep her balance. The place has become crowded in the time she's been here. Men shout over the music and slam drinks on tables, eyes wild with the night, on fire and ugly when they look at her. She makes it to the place where she must go towards the door to her left rather than the washroom along the right wall. Casually, carefully, she peers over her shoulder to the bar. The cowboy faces away from her, talking and gesturing with the bartender. The bartender's eyes catch Sylvina's. He winks. She slips out the door.

The snow has finally come. Huge flakes fall thick and quick all around her. Seeing snow for the first time this season makes Sylvina smile. It has already covered the ground. She knows the night's cold, but she only feels it tingle in the small of her back and harden her nipples. Her tongue is warm with the sweet booze and she can't feel her toes at all. Her head floats above her shoulders and she ploughs along the snowy sidewalk a block, then two, away from the bar. Tomorrow she will see her girls.

"Hey little darlin'." The cowboy's voice is behind her, startling her. "Are you heading back to Arizona already?"

She turns to face him. "No" is all she can think to say.

"No thank-you's for all the drinks, bitch?" he asks, his voice still low and pleasant.

"I had to leave. I'm not feeling good," she answers. He raises his hand to cut her off from saying more. With his other hand he pulls a long thin blade from his pocket and walks towards her, making her back-step into the driveway of a small, dark house.

"Take your jeans off, squaw," he says, smiling. Sylvina isn't sure if he's joking. She wants to believe it's his bad sense of humour, but he reaches out and pushes her hard so her ass hits the ground and her breath hitches. "What I tell you to do?" he asks her.

Sylvina is frozen. The cowboy steps closer. A pickup truck crunches by on the snowy road behind him. Sylvina wants to cry out. The cowboy is kneeling and in her face now, and she can't tell where the hand with the knife is. She holds her breath for the pierce and pain. "Take your jeans off, squaw bitch," he hisses into her face. All the casualness has left his voice.

Sylvina sees the pickup truck suddenly behind the cowboy again. It honks its horn. The cowboy jumps, then turns and stands. "You OK, there?" a familiar voice shouts from the rolled-down window.

"Yeah. Girlfriend's just feeling a little sick, is all," the cowboy answers.

"No!" Sylvina screams, not even aware it's her own voice. Her shout sets the cowboy in motion, like a grouse scared out of the bush by a shotgun blast. He rushes awkwardly down the drive, his boots slipping and skidding as he cuts left onto the sidewalk, just as Drew opens his truck door. The look on his face is confused, unsure, as he watches the cowboy run away. He walks to Sylvina and helps her up.

"You're frozen," he says. "Get in the truck."

His heater is running full blast. Sylvina reaches her hand to the vent and begins crying. Drew reaches across her to the glovebox and hands her some Kleenex. "Here," he says. "What was all that about?"

"He followed me from the bar," she says. "He had a knife."

"It's all OK," Drew says. "I won't tell him."

Sylvina is confused for a moment. For a second she thinks Drew is talking about the cowboy, but soon realizes he's referring to the pilot. "No, Drew, that's not a worry. We're basically broke up now," she says, her fingers thawing, aching and burning. She shivers, watching the snow cover the truck windows.

"You two didn't seem a good match anyway," Drew says after a while. A Shania Twain song plays quietly on his radio.

"I love this song," Sylvina says to break the uncomfortable silence.

"I love you," Drew answers. Sylvina bursts out laughing. This is all just too much. She's laughing and crying and just wants to be back home. She looks over at Drew and can see he's hurt and she wants to explain to him that her laughter is release, not aimed at him. She's just happy she isn't getting raped right now by that pig.

"Sylvina," Drew moans and reaches over to her, hugging her hard.

"No, Drew," she says, her laughter drying up. "It isn't what either of us wants."

"I love you, Sylvina," Drew says again, beginning to cry. "And all you do is hurt me. You can't even wave to me in the bar." Sylvina is twisted towards him in her seat, her arms pinned at her sides. It's hard to breathe.

"No, Drew," she says again, worried.

"I want you, Sylvina," he says. "I didn't want to share you with him. That was his idea."

"No, Drew," she repeats. She struggles against him now. He reaches up with his left hand and punches her hard in the temple. A sharp pain shoots in her head, ricocheting and popping. She sees black spots.

"Now don't you try to hurt me again, Sylvina," Drew says. "Don't you go embarrassing me in front of my friends." Drew punches her again in the same spot, one knuckle digging into the soft circle of flesh. Her head feels like it's been split. She blacks out.

What follows comes in flashes. She is on her back in his seat. Her eyes open to his face just above hers, grimacing and crying, kissing her mouth. Her body is numb from his weight. She sees snowflakes hitting the passenger window, sees his vinyl dash. She goes back into darkness. She comes awake again, tugged back by yanks at her legs. She looks down to Drew struggling to pull her jeans off her. She kicks at him and he shoves her hard so that her head hits the metal of the passenger door handle. Lights and dots explode all around her and she fades out again. There's a stabbing pain and a burn in her groin and she knows in the darkness what it is. She swings out at the weight on top of her and again feels the knuckles on her temple, sending her this time deep into the warm black liquid of the truck's seat.

After a time, the warmth begins to turn icy. Something is tickling her face. It's Grandpa, her mother's dad, Prophet, tickling her face with a goose feather, telling her a story so she isn't too lonely. "One time I was out hunting with my brother," Grandpa says. "My brother liked to make fun of me because I liked sleeping naked in my blanket at night. He didn't believe it was warmer than clothes. Well, one morning I woke up and my brother was gone and so were my clothes. I went outside to look for them. Nothing. Only my boots and my blanket. It was much colder than this, you know. Crazy brother. I had to walk five kilometres home through the snow with only my blanket.

When I got back to the reserve, everyone came out and laughed at me. Someone said I looked like a prophet, and that name stuck." Sylvina can feel herself smiling. She'd always thought that was his birth name. "Get up now, Sylvina," he whispers to her. "Get up now before you freeze." He gently tickles her face with the goose feather again and says, "Hey. Hey."

Sylvina opens her eyes, but everything is fuzzy, like a TV left on too late at night. Snow falls in fat flakes, tickling her face. Her eyes focus. A woman's face is above her. An Indian, silhouetted by a streetlight. "Hey. Hey," she says. "You better wake up, you. You're going to freeze there." Sylvina recognizes her. She's from a little reserve, Fort Albany, up north of Moose Factory. The woman is drunk.

Sylvina tries to sit up. The woman helps her. Sylvina shivers violently. "Somebody's hurt you," the woman says. "Look at you, *Anishnaabe* woman. You wait here, you. I'll get help."

The woman is gone a long time. Sylvina looks around but doesn't recognize where she is. A pickup truck passes farther down the street. Suddenly, Sylvina is more afraid than she has ever been that Drew will come back. She stands up and her head explodes with pain. She tries to walk but trips. Her jeans are around her ankles. It takes forever to pull them up and button them. She sits huddled on the curb, shivering crazily and crying.

A car pulls up and a bright light shines in her eyes. The pain makes her cry out and throw her hands up. Two policemen get out, hands casual in their coat pockets. "What's the problem here?" the taller one asks.

"Looks like this one's been brawling," the other says. Sylvina stands up, swaying, light-headed and stunned. "Maybe she got in a fight with that other crazy squaw we just talked to," the cop continues, pointing and walking towards Sylvina, his hands out of his pockets now.

"This one's definitely had a few too many as well," the taller cop laughs, approaching her from the other side. "Makes ya wish they'd just stay on the reserve."

The idea of more rough hands on her makes Sylvina go grey, makes her stomach rock. As the tall one grabs her arm, Sylvina reaches out and strikes at him, slapping his cheek hard with her open palm. "Hey!" the other shouts as he pounces and grabs her, pulling her arms behind her back. The slapped policeman, red-faced and shaking with anger, grabs her by the hair and drags her to the police car. Sylvina's legs give out and he drags her weight, grunting.

"Stupid bitch," he says. "Resisting arrest, assault on an officer, public drunk." Sylvina throws up from the pain onto the side of the cruiser.

"Assaulting a police cruiser," the other cop says, guffawing. "We got a real live one here." They get her into the back of the car. Her crying almost sounds like a laugh.

Sylvina remembers flashes of the drive in the car, being taken inside the police station, the place so brightly lit that she throws up again. Shouting. Laughing. Being fingerprinted and asked many questions, none of which she can make sense of. Her head screaming, pounding, her brain trying to break out of her skull. The bright, sick lights. The policeman takes her wallet, her belt, her shoelaces, her beaded eagle hairclip. He puts her in an eight-by-eight cell with a cot and toilet and nothing else.

"Sleep it off," he says to her. She wishes she could. Thirsty. So thirsty. She considers drinking out of the toilet like a dog. "I'd like to die," she says out loud. She considers hanging herself. Sylvina lies down, wondering if she'll wake up again.

Minutes? Hours? How long has she slept? The bright fluorescent light of the cell gives nothing away. The police have forgotten about her. The pilot doesn't care. Her mother doesn't know where she is. Pounding head. She can feel the swell of bruise on her right temple. Her vagina is on fire. Sylvina's afraid to touch it, scared of what she will find, some disgusting leftover of Drew. Her shaking sobs hurt. Just a drink of water, a shower, darkness. She can tie one leg of her jeans around her neck and the other somehow to the vent above. Then it would be easy. Stand on the cot. Step off.

The cell door clanks open. A new policeman holds out a sandwich in wax paper and bottled water. He places them on the edge of Sylvina's cot. She looks at his eyes for a brief second. The look in them surprises her.

"I'm sorry," he says. "It seems that the officer doing shift change forgot to mention your presence. Can I get you something?"

There is so much that Sylvina wants right now. The last day to disappear. To be home. She can't find words to answer him. She feels sick and ugly under his gaze and turns her head away.

"My advice is to go along with what is asked of you for the next couple of days, until the court backlog is eased, and not make any waves. Your hearing should be before this weekend but, if not, this is your home for the next little while. Hitting Officer Whitt was not a good idea." Sylvina listens with her head to the wall. "Volunteering information like your name and address can only help, Sylvina," he continues. She looks over to him quickly. How does he know her name? Then she remembers they have her wallet. "My name's Officer Johansson," the policeman says. "I'll be in to check on you every hour during my shift."

She wants to ask him for something for her headache, but in the time she searches for her voice, he leaves.

A fitful sleep. She dreams of her girls, of them dancing at the spring powwow in jingle dresses, in moccasins that Sylvina has stitched and elaborately beaded herself. Theresa dances a competition dance. So pretty. Long black braids tied tight and shining. Her dress flashing and tinkling its hundreds of little bells as she spins and taps the balls, then heels, of her feet in the dirt of the circle. Peneshish following her big sister's lead, spinning and jingling, dancing and clapping and laughing and winning.

Her coughing wakes her. Her throat feels shredded. Sylvina reaches down and picks up the water, opens it and drinks it all at once. She fights the urge to throw it back up. Her body needs this one thing.

She sleeps again, and her husband comes to her. His eyes are very sad. "Forgive me," he says. "I'm sorry." He holds his hands out to Sylvina. He's crying. She's speechless. She's never seen him cry before.

The sound of the cell door brings her quickly back to consciousness. Johansson hands her another bottled water. "You should eat something," he says. "How'd you get that bruise? You have to inform me if you want to see a doctor." The thought of a stranger's hands on her makes her feel sick. She shakes her head. Johansson hands her some white pills. "Aspirin," he says. "Are you allergic?" Sylvina shakes her head again. "I have to watch you swallow them," he says. She puts the Aspirin in her mouth, followed by water. She opens her mouth to show him they're gone. He leaves.

Sylvina knows a new day has come when she's escorted to the showers, a cavernous, tiled room with faucets sticking out of the walls. A big woman escorts her. Other than this woman, Sylvina is the only person in this place. The sound of the water echoes loudly. She scrubs and scrubs until the woman tells her it's time to go back to the cell.

The days pass. Three showers and she thinks she can still smell Drew's cologne on her. Johansson is the only one who speaks to her. He lets her know what day it is, what the time is, when the court might hold her hearing. "Only a couple more days," he tells her. "Monday morning, first thing. The Crown will most probably drop the resisting arrest and assaulting an officer in exchange for time served. But he'll hit you with public intoxication. Pay the fine, you'll be free to go."

Sylvina spends hour after hour sleeping. She doesn't have to think when she's dreaming. When she's awake, she traces her finger along a crack that runs the length of the wall. River ice. Pressure cracks. She pretends she pilots a plane high above the river. She's a good flier.

On Monday morning Sylvina is taken to the shower, then given her clothes back, washed overnight and folded neatly. She dresses and goes to see the judge.

"I'm mad at you, Mommy," Peneshish says to Sylvina. They're sitting on the riverbank looking out to the mainland. The sun is warm for April. In the four months she's been back home, she's been re-teaching herself to bead leather and has pricked her fingers enough times that the tips are becoming callused. A drop of blood for each row of beads, she figures. She's not enjoying the experience. "Mommy, I want you to play with me!" Peneshish says. In the course of this winter,

Peneshish's throat, her vocal cords, have learned freedom. She is constantly surprising Sylvina with new words and expressions. Sometimes, Sylvina can't keep her quiet. The ancestors must have whispered in Peneshish's ears over the winter that this would be good punishment for Sylvina.

Theresa refuses to stay with or even talk to Sylvina. When the girl spotted Sylvina and Peneshish at the Northern Store the other day, she made a scene of turning and walking the other way. She can hold a grudge, for sure. Theresa stays with Sylvina's mom, for the most part. Her mother won't talk to Sylvina either. This stubborn line runs in the family, Sylvina thinks.

"Play," Peneshish says, stamping her foot and looking at her mother.

"In a minute," Sylvina says. "I've got to finish your moccasins for the powwow."

"Stupid moccasins," Peneshish says.

When Sylvina returned to the reserve, her husband had disappeared as well. Four months later now and the afternoons warm enough to sit by the river and he's still not home. Nobody admits to knowing where he is. Someone must know, Sylvina thinks. There are no secrets among the people of this island. Peneshish has stopped asking where Daddy is every day. Now it might be once a week. Maybe it's better this way.

"OK, Mommy. Time to play," Peneshish says. Sylvina ignores her chattering. For Sylvina to give in is to admit defeat, and both of them know it.

"Come here," Sylvina says after a while. Peneshish is busy throwing sticks into the river two at a time, watching them race, talking happily to herself. "Come here, Peneshish," Sylvina says again gently. Peneshish looks to her, then walks up the bank towards her. "These flowers are for you, for your feet," Sylvina says, holding out the finished beadwork to her little girl. Peneshish looks at it, then runs a finger over the hundreds of tiny coloured beads stitched onto the moose hide.

"Ever nice, eh?" Peneshish says.

Sylvina looks at her own work. "It definitely isn't Mrs. Metatawabin's work, but it's OK, I guess," she says.

"What do you mean?" Peneshish asks, her eyebrows arched.

"Mrs. Metatawabin is the best bead-worker on the reserve," Sylvina explains. "I'm just saying I'm not perfect." Peneshish looks at her with squinted eyes, looking for words. She turns and walks back to the river. Sylvina isn't surprised to see her own mother in her daughter's eyes. Peneshish resumes talking to herself and throwing sticks into the river. Sylvina can't help but smile at her awkwardness, her strong little arm.

WEST
Running

KUMAMUK

Buzz on the reserve was that the wrestlers were definitely coming. The chief had worked it that eleven of the monsters would stay and do battle in three events spread over seven days. Every Cree on the James Bay coast was invited and with the ice road melted to thick mud, the only way to the reserve was by air. Air Creebec had already added extra flights. People for three hundred kilometres were coming. Such an event had never been attempted in so remote an area, and the council and promoters stood to make some very good money.

But money was not what interested young Noah. He'd seen the names on the card. The one and only Chief Thunderbolt, Protector of the Indian Nations, was coming. He was the warrior who'd developed the Strong Bow, and that move was feared by all his opponents. Although Noah had not heard of the other wrestlers, he'd seen Chief Thunderbolt on television before; the children had been allowed to meet in the community hall every other Saturday, if they'd done well in school that week, to gaze at the television and the wrestlers battling on the screen. And now next week, real live wrestlers were going to be in that very same community hall, fighting it out right in front of Noah. Not many events in Noah's eight years of living had seemed so exciting. He couldn't wait.

The day of the match, all of the smaller children were horrified, Noah among them. The wrestlers had brought bright lights and very loud music and an announcer shouting through a microphone. Nearly-naked men paraded into the packed room, hollering and beating chests and slapping hugely muscled arms. For the most part their flesh was ghost-white, but a few were bronzed dark as the Indians who surrounded them, and there was one as black and shiny as a Canada goose's beak. Everyone had expected them to be larger than normal men, but here in real life they seemed as monstrous as *windigos*, and their howls and shouts were just as scary.

The announcer continued rumbling into his microphone. Children clapped their hands over their ears at the booming voice. Noah looked around him at the crowd, at the children retreating from the front rows as the huge men scrambled up into the ring and continued their shouting and slapping. Noah was the only one to move forward. He stood in the third row all alone, transfixed.

There was a fat monster with a straw hat and overalls; the announcer called him Giant Haystacks. Another had long greasy hair and black makeup covering his eyes and was called the Diesel Machine. Another wore some kind of fancy army uniform, skin tight, with tall black boots. He had a tiny moustache and in his hand he carried a short stiff whip. The announcer called this one Fritz Von Schnitzel.

The next had a crewcut that was dazzling white. He seemed as if he were made of bronze and his arms and legs were as big as some of the kids watching. His stomach looked to Noah like the rippled wake his father's motorboat left in the river in summertime. This man the announcer named Beef Wellington. Beef Wellington looked straight at Noah, curved his arms in front of him till all the muscles in his neck and shoulders and chest and arms bulged, and roared. Noah couldn't help but smile at the attention. He wanted to lift his arm and wave back to Beef Wellington, but he was too shy.

The next giant wore a scarf made of pink feathers wrapped around his neck and a tight pink bodysuit. His eyelashes were long and black. His cheeks were red. When the announcer introduced him as the Pink Panther, he ran his hand over his long blond hair as if to make it neater than it already was. Then he carefully lifted one hand to wave as he blew kisses with the other. Noah heard some of the grown-ups behind him giggle.

The announcer's voice boomed out again, "One of the natural wonders of our modern world, the Orderlies!" Two men, identical, jumped up onto the ropes at the same time. Everything about them was exactly the same — their blue doctor pants, the doctor masks hanging around their necks — and each had the same tattoo of a naked woman on his left bicep. Then came the black man. His skin glistened with oil; his muscles flexed, detailed and massive; his bald head had a single vein standing out on the front of it. The announcer called this one De Stubborn Headache. Noah had never seen a live black man before, and remained as silent as the rest of the crowd in the gym.

Next to take centre ring was a mountain of flesh. He too was bald but, in contrast to the other bald one, he was white as the underbelly of a fish. Two small eyes peered out from his huge head. Noah wondered how this one could move in the suit of fat that covered him. The announcer simply called him Bulba. But it was the last two that most caught Noah's attention. The first one, Kid Wikked, wore a sequined mask and a white cowboy hat, white boots and white bikini bottoms. And then there was the other. Noah's idol, brown as the crowd, wearing a loincloth and tall moccasins. On his head was a war bonnet, the eagle feathers reaching down his back to his knees. On his cheeks were colourful lines of war paint. When the announcer shouted the name Chief Thunderbolt, the wrestler let out a war cry that shot straight to Noah, straight into his heart. Suddenly, Noah saw his whole fantastic life sprawl out in front of him. It was at that moment that he knew exactly where his life would take him.

Before the children and adults in the gym had a chance to recover from this onslaught of muscle and tight shorts and makeup, most of the men jumped from the ring and retreated, whooping, to their dressing rooms in back, leaving two warriors, Fritz Von Schnitzel and the Pink Panther, with the announcer between them.

"Ladies and gentlemen," the announcer boomed, stretching each word to breaking point, "our first match of the afternoon is a grudge match extraordinaire." Each of the men stood restlessly in his own corner, shaking out his arms and legs. "It's not a secret," the announcer continued, "that there's no love lost between these two men. In fact, Fritz Von Schnitzel claims there's no room in the wrestling world for, as he puts it, such an abomination as the Pink Panther." At the mention of his name, Von Schnitzel clicked his boot heels together and looked down his nose at the audience. "Von Schnitzel comes in weighing a respectable 238 pounds. The Pink Panther, 252."

The Pink Panther turned and waved daintily to the crowd, flipping his scarf of feathers behind him. Von Schnitzel strode quickly across the ring and pounced on the Panther's back, driving his elbow into the pink man's shoulder. The two fell to the mat with an echoing boom. Noah gasped. Von Schnitzel knelt across the Pink Panther's body with his knee. Each time he landed, the ring shook and a mighty *bam!* erupted. Noah didn't know how the poor Panther was able to take such a savage beating. He looked behind him at the children covering their ears and eyes. Some of the teenage boys smiled, and John Goodwin even shouted out, but other than that, the audience was silent and staring, as if they weren't sure they should be witnessing this.

Fritz linked his own arms under the arms and over the neck of the Pink Panther in a full nelson and arched the Panther's back up in an unnatural bend. Noah recognized this from TV as the dreaded Nazi Clutch. The Pink Panther's face twisted in pain. His makeup was a mess from the sweat, or maybe tears, Noah couldn't tell. The ref knelt and watched the battle carefully from up close. Von Schnitzel released the Panther, rolled him onto his back and lay across his chest. The ref, down on his stomach now, pounded with his palm on the mat, "One ... two ...," and then the Pink Panther roared to life, arching his back like a salmon leaping rapids, throwing Von Schnitzel from him. The Panther was up now, driving his pink boot down with echoing thumps onto Von Schnitzel's chest. After what seemed to Noah an unbelievably long torture session, the Panther dropped to his knees, straddled Von Schnitzel, held his shoulders down on the mat and listened as the ref counted. When he shouted, "Three!" the Pink Panther leaned down and kissed the knocked-out Fritz on the cheek. Noah heard the crowd gasp. The Pink Panther pranced around the stage as Von Schnitzel groggily pulled himself up and retreated to the dressing room.

The other matches came just as quickly and as furiously.

Giant Haystacks battled Bulba, two mountains of flesh colliding and falling with such a shaking crash that Noah was worried the ring would collapse. Bulba was disqualified for gouging Haystacks' eyes. That bothered Noah. Haystacks seemed like such a friendly man.

By the third fight, Noah was keeping a tally of the good guys versus the bad. The Pink Panther was funny. Therefore he was clearly good. Fritz Von Schnitzel reminded Noah of Mr. Daguerre, his French teacher, who had moved up here from Montreal and was mean and spoke with a thick accent. Von Schnitzel clearly fell into the bad category. Giant Haystacks was very friendly, calling out, "Howdy, y'all!" to the crowd and waving his straw hat. He was good. Bulba was ugly and a cheater. There was no question where he belonged.

The last fight of the afternoon was not so easy to weigh. Although the Diesel Machine had greasy long hair and black makeup that made him look evil, Beef Wellington, whose hair shone like the sun and skin glowed, strutted around, shouting to the crowd and bragging about himself. Noah didn't want to judge these two too quickly.

They were by far the strongest and most athletic, climbing to the top of the ropes and soaring off them like birds. And they were well-matched. As soon as it appeared that one was doomed, on the verge of a three count, he would arch his full body and throw the one on top into the air. The momentum of the battle switched many times. As the match neared its time limit, there seemed no clear winner to Noah. Beef Wellington grabbed the Machine's arm and whipped him incredibly fast into the ropes, but he came slingshotting back, running full force into Beef with a slap and the two would go crashing down.

Noah saw that by now the crowd was captivated, and in

watching intently they remained very quiet. Grandmothers leaned to one another and whispered in Cree, the children covered their eyes when the action became too fierce, the older hunters watched and nodded among themselves when an especially athletic move was made. But everyone remained respectfully quiet with the final bell. The ref announced a draw, and both men shouted and made menacing movements towards each other before stalking off to their rooms.

"The second of the three matches this week will be Wednesday evening," the announcer called as the Indians stood in the rows of chairs, wondering whether it was time to leave. The announcer climbed from the ring.

As the crowd filtered out, Noah tried to build up his nerve. Gerald and Thomas ran up to where he stood, close to the ring.

"Ever brave, you," Gerald said.

"Ever crazy! Did they get their sweat on you?" Thomas asked. Noah shook his head proudly.

"No. It was real loud, though," he answered.

"Come on, you," Gerald said. "We're going to the river. Breakup's any time now."

"We can play wrestling there," Thomas continued.

Noah just shook his head again. "I'll meet you later," he told them. "I got to do something right now."

The other two shrugged and ran off, excited from the action they'd just seen. The long winter was finally gone and the air was warm enough for sweaters or long-sleeved shirts. Winter's only reminder was the river, wide and white, still a couple of feet of solid ice but threatening to bust open any time now, as it did every May.

Noah walked around the foot of the ring, running his hand along its canvas floor that stood to his chin. He saw himself pacing like a wolf in its centre, waiting for the foolish opponent who would challenge him; saw himself launching on Bulba or Von Schnitzel and staring into their scared eyes as he sunk his claws in. Noah broke from the ring and headed to the wrestlers' dressing rooms.

"What's with the quiet crowd?" he heard Diesel Machine ask from behind a half-open door.

"That's the spookiest fucking thing I ever witnessed," another voice spoke out, one that Noah didn't recognize.

"Must be an Indian thing," someone else added. "They ain't never seen anything like this before. Half of them have never even been to a city."

Noah walked in. The men stared down at him. Most of the ones who'd been introduced were here in the big room. Almost all of them stood around in normal clothes now, but they still looked gigantic.

"Hey," Bulba said. His voice was high-pitched, almost like a woman's.

"Hey kid," Beef Wellington said, followed by the others. Noah just stood and stared up at them.

"You want an autograph or something?" Diesel Machine asked finally, the other men laughing.

"Maybe he doesn't speak English," Beef said.

"I want to join you," Noah blurted. The men looked at him and laughed louder.

"You might want to gain a little weight first," Giant Haystacks rumbled. He was still in his overalls, but with a shirt on underneath.

"How much you weigh?" asked Beef Wellington. "Seventy, seventy-five pounds?"

"Almost eighty," Noah lied. The men looked to one another.

"Let's see your muscles," Bulba said.

"Yeah, make a muscle for us," Von Schnitzel said. His accent didn't seem so strong up close. Noah took off his jacket, pulled up his sleeves and made a muscle with each arm, shaking from the effort. The men whistled.

"Not bad, not bad," Diesel Machine said.

"You look like a strong young brave," Chief Thunderbolt spoke. He had been sitting behind the other men, but now stood up. Noah stared at the big brown man, his war paint gone and his black hair slicked back. Noah had never been called that before, but he remembered someone saying it in a cowboy movie once.

"I'm pretty brave," he answered.

The Pink Panther walked in from behind, asking, "Who's the punk?"

"A kid from here. Says he wants to become a wrestler," Diesel Machine answered. The two men walked to one another and briefly touched hands.

"That's real cute," the Pink Panther said. "You're not big enough yet," he continued, squatting down on his massive legs to look at Noah. "Just eat a healthy diet and in a couple years you get back in touch with us."

"You got a restaurant on the reserve?" Bulba asked. "I've got to feed the beast." He patted his gigantic stomach. Noah nodded, staring at it.

"Yeah, we do. It's in the council building. I'll show you where it is." The men all stood and Noah led them out of the gym and down the gravel road to the restaurant. As he walked in front, leading this procession of giants past the little houses and the cemetery along the river, he felt as proud and important as he ever had.

Sunday morning before church, Noah's grandfather took him on their walk. They walked where they always did: along the Attawapiskat River; south along a path that Grandfather told him stretched 600 kilometres to the nearest highway, which in turn supposedly ran the whole length of Canada. Noah had traced the route on an atlas in school, from his little dot of a reserve on James Bay down to Moosonee and then farther south to Cochrane and the fabled highway. It really did stretch in either direction from Cochrane, like Grandfather said. Going east, Noah followed it as it dipped down to Toronto, then Montreal to New Brunswick to Halifax and the ocean. Going west, the highway stretched out to Thunder Bay, then Winnipeg, where an uncle lived. The highway's red line ran on through the prairies, then the mountains, before disappearing at Vancouver and the other ocean.

On today's walk, he and Grandfather watched the ice's movement on the river. Although the weather was warm, the ice refused to give up its hold over the water. "Any day now," his grandfather said, "you'll hear the cracking from kilometres away and think it's thunder, and if you don't run, you will miss saying goodbye to the ice for another year."

Grandfather pointed out some early geese arriving at their summer grounds, a small v that looked tiny so far up in the air. "We'll go to goose camp soon," he said, and Noah thought about the white canvas tent the family would live in for a week and the goose blinds he would help to repair and then sit quietly with Grandfather, waiting for geese to see the decoys set out in the water a few yards from the blinds.

They walked farther down the river without saying much, and Noah wanted to tell his grandfather about these wrestlers who were on the reserve for a full week and about the excitement of that first show and how Noah wanted so bad to become one of them. But Grandfather wouldn't understand. Maybe he could get Grandfather to come to Wednesday night's show to see for himself. After all, this was such a rare thing, such a special event, that people from other reserves had flown in to witness it, and every house, practically, was keeping a visitor.

"I have to get you back home so you're not late for church," Grandfather said. Noah hated church as much as Grandfather, but both of Noah's parents were members of the Pentecostal mission now. The only thing Noah liked about church was when someone got touched by the Holy Spirit and began speaking in tongues. Whoever it happened to either stood straight as a board and babbled, or shook and sweated and spat with every strange word. This didn't happen often, though. One man who came to speak at the church from somewhere down south spoke of a snakepit where the preacher would stand and never be bitten by the writhing, poisonous creatures. If his preacher would do that, then Noah would have no problems going.

Grandfather told Noah that he didn't like the church because it didn't seem to be doing them any good. There was hardly anyone anymore who did the sweat lodge or knew of the shaking tent or feared *windigos*. Grandfather said he had probably been the last one on reserve to go on a vision quest in order to become a man. He had gone out for six days without eating or drinking anything. A lynx had come to him on the next day and told him everything he would need to live life properly. The lynx had just sat down and begun talking to him with a human voice. Grandfather had wanted Noah's father to do a vision quest, but the residential school had forbidden it. Grandfather talked to Noah now of the same thing. He was trying to prepare him, Noah knew, and Noah waited anxiously for the time when he would be ready.

All of the boys at school on Monday played wrestling during afternoon recess. Everyone wanted to be either Diesel Machine or Chief Thunderbolt. Noah worked hard on his Strong Bow and got so good at it that he made Gerald cry.

"I saw you with the wrestlers on Saturday," Thomas said to Noah. "Ever crazy, you! You look like a midget beside them!" Gerald and Thomas laughed at that. It didn't bother Noah. He was growing. Last night after church he had eaten so much dinner that his mother told him to stop.

At the end of recess, one of the older boys pile-drove one of the smaller ones, so the principal banned wrestling in the schoolyard. He came on the intercom just before school let out. "An important announcement to students," he said. "Nick Lazarus was hurt in the yard today when another student attempted a wrestling move on him. Keep in mind, students, you are not professionals. From here on in, you will face suspension if you are caught wrestling on school grounds. Tomorrow we will have professional wrestlers currently staying on reserve come to our classrooms to discuss the dangers of their job."

Gerald and Thomas and Noah turned in their desks and looked at one another. Noah gave the other two a thumbs-up.

At dinner, Noah told his parents of the upcoming visit. "They're going to come to our class and talk to us," he told his mother between forkfuls of baked beans. "Maybe they'll show us how to properly do some moves."

"You're not allowed no wrestling moves at school anymore," his mother said.

"John Goodwin pile-drived Nick Lazarus and gave him De Stubborn Headache," Noah said. He looked at his parents but they didn't get it. "Are you going to come with me to wrestling on Wednesday night?" he asked after a while. His father looked up at Noah from his food.

"We got church on Wednesday night," his mother answered. "A preacher's come all the way from Toronto to preach the Lord's word."

"Oh," Noah answered. "You'll miss the wrestling match."

"You're coming to church too," his father said with the tone dangerous to argue with. Noah felt his heart sink.

The days were already longer. Noah got out of his house as soon as he could. He wanted to sneak around, see if he could spot any of the wrestlers wandering about. Some of the men had taken the wrestlers out all day Sunday to ice fish for pickerel. Although they were staying at the trailers by the council office that the chief called a hotel, Noah hadn't spotted them around. Word was that they were working out at the school gymnasium. Noah rode his bicycle that way, but as he passed the restaurant he saw a glimpse of Chief Thunderbolt. Noah got off his bike and quietly walked in the door. There at tables were Chief Thunderbolt, Kid Wikked, Beef Wellington and the Orderlies.

Noah couldn't believe who was sitting there with them. His teacher, Miss Crane, the grade five teacher, Miss Nelson, and the grade eight teacher, Miss Reynolds, sat laughing and smiling, looking like three dwarves surrounded by the five big men. Noah took a seat by the counter and watched them. The teachers giggled like the little girls did at recess, then stared up with big eyes at the men. Noah strained to hear what they were saying, but could hear only the laughing clearly. After a while, the Orderlies got up and left. "We gotta quit hanging out together," one said to the other. "Together we creep them out. We're never gonna score this way."

Noah looked back to the others, all paired off now: Miss Crane with Chief Thunderbolt, Miss Nelson with Kid Wikked and Miss Reynolds with Beef Wellington. He decided to chance it and moved behind a fake bush close to the couples.

"How about cocktails at my trailer?" Miss Reynolds spoke up. She whispered the words loudly. All the others seemed very happy with the idea.

"Don't spread the word around," Miss Crane said. "This is a dry reserve after all, and even if the chief throws the best parties around, we'd be in a world of trouble if anyone found out." All of them laughed quietly. Noah wished he knew what cocktails were.

"Let's go," Beef Wellington said, slapping the table and standing up. Noah moved quickly back to his chair.

"What tribe are you?" Miss Crane asked Chief Thunderbolt as they all stood and moved to the door.

"I'm Puerto Rican, actually," he answered.

"Yeah, he's a spic," Kid Wikked said, and they all laughed. Noah hadn't heard of the Spic band before. As they passed by, Noah watched Miss Crane holding Chief Thunderbolt's arm, staring up into his eyes. Chief Thunderbolt looked straight down at Noah and gave him a big thumbs-up; then he walked out the door with Noah's teacher and the others into the night.

Gerald and Thomas and Noah sat by one another in class all day, passing notes about which wrestlers they wanted to come visit their room. Gerald was hoping Giant Haystacks and Bulba would show up because he wanted to see if they could fit through the door. Thomas wanted De Stubborn Headache to show up because he wanted to look up close at his black skin.

Noah had told him that Headache's palms were light-coloured like theirs, but Thomas wouldn't believe it. Noah sent a note saying that Chief Thunderbolt would show up because Miss Crane had a crush on him. He drew a picture of the two of them kissing, but Gerald said he couldn't tell what it was of.

At recess, Noah and some of the other braver boys went down the hill by the fence where the teachers couldn't see them and worked on their wrestling moves. Noah easily defeated the younger boys and with only a few minutes of recess left, found himself facing John Goodwin, who everyone called Pile-Drive King now. John tripped Noah and jumped on him, his weight easily holding Noah down. He placed his hands around Noah's neck and squeezed.

"Say uncle," John said, staring down. "Tap out or black out." Noah struggled for air and, on the verge of panicking, tried to see in his head what Chief Thunderbolt would do. Then he lifted his legs high up and caught one over John's head. With a sitting-up motion, Noah leveraged the Pile-Drive King down so that he was on his back with Noah's legs snaked around his neck. Noah squeezed and John tapped the ground frantically. The other boys cheered as the school bell rang, and Noah jumped to his feet. He'd beaten John — John who weighed much more and who all the younger children were scared of.

During math, Miss Crane interrupted the students. "Our special guests have arrived," she said. Noah looked up to see Kid Wikked and Chief Thunderbolt walk in. All the kids stopped what they were doing and stared up with big eyes.

"How," Chief Thunderbolt said to the kids, raising his hand to them. Everyone stared back.

"Howdy, y'all," Kid Wikked shouted, making a six-gun

with each thumb and forefinger, shooting the children with imaginary bullets.

"How do your people give greetings?" Chief Thunderbolt asked the class. The children stared back at him, too afraid to answer.

"We say, 'Hiya, how are you?'" Annie finally said, looking to Miss Crane nervously, not sure if she should have raised her hand first.

Chief Thunderbolt looked at Kid Wikked. "No, he means in your language, in Cree," Kid Wikked spoke up.

"They say, '*Whachay, dannee dotamin,*'" Miss Crane answered, smiling at Chief Thunderbolt. "It means 'Hello, how are you?'"

"I am fine. And you?" the chief answered to Miss Crane. They both giggled.

"So what questions do you little redskins have for us today?" Kid Wikked asked, slapping his hands together and looking at the class. The children stared back at him.

"What band are you?" Gerald finally blurted, looking at Chief Thunderbolt.

"I prefer to think of myself as belonging to all tribes," Chief Thunderbolt answered.

"How do you say hello in your language?" Sal Enosse asked.

"Well, today I say, '*Dam doman,*' but normally I would say '*¿Hola, como está?*'" The children smiled at the strange words.

"Can you kick Kid Wikked's bum?" Thomas asked.

"Thomas!" Miss Crane blurted, her face turning red.

"It's OK," Chief Thunderbolt said, raising his giant hand. "Actually, Kid Wikked and me, we're partners. We represent what is good and honourable in our society." He lifted his arms in a big circle for the children. "We are the alliance of the old ways and new, of cultures, of what made this country what it is today."

The children stared at him some more. Noah didn't know what to think. The words sounded big and good, but he really couldn't figure out what they meant. Kid Wikked kind of looked left out to Noah.

"Are you an honorary member of the Spics?" Noah asked Kid Wikked.

"Noah!" Miss Crane squealed.

The two big wrestlers looked confused, like they'd been given back-to-back Atomic Drops.

"I think that's quite enough," Miss Crane announced sternly to the class. "Please accept my apologies, Chief, Mr. Wikked. The children don't get many visitors."

"That's quite all right," Chief Thunderbolt answered, touching her shoulder, making her blush. Noah wished he knew what he'd said wrong.

"Make sure you eat all your vegetables," Kid Wikked growled to the kids, bending and making a crab with his arms so his huge muscles bulged from his T-shirt.

"And make sure to say your prayers to the Great Spirit," Chief Thunderbolt bellowed, lifting his arms and making the muscles bounce like softballs under the skin.

Noah spent all of Wednesday trying to figure out how to get out of church. He could pretend to be sick. No, that was no good. His mother would stay back with him. He could pretend to have a big homework assignment and maybe his parents would let him stay home alone to complete it. That wouldn't work either. They'd ask all kinds of questions he couldn't answer. There was only one option.

As soon as they walked to their pew Wednesday night, Noah pulled his mom's arm and whispered, "Gotta pee." He walked slowly down the centre aisle, and when he reached the door, he bolted out and down the road to the community centre. His parents would be so caught up in their hallelujahs and tongue-talking that they wouldn't even notice him gone.

Inside the community centre, all the seats were taken except for the first three rows around the ring. The first match was already going. Noah made his way to the very front row, his eyes glued to a tag-team match between the Orderlies and De Stubborn Headache and Giant Haystacks. The Orderlies were far outweighed, but Noah saw right away that they were much more agile, one of them jumping away to avoid Giant Haystacks' clumsy swings and bouncing off the ropes, sling-shotting himself into Haystacks' soft mountain of a belly. When Haystacks could take no more punishment, he made the reach to a frantic Headache. The two men touched fingers and Headache was in the ring. The ref was trying to be a good one, Noah saw, but the Orderlies were so identical that he couldn't keep them straight. When it seemed that one Orderly was out of gas, the other would trick the ref into looking elsewhere while they quickly switched places. The crowd whispered their praise of the Orderlies' cunning, and agreed that it was just a matter of time until they had Giant Haystacks and De Stubborn Headache gasping for breath. In a daring two-man ricochet, one Orderly flung the other with such force that Noah winced at the slap of muscle on muscle as the Orderly careened into Headache, knocking him out. The ref gave the three count and the crowd clapped a little.

Noah whooped when Kid Wikked took his corner to face Beef Wellington. Miss Crane and Miss Reynolds and Miss

Nelson had come up to the front row now and were cheering for the two men. The fight seemed to last forever. Both men growled and fell and hollered and, just when it seemed that one had the other in an impossible situation, he would break free. Suddenly, Diesel Machine appeared at ringside, making threatening gestures towards Kid Wikked. At one point he reached under the rope when the ref wasn't looking and tripped the Kid up. Beef Wellington pounced.

That's when Noah saw Chief Thunderbolt dash down the aisle, diving and sliding into the ring to come to Kid Wikked's aid. The ref tried to pull the three men apart and, when he threatened to disqualify Kid Wikked, Chief Thunderbolt stood up and argued loudly with him in the corner. Noah watched in horror as Diesel grabbed a folding chair behind the ref's back and climbed into the ring. Beef Wellington held a dazed Kid Wikked. Diesel Machine raised the chair and brought it down with a metallic bong onto the Kid's back, then threw it out of the ring and dove out. It all happened so quickly. By the time the ref turned from arguing with the Chief, Beef Wellington lay with Kid Wikked unconscious beneath him. The ref jumped to the floor and slapped out a three count. Noah wanted to shout to him that the bad men had cheated, but couldn't find the words. Kid Wikked opened his eyes for a second and stared straight at Noah. Noah waved, but the Kid closed his eyes quickly and went back to sleep.

"Stupid ref," Noah whispered under his breath. He watched the Chief help a woozy Kid out of the ring. Noah gave the Chief a thumbs-up, and the Chief gave him one back with sad eyes. It was clear now. The Chief and Kid were better than good guys. Beef and Diesel had chosen the dark side.

When the hall had cleared, Noah again went to the

change room. The men who had battled were sitting tired with towels over their shoulders. Noah was surprised to see that all these enemies sat and laughed with one another. It was good that they didn't hold grudges. He walked in proudly and made the biggest muscle he could with each arm. The men ignored him.

"I want to join you," Noah said quietly. The men laughed at him.

"You ain't old enough, kid," Kid Wikked finally said. "It's a shitty life anyway. You don't want this."

I *do*, Noah wanted to say. The men went back to talking with each other. Noah walked out and down the road to face his parents.

Noah's face still stung from where his father had slapped him. Hitting Noah was something his father had learned when he became a Pentecostal, Noah figured out. He walked along the river and turned this over in his head. It was Thursday morning, and Noah figured that if he walked fast, he could make the highway in a few days. The morning was warm and bright. His friends would just be getting to school. Noah's parents wouldn't even notice him missing until dinnertime, when he didn't turn up. He would show all of them — his parents, his friends, the wrestlers. He'd make his way to some big city where they were sure to have a wrestling school. Noah would work hard, grow strong and become great.

Last night his father had said, "No more wrestling for you," and by the time he finished that sentence Noah'd made his decision to run away. He'd filled his knapsack with crackers and pork and beans and a can opener this morning without his mother seeing. Those wrestlers would be sorry they hadn't taken Noah, especially on that day in the future when he held up the championship belt. Noah walked along the frozen river and formed and re-formed his plans.

By lunchtime, Noah's pack felt heavy. He sat by the river, on a large flat boulder that was warmed by the sun. He opened a can of pork and beans and realized he'd forgotten to pack a spoon. He scooped the beans out with his fingers and looked at the ice and water. The first clouds of doubt skittered across the horizon. The nights were still cold and they were very dark. Noah lay on the rock and let its warmth sink into his skin.

He wasn't sure how long he'd slept. Something tickling his face woke him. He opened his eyes to a great swarm of butterflies above and around him. Many had landed on the rock and on his body, their wings beating slowly. The ones that still hovered were so great in number that their wings made a low whirring sound. Noah's heart quickened at the sight. Some of the butterflies were as big as his hand. Their colours were amazing in the sunlight, orange and glistening black and deep red. Their wings made such a sound that it seemed to Noah that they were whispering to him in some strange language. He watched and listened to these tiny tongues of fire. Hundreds of butterflies. Thousands. They continued their whispering until Noah began to make out a pattern, began to understand them, began to grasp the meaning of this event.

It could have been minutes, it could have been hours. Slowly the butterflies dispersed until Noah was left alone again. He thought of Grandfather. Grandfather called these little creatures by their Western Cree name. *Kumamuk*. Grandfather admired them for their beauty and grace, for the strength that enabled them to fly thousands of kilometres. Noah knew now what he had to do. He'd experienced his vision.

He made it back to the reserve before dinner. No one seemed to know he'd been gone all day. Miss Crane wasn't her usual self with Chief Thunderbolt around, and she'd not even reported Noah's absence to the principal. His butterflies were already protecting him. That night he began his preparation for Friday evening and the last match. He raided his mother's old box of powwow materials which she hadn't touched since becoming a Pentecostal. He also swiped two of her old pairs of pantyhose. If he worked hard, he'd have it complete in time.

Grandfather came for dinner that night. Noah wanted to tell him about the butterflies, but knew that would have to wait. Tonight's match was on his mind, and Noah was ready to sneak out and get in trouble later if he had to in order to see it.

"I got some plans with Noah tonight," Grandfather said to Noah's parents. They looked mad that Grandfather wanted to take him and do something. He was supposed to be grounded.

"All right," Noah's father said, then got up and helped Noah's mom with the dishes. Grandfather leaned close to Noah and whispered that he'd better get ready for the wrestling match or he'd be late. Noah ran to his room and changed. Even though it wasn't cold out, he pulled his coat on. He met Grandfather outside.

"Me, I'm too old for the crowds," Grandfather said. "Get going."

Noah ran into Thomas and Gerald at the hall. "Ever dumb you," Gerald said. "You're going to melt in your coat."

"Are you going up front?" Thomas asked.

"Yeah. You come too," Noah said. "You don't want to miss this tonight." The boys followed him to the nearly empty front row. The card tonight was excellent. Bulba was fighting De

Stubborn Headache to get things rolling. Then there was a rematch between Pink Panther and Fritz Von Schnitzel. But the highlight was the final bout. Diesel Machine, in what the announcer called an unholy alliance with Beef Wellington, was scheduled to battle Kid Wikked and Chief Thunderbolt. Noah fingered part of the creation he'd carefully placed in his coat pocket.

He had a hard time concentrating on the first match. De Stubborn Headache attempted to lift Bulba off the ground but collapsed under his immense weight. Bulba lucked out and got an easy three count. Noah looked around him. The crowd had become braver. Kids and adults alike had filled up the third and second rows, and even part of the first. They'd also started making a little noise, but not much. Pink Panther laid out Fritz Von Schnitzel with rapid machine-gun punches, then climbed to the top turnbuckle and flew off, landing with a slap on the convulsing Schnitzel. Victory once again was the Panther's, and Noah was happy to see the good side winning.

Noah watched his hero climb into the ring alongside Kid Wikked. They faced off with Beef and Diesel. Noah's heart pounded. The bad guys dominated the first part of the match. Every time the ref wasn't paying attention, one of the bad men did something dirty. One time it was an eye gouge, another time a kick below the belt. But then Kid Wikked came back from a near tap-out, picking Beef high up into the air, then dropping him straight onto his own back, slamming Beef onto the canvas with a great boom. The crowd actually shouted out at that one.

The Kid tenderized Beef with foot stomps to the stomach, then tagged Chief Thunderbolt. Noah had never seen such a sight as Chief Thunderbolt dashing into the ring, landing furious blows and tossing Wellington around like a doll. It was obvious that Beef was cooked. He had nothing left. But in the bad guy's corner, with the Chief's back to Diesel Machine, Diesel crashed his forearm onto the back of Chief's neck, a totally illegal move. Chief Thunderbolt dropped stunned to his knees, and Beef tagged out to Diesel. Diesel entered the ring and paced around Chief Thunderbolt like a lion, making faces at a frantic Kid Wikked. Then he began kicking Chief with loud stomps. The Chief fell onto his back, hurt bad. Noah's heart pounded. He could hear the butterflies in his ears. Diesel knelt on Chief's chest, his back to Noah, and raised his arms to the crowd.

This was Noah's chance. He pulled the stocking he'd carefully painted in the bright colours of the butterfly from his coat pocket and pulled it over his head, adjusting it so he could see through the little holes he'd cut for his eyes. He tore off his coat and kicked off his jeans to reveal the costume he'd created, ran from his seat and pulled himself onto the side of the ring. He quickly scrambled up the ropes and balanced himself on the top turnbuckle, lifting his arms wide to reveal the cape he'd painted orange and red and green, the wings of the butterfly. His wings. "I'm doing it" was all he could think. His ears were filled with the roar and rush of his blood, with the butterflies whispering to him, "You're doing it!" Beneath his cape Noah wore another pair of his mother's pantyhose, these ones black like a butterfly's body, and pulled up to his chest.

For the first time he could hear the crowd. He could make out Thomas' and Gerald's voices in the shouting. Some of the women screamed. Others were laughing with excitement. Noah looked across the ring at the awestruck face of Kid

Wikked. He raised his arms higher for the crowd to drink in his costume and shouted, "I am Butterfly Warrior!"

With his back still to Noah, Diesel Machine was completely unaware of his presence. Noah looked down at Chief Thunderbolt. The Chief looked surprised. He slowly, haltingly raised his arm from the mat and gave Noah a thumbs-up. Noah tensed, then leapt. It felt like he was in the air for ever. The orange and red and green cape made of his father's old dress shirt flapped behind him. He had just enough time to watch Diesel's head turn up to him. Diesel barely had time to shout, "Whoa!" before Noah landed on him, Noah's knee sharply striking Diesel's forehead and sending him off Chief Thunderbolt.

Noah landed with a whomp on the mat, and it was much harder and hurt much more than he had imagined. The crowd roared now. He rolled over, the wind knocked out of him, and stared at the lights above him. His knee ached bad, but his friends shouting his name excitedly helped ease the pain a little. Noah sat up just in time to watch Chief Thunderbolt put Diesel Machine in the Strong Bow before pinning him. An egg had risen already on Diesel's forehead and his eyes were closed. Noah raised his arms up in victory. They had won. The Indians had won.

LEGEND OF
THE SUGAR GIRL

White men gave Indians a lot of gifts. Guns and outboard motors. Television. Coffee. Kentucky Fried Chicken. Road hockey. Baggy jeans and baseball caps. Rock-and-roll music and cocaine. But there is one gift that no one ever really talks about.

Once there was a young girl. She lived far up in the bush, past the Canadian Shield, so far up that deer could not survive in that harsh place. Her father was a hunter and trapper. Her mother made her family's clothing and cleaned the game that the father brought home, and she stretched and tanned the hides. They traded these pelts at the Hudson's Bay Company post for some of the *wemestikushu*'s, the white man's, goods — goods that the *Anishnaabe*, the Indians, found made life a little easier in that cold place. They traded lynx and beaver, moose and marten and snowshoe hare and mink for flour and bright cloth, bullets, simple tools and thread.

The young girl had many brothers and sisters, and all of them helped their parents with cooking and sewing, hunting and trapping. In the winter they kept their home in the bush by the father's traplines, and in summer they moved camp to the edge of a lake where fish were plentiful. This young girl wasn't so different from other young girls. She had a doll and her brothers and sisters to play with. Sometimes they would argue, but most of the time they got along. The young girl had a good life, especially in the summer, when it stayed light until late in the evening and the family would stay up with the light, playing games and telling stories.

But as all things must, this good life would soon come to an end. One day, after a visit to the Hudson's Bay Company post, the father came back with an ashen face. He sat with his wife and explained to her what he'd been told by the white traders at the post. A residential school had been built near the post, and the government had made it law that all *Anishnaabe* children must leave their families' camps and live at this school. "It won't be so bad," the white traders told the young girl's father. "Your children can come back and live with you for two months every summer. Think of it this way," the white traders said. "They will live in our world and learn our ways."

"And what if I do not send them to your residential school?" the father said.

"Then we are no longer permitted to trade with you, and the government will send the Mounties and they will take your children anyways," the white traders answered.

The young girl's father told his wife all this, and she cried. She knew they had to do what the government told them.

"We will go deep in the bush where they cannot find us," the father said. "We will live the way the grandfathers did, and forget about these white men."

"Even this country is not big enough that we can run away from them," his wife said. "They have airplanes that will spot our fire smoke. You won't have bullets for your gun. You can no longer shoot a bow well enough to feed all of us. What kind of life would that be for our children? Running and hiding the rest of our lives like rabbits."

So the young girl's parents had no choice but to do what the government told them. When the geese left that autumn, they took the children to the residential school, where nuns in black habits, with stern round faces, waited for them.

The first thing the nuns did was cut the children's hair. The boys had their hair cut short so that it poked up from their heads. The girls' hair was cut in straight bangs, the rest of it hanging above the shoulder so that they could no longer braid it as their mothers and grandmothers did.

The next thing the nuns did was dress the children in stiff, itchy clothing. Then they told them that they were no longer allowed to speak Cree. If they did, their mouths would be washed out with soap and they would be struck with a switch. Some of the children laughed, the young girl among them, for they thought the nuns were joking. Who would hit children, especially with a switch? They were not dogs! The young girl was shocked when a nun dragged her to a room, put the young girl over her knee, hiked her schooldress up and beat her bare skin until she cried.

That night, and for the next several months, the young girl fell asleep to her own crying and the sound of the other children crying in the large room lined with beds. They missed their parents and the cook-fire and the smell of tanned leather.

Besides the haircuts and clothing and days filled with clocks and classrooms and spankings and schedules, the oddest thing the young girl experienced was the food that the nuns made her eat three times a day. In the morning, she stood in a line with the others and was given a bowl of grey mush. Then she was given a little milk to pour on the mush. But the most interesting thing was that she was expected to place a spoonful of sugar, white as snow on a lake, onto the mush and milk. The sugar made the bland food taste good. The young girl learned to like her breakfast because of it. It made a grey morning bright for a while. Soon, the girl got in the habit of sneaking a spoonful of sugar into her schooldress pocket. During the day, when she was bored or felt like a treat, she licked her finger and placed it in the sugar in her pocket, then stuck her finger in her mouth without any of the nuns noticing. She was very careful doing this, for if the nuns saw, they would surely beat her with a tamarack switch.

The days turned to weeks turned to months. The children became better at speaking English, but many still spoke their own language, sometimes accidentally, sometimes on purpose. Always, when they were caught, they had their mouths washed out with soap and were given a switching on the bare skin of their behinds. The young girl noticed that even the bravest boys, who on a dare would look a nun in the eye and insult her in Cree, could still be heard crying quietly as they fell asleep. The nights were the worst; nuns creeping like ghosts between the beds, hushing children with their bony fingers to their lips. The young girl looked forward to mornings.

When the children were very good, they were given a hard candy, sweet and brightly coloured, that they sucked on until the candy became a sliver, then disappeared. These were even better than white sugar to the young girl. The flavour was deeper, thicker. It made her think of warm sun on her skin, and made her feel the way you feel when you wake up in the morning and realize the day is all yours. The grey days of residential school passed more quickly with hard candy.

Spring came, and the children talked about soon going back to their summer homes by the lakes and rivers. This prospect made the children happy and, when they were happy, they behaved well. The nuns in turn handed out a little more candy. The young girl thought it would be a good idea to bring some of this candy home with her. She began doing favours for the other children, making their beds, tickling their backs, even giving away part of her dinner in exchange for the candy.

It wasn't long before she became possessed by the idea of hoarding candy. If she could get enough of it, she could have candy all the time and her days here would be much happier. She begged and finagled and traded so much that soon the other children began to call her by a new name. They began calling her the Sugar Girl. Some of them meant it to tease her, but the Sugar Girl was proud of her new name. The other children began to admire her intensity and focus on this sweet substance. Before long, they called her this name as a sign of respect.

Summer was a strange time for the Sugar Girl and her brothers and sisters. They had only spoken their language in secret and in whispers all year, and for the first long part of the summer, whenever they spoke Cree out loud, something inside them flinched tense for a beating.

Summer passed quickly, as summers do. Years passed quickly, as years do. Each summer as the children grew, they came back home remembering a little less of their language, until a time came when the Sugar Girl and her brothers and sisters could barely talk with their parents anymore.

During these years that the Sugar Girl was gone to residential school, her mother and father tried to live life as they'd always lived it. Father went out on the traplines or moose hunting, and Mother kept their home. But they were growing older, and with age comes weakness. To cut and clean a moose is a young man's work, and hauling its weight back home is many young men's work. With no children to help them, the Sugar Girl's parents finally admitted that they had to do what other parents were doing. They moved to the reserve where the residential school was and, with the little bit of money the government gave them, they bought expensive food and necessities from the Hudson's Bay Company. The Sugar Girl's father had no choice but to laugh when he thought about how well the government and company worked together, how they were like two hands of the same body. One hand would give him something, and the other would just as quickly snatch it away.

The years passed, and the Sugar Girl grew up and eventually came to call the residential school home, just as the nuns and government had planned. As she grew taller, the Sugar Girl grew plumper. The nuns' food was very different from her family's food. The sauces, the desserts, the sweet teas and soda pops she discovered — all of them were thick with sugar. In some strange way, this food that she ate and grew to love replaced what had been taken away from her, and when the Sugar Girl felt sadness, the sadness that comes from deep in the stomach, she smothered it with her sugar foods.

The day finally arrived when it was time for the Sugar Girl to leave the residential school. Although she would never have imagined it when she first came there, she was scared to leave. Even though the nuns were generous with their whippings, they also gave her things she needed — her clothing, her food. But what they had neglected to give her was the ability to find these things on her own.

The government gave her a little money, just as they gave her parents a little. It was strange to realize that, now that she was free to see her parents, she rarely did. She spoke a different language, liked different things. This fact made her sad sometimes, made her feel as though she'd lost something very important, and when the sadness swelled up from inside her, she blunted it with sugar in its many forms.

For all the pleasant feelings that these sweet things brought her, the Sugar Girl began to notice bad effects. Her teeth were turning brown and hurt her horribly. Her skin had suffered too, as the poor diet ate away at that as well. She noticed that when she didn't eat sugar she felt run down and got horrible headaches. She kept eating it.

On her twentieth birthday, the Sugar Girl's friends gave her her first taste of alcohol. That night she felt once again the way she had as a small girl when she'd been given her first taste of sugar. It made things seem brighter, warmer. It made her happy and made her laugh. It made her forget. She didn't know that alcohol was sugar in its fermented, purer form. "Think of it as candy for adults," one friend said to her that night, and she laughed and laughed until the tears flowed.

And so it was that alcohol became her new candy. But the effects of this new candy were stronger. She felt its effect soon after she drank it, felt it the next morning. Worse than that, she did things while drinking that she normally wouldn't do. For the first hour or so she and her friends would talk more and laugh more than normal, and that was nice. But when they continued to drink, the laughing turned to sadness or anger. She never knew for sure which way it would go.

She wanted the warm feeling of happiness that first came upon her to last, but the alcohol wouldn't allow it. When the Sugar Girl drank too much and the sadness or anger came, she tried to figure out where it came from. She was angry with the nuns. They'd threatened her and hit her until she'd become what they wanted. But she didn't really know who or what this new person was that she'd turned into.

There were mornings when the Sugar Girl would wake up sick, never wanting alcohol again. Sometimes there would be a man she knew, or even one she didn't know, lying beside her. On these mornings, the Sugar Girl wanted the life of her childhood back. The fire at night. The sound of her mother singing an old Cree song. Her father's stories, the games with her brothers and sisters. But her parents were too old now to go back and live in the bush, to teach her brothers and sisters how to hunt and trap and make Indian clothing and prepare game for eating. That life was gone.

As those awful mornings turned into afternoons on the reserve where she lived, and her body began to feel better, the Sugar Girl questioned whether she even wanted that old life back. She'd gotten used to and learned to like what the nuns and government had given her. The soft bed, the radio and its music, the food that was as available as the Hudson's Bay store. Life was easy. If she was careful with the money the government gave her each month in exchange for her family's old hunting grounds and life, she could just get by. But there was still the nagging worry, like a mosquito buzz late at night, that her life was missing something.

When the day came that the Sugar Girl found she was pregnant, she thought maybe this was the thing she had been missing. The white doctor informed her that not only was she to have a baby but she had a disease, something wrong with her body and how it dealt with all the sugar she'd consumed since childhood. "You should take better care of yourself," he said. "Many of your people have this problem. Your bodies can't deal with the awful diet you subject it to. If you're not careful, if you don't change your ways, it will kill you."

And so it came to be that the Sugar Girl gave birth to her sugar baby. She gave him a Bible name, in the hope that this would help him in his life with the white people, and raised her boy as best she could. She thought back to her own childhood and what her mother would do when the Sugar Girl was sick or acting up or needed help. But that seemed so long ago. There weren't too many memories of that time left. Sometimes it was easier to do what the nuns had done to her, and spank her boy when he was naughty, and quiet him with candy, and feed him the same things she ate.

For a short time when she was pregnant and when she was breastfeeding her baby, the Sugar Girl felt as healthy and happy as she had as a child. But it wasn't long after that time that she fell into her old ways again. She saw it in the grocery store, at the restaurant, in her home. It had made itself a permanent part of her. It was impossible to separate herself from the thing she had become.

So she raised her child as best she knew how and lived as best as she knew how. But the Sugar Girl got sicker and sicker. The same sugar that had befriended her and comforted her as a child and helped her live as the nuns demanded, was her enemy, had been her enemy from the beginning, eating away at her from the inside out. And by the time it was the son's turn to help look after his mother, he too was taken away to the residential school. The Sugar Girl had lived long enough to feel the same pain her mother and father had felt. The son suffered the fate of a residential school child, and in painful ways, at the hands of certain sick men, that his mother had fortunately never faced.

But legends are not meant to be sad stories only. They are told to express a people's magic, to make victors out of weaklings. The Sugar Girl died, but a part of her was carried on in her son — that good part that the nuns couldn't take out of her, that had been in her all along though she didn't know it.

The Sugar Girl's son was strong. After all, his blood was Cree. He left the residential school and watched it crumble at the hands of the ones who had built it, watched it rot and collapse because of their physical and mental and sexual abuse. The Sugar Girl's son went on to learn everything he could about the dangers that had silenced his mother, and in turn he taught some of his people about the dangers of the sugar disease.

White men gave Indians a lot of gifts. Hockey and electricity, prefab houses, snowmobiles, running shoes, pickup trucks, pavement and reserves.

In turn, Indians gave white men some gifts back. Lacrosse and long hair. Corn and the peace pipe. Names for professional baseball teams. Powwows, Tonto, Custer's Last Stand. Land. Lots of land. Thanksgiving.

It's the gifts that are never mentioned, though, that we all feel the most.

ABITIBI
CANYON

When Richard, my second cousin, told me he was here to arrest Remi for suspicion of involvement in the Abitibi dam getting blown up, I laughed at him till his red cheeks blushed purple. Richard's the tribal police sergeant, the big one sent when a drinking party turns violent or there's a standoff between an abusive husband and his wife's brothers. They send him when the situation calls for muscle. We call him the Equalizer. That he was here for Remi, his own blood, it didn't make sense. Remi's the first frog child. He can't comprehend what a dam is for, never mind how to blow it up.

Four of us on the reserve had frog children. You have to have one to be a member of our club. *Anigeeshe awasheeshuk.* The Cree word for them. My son Remi was the first. Born nineteen years ago. Big bulging eyes. Thick, muscled limbs. A long sloping back. His voice a croak. The old ones on the reserve, they named him first. *Aneegishush.* Little Frog. And when more came, over the years, to different women near the Abitibi Canyon, *anigeeshe awasheeshuk.* Frog children.

You see the Abitibi Canyon from the Little Bear Express, appearing like a *windigo*'s grave out of the trees, dipping slowly at first, then shooting straight down, the rock cliffs dropping for a lifetime until the brown water of the river licks them and swallows them up. Long fat pike there. Sturgeon big as my husband, Patrick. Old Isaac Tomatuk, who's dead now, lost part of his finger to a pike there, years back. The odd part is, Isaac swore till he was gone for good that the pike had a man's eyes. No one doubted him. If there's a sacred place still left for us, it's Abitibi Canyon.

Me, I didn't want another after Remi. Not because he looks like a frog. Children are too much work. My life is full enough. I sound selfish now, and I guess I am. I do love Remi. I've fought for Remi. Big fights. Hair pullers. Nose bleeders. Cheek bruisers. It got so that they called me the freight train. No man or woman was safe if they insulted Remi. It soon got, though, that he could defend himself. At least make others think twice when they saw the size of him.

All the trouble, Remi's trouble, began with work in the canyon. The band council had been battling over whether to let the hydro people build a dam for power. It was a big project being proposed. A year of construction. More money than I'd ever heard of was involved. How much the band would ever see was questionable. One side loved the idea — especially the chief, Jonah Koosees. Big money for all of us, he said. New schools. New houses. Prosperity. The down side is that thousands of hectares of traditional land will be swallowed up by water. No more hunting. No control in our own country. Negative environmental impact. My husband, Patrick, he's against. He's on council. *Hookimaw* of the ones who are against Jonah. Give the *wemestikushu* a little, he knows, and they find a way to take it all. Thing is, Patrick's got a lot of history, a lot of examples to back him up. We might lose hunting ground, Jonah said to

Patrick at one meeting, but just think of all the new fishing area we'll gain. Jonah's humour isn't so funny.

This battle has been going on for two years. It's split the community. It's good for our side that more on the reserve are wary of giving so much land away in return for promises. We've seen it before. No one trusts handing over all we have in return for paperwork. That's what treaties are for. Jonah Koosees, he knows he's in a losing battle. Election for chief is in a few months and the majority here don't trust him. The way things are going, my man Patrick will be the next chief.

Me, I'm against it for a more selfish reason. Me and Shirley and Mary and Suzanne, we get up there twice a year to camp with our *anigeeshe awasheeshuk*, where we keep the idea of the Abitibi Canyon Ladies Club alive. It's a simple club. We just leave the reserve behind for a little while and camp with our children up in the canyon. Where else could we meet that has the same meaning to all of us? Strong magic there.

It's pretty much an accepted fact around here. It's what the older ones refer to as a place of power, a place where the manitous live. Lots of boys been sent there by their fathers for a first fast and vision. Many girls for their first blood of womanhood, their strawberry ceremony. Strange lights have been seen there at night. Everybody here knows someone who's seen them. Government men in red parkas came to investigate that. Said it was the northern lights playing tricks. Wasn't no northern lights. It was manitous. Sky children. At least these manitous were. They come out and run around like that when they're unhappy. With what's been going on around the canyon lately, I expect people will see a lot more of them soon.

This one time when Remi was no bigger than a goose, I left him with my mother, his *kokum*, while I went to the bingo.

I still remember winning a hundred dollars. Big money back then. Not anymore. Pots in the thousands now. New cars, snowmobiles, trips to places where snow has never fallen. When I came back, Remi was sleeping on the couch, his sloped naked back shining in the lamplight like a wet piece of driftwood. My mother, she wasn't sleeping. She'd sat up watching Remi, waiting to tell me.

"He spoke," she said. Nothing new. He'd been putting his mouth around certain words in Cree and English for a whole year. "No," she said. "He spoke whole sentences. He spoke like that priest does, about water covering the land." At the time I didn't think much of it. I brought Remi to church since he was born. Had him pray right along with me to keep winning bingo. Maybe he had a gift for repeating. But mother — old school. From then on she had Remi to every medicine man, every circle, every feast, every sweat when his lungs got strong enough. It got so that I teased him, though he couldn't grasp that. Called him *aneegishush dekonun*. Little frog medicine man. He smiles and shows his crooked teeth when I call him this, even now. I like that he likes it.

He spoke strange words for a while, talking like a slow minister on a roll. I remember the first time I myself heard him speak like that. He was six. We'd just fitted him for glasses. Black, thick-rimmed things. He was angry and hated them. "The Lord says, Repent!" he shouted at Patrick and me when we got him home. "Heed my word and be saved!" Then he went back to talking like he always did. Slurred words and lots of smiling. I was never quite sure if he was acting or not, wasn't sure where it came from, but I got used to it. You get used to anything after a while. Right about the time he turned twelve, he quit talking like a minister. We don't know why. He just went back to being a handicapped kid, his tongue thick when he talked, his mind searching hard for the words.

Mary and Shirley and Suzanne are the three others with *anigeeshe awasheeshuk*. None of those kids ever talked like prophets, though. They are all younger than Remi. All born in the Abitibi Canyon. All of us lived in Abitibi Canyon when our husbands worked on the railroad crew. All of us who had frog children conceived them while we were living there. Doesn't take a genius. Again, government men came in to investigate. These ones had green parkas. Lots of needles. Lots of questions that made the other girls blush. Lots of prodding. Lots more blushing. Results are inconclusive, the government men finally said. Possible coincidence. Possibly eating the same fish poisoned by a sunken Soviet nuclear sub thirty-five hundred kilometres away. Lots of possibilities.

"What about the possibility that these children are gifts from manitous?" Mother says. "Lots of possibilities," I say like a government man. "Results are inconclusive."

When Remi started growing, he didn't stop. At eight, his frame curved like a bow, he was still a head taller than the others his age. At twelve he could carry twenty-five geese for kilometres, on a pole slung across his arched back. At fifteen he was as big as his father, one of the biggest men on the reserve. This in a band of big people. To top it off, Remi will always have to wear those thick black glasses that magnify his eyes. He breaks all the others. There's no getting past the fact he looks like a big, crazy Cree.

Remi's father is what they call an activist. He's always filled Remi's head with stories of how we're an Unceded First Nation, how our particular band never signed a treaty. I thought Remi didn't understand any of it till one night, just before all hell broke loose on the reserve, I told him to help me with dinner and he shot right back, "No. I'm not seeded." I sent him out hunting with his father. That trip changed things for good.

When they came back, my husband told the reserve of bull-dozers being unloaded and work crews scurrying around like ants upriver of the canyon. Most were shocked that we hadn't been told of this latest venture on what everyone considers tribal land. But I wasn't. I've known Jonah Koosees for a long time. I knew as soon as my husband told me about new work crews up there that the OK had been given by Jonah, without council even knowing about it. Rumour is Jonah's got a bank account down south that would make the Pope jealous. It's obvious by his clothes mail-ordered from Toronto and his car that he lives by other means.

Jonah might as well have admitted his guilt when the next day he didn't show when half the band boated upriver to see for themselves and make a plan of action. My man was there, Remi beside him, grinning and drooling. Didn't fit the mood. I came too, sad to see my special place with so many people on it, white and Indian alike.

We set up camp and started cook-fires along the river-bank. Just like the old days. The workers watched nervously from their camp downriver, images of scalpings and savages dancing around campfires all night, I'm sure. Just like the old days. I make sure that Mary and Shirley and young Suzanne, the newest Abitibi club member, have their tents right by mine. Maybe if the four of us try hard enough, we can pretend there isn't anybody else around. Nobody's really got a plan at this point. The young warriors want to force a standoff and stop construction, with violence if necessary. Patrick heads back to the reserve, to a phone, so he can call lawyers and get an injunction until we can sort out exactly what's happening.

We sit and drink hot tea and cook bannock for our children over the cook-fires. The smell of the raisins and fresh dough makes me hungry. I watch Remi play with the other women's children, his big, awkward body hulking over the two little ones, his paw hands gently picking them up and dipping them, giggling, into the river like something I might have read in the Bible once. Remi does this over and over. Picks up Mary's little boy, Jacques, who's only six and round like a black-haired piglet, under the arms and raises him over his head until Jacques squeals. Then Remi, with a look of deep concentration and his tongue sticking a bit out of his mouth, dips Jacques into the cold stream of brown river up to his waist, Jacques' face contorting from a grin to the surprised O of shock, a whine like a fire truck coming from his mouth.

Remi then picks up Albert, who's thirteen and much bigger, and Remi must strain to do this. Albert is thick-limbed and stronger than he knows. Shirley is always complaining of bruised arms and strained muscles. Remi knits his brows, squats like a weightlifter, heaves Albert into the air, holding him there like a prize or an offering, then splashes him down into the cold water, where Albert moans with a child's happiness.

This is when Jacques runs up and Remi begins the whole process again. He would continue this cycle until he dropped from exhaustion if I didn't interrupt him. Remi needs these cycles, lives for the repetition of events and daily grind. Mother says he is the old Cree epitomized, his desire for cycles and seasons and the healing circle.

I see that there are a couple of white workers standing by

a pickup truck on the new little gravel road that's been carved out of the bush in the last few weeks. They lean against the truck and watch what's becoming most of the reserve set up camp.

Suzanne's little boy, he's still just a tiny thing. Suzanne breastfeeds him discreetly and watches the boys play. She is scared of the intensity, the complete focus that Remi exhibits in his actions. He's like a machine. Or an alien, she thinks — I can see it in her eyes. Suzanne will get used to it. Maybe one day it will even become a calming thing for her.

I watch the two workers' eyes glide to Remi and the boys. First one man stares, then he nudges his friend in astonishment. Both talk and laugh, pointing like they are the only ones who exist here. I hope Mary doesn't notice this. She will stomp over, and then stomp over them. Mary's a hothead. Although one of the workers looks Swampy Cree, I don't think he is. He would never be so obvious in his rudeness. Suddenly I see that Mary does notice. My stomach tightens.

"What's this all about?" she growls, looking at the men. Mary stands up. The men see her. They stop laughing. She walks over to them and I can see her exchanging words. The two men look down at their workboots, hands in pockets. They nod and the Indian-looking one answers. He looks up into Mary's eyes briefly, then down again. She walks back, the two men following.

"Rather than them making fun, I told them to come meet the kids," she says, dropping her weight onto her haunches. The two are nervous. Scolded schoolboys. We women sit and look up, wait for them to introduce themselves.

"I'm Matthew," the skinny white one says.

"I'm Darren," the other says.

"You *Anishnaabe*?" I ask Darren. He just looks at me. That answers it. "Are you Indian?" I ask.

"Oh," he answers. "No. My parents were born in Japan, but I'm Canadian."

"I'm not an Indian either," the skinny one says. No shit, *kemo sabe.*

"These are our children," Mary says. "Funny, eh?" The two men look down at their boots again.

"It's just that I've never seen retarded Indians before," Darren says. Mary stares at him.

"We don't call them retarded," I say. "We call their condition an environmentally induced mental handicap. The doctors came up with a name for this particular condition. Abitibi Canyon Syndrome."

"Yeah," Shirley says. "You work here long enough, your kids might turn out the same." Darren and Matthew stare at one another.

"Go play with them," Mary says, shooting her thumb towards our children. Suzanne looks up, panicked. Quiet girl isn't used to Mary's strong personality. Shirley laughs.

"Yeah, get yourselves acquainted," she says. The two really look nervous now, but they follow her command, not strong enough to resist her will.

For the first long while, the two men stand behind the children, not sure how to enter their circle of play. The children know they are there. I can see their sidelong glances. If you want in, they seem to say, we're not going to make it easy. Good boys. Eventually, Matthew sits and removes his boots and socks and rolls up his pants. He walks into the river carefully and says, "Hi," to the children. They ignore him. Matthew walks out a little deeper, then suddenly slips, disappearing into the water. Remi and Albert stare, concerned, but when Matthew's head pops up from the water, grinning, they begin to laugh, their laughing turning to howls, eyes squinting, mouths wide open. Makes the rest of us on the bank laugh too. Jacques looks at all of us, not sure what's so funny, but then joins in, not wanting to be left out. Matthew stands up and bows to us.

It isn't long before Darren is sitting with the boys, carefully explaining to them how the dam is going to be built. He used the sand to construct a model, and the boys watch, transfixed. Remi looks from the sand model to Darren's face. He's completely mesmerized by the talk, by Darren. After a while, Remi grabs Darren's hand and holds it in his. Darren looks surprised, but continues talking. Remi's never taken so quick to a stranger before. Darren will say something, and Remi repeats the last word or two, squinting behind his glasses and smiling. "Dam," he repeats, and "construction," and "dynamite."

"Oh shit," Matthew says, tapping Darren's shoulder. "Here comes the asshole." They both turn their heads and watch a large man with blond hair stomp through the sand towards them. He carries a hard hat, wears a white T-shirt under a long-sleeved shirt. Looks important.

"What the hell are you two dipshits doing here playing with kids? You asking me to dock your pay?" Darren and Matthew turn their heads from him like it isn't important what he's saying. "Better yet," the hard hat says, "I'll stick you on that train and you can crawl back to wherever it is you crawled from." Matthew's eyes sparkle with hate. Darren continues to stare calmly out at the river. "Don't dare give me that look, son," the hard hat says.

"I ain't your son," Matthew spits back. Darren stands up and pats Matthew's shoulder to calm him before things go too far. They get up and follow the man back to work. Remi waves to Darren's back.

For the next days we all camp and burn great fires at night. We send sparks and smoke into the sky high as we can. My man remains away, working on an injunction. Small stones to stop a river. Rumours fly through the camp, worse when it turns dark. The government will flood our reserve and move us to a barren place down south. The army is being called in, fearful of another Oka. The dynamite will blast soon and the construction crews don't care whether we're in the way or not. The worst of it is that we all know these are real possibilities. The great fires at night, tree trunks stacked in teepees ten metres high, are our sign to the crew and the manitous watching that we are still out here in Abitibi Canyon, in the same bush by the same river we've lived by *mawache oshkach*, from the beginning.

Patrick visits on the third day to bring news and some supplies. He calls us all to a meeting on the riverside and tells us it's important to stay. "We have to slow down work in any way we can," he says. "In any lawful way we can." The warriors grumble. "It could be a week before we have an injunction," he shouts to our crowd. "Historically, the more work the crew does before an injunction, the smaller our chance of stopping the dam being built. If the court sees not much was built, they are much more likely to rule against more building."

"And what of Jonah Koosees?" one of the women calls out in Cree.

"He's still disappeared," my husband answers back in Cree. The crowd talk among themselves. "That is the best news we can have," Patrick shouts. "It will be a damning thing to see that the chief who secretly made this deal has run away. Just focus on ways to legally slow down their work. We can win this court battle."

So we devise ways to slow things down. One morning a barricade of trees appears on the work road leading to the river. Every evening we stay up late into the night, playing loud music and screaming and laughing like drunken Injuns until dawn to keep the workers awake and nervous in their beds. We are good actors, having outlawed liquor on our site. From what I can tell, everyone obeys. We invite workers who are brave enough to come for tea and bannock during their breaks, and keep them talking with us as long as we can. From what I can see, our plan is working. It is hard to tell of any progress, other than the work road that leads to the river and the litter lying around.

But on the sixth day all of us are shocked to see great mounds of dirt being bulldozed into the river from either side. At first we think the fools are making a dam of mud, like children do in small streams, but we quickly find out that this is simply the first of many foundations to slow the river's course. One old fellow who's worked on dams before says that men would actually slow the great Abitibi to a trickle for a time by shutting dams farther up the river, and from these mounds of dirt that we now see built up and falling into the river they can build further foundations, and pour tons and tons of concrete. So this dirt is how it all starts. I can't picture my stretch of river here running dry. I push from my mind the image of a concrete monster lying in our river and controlling it like some greedy giant.

I sit with Mary and we debate how much slower the river runs now due to the mounds of dirt that stand like giant breasts on each side. "It isn't important that the river is slower right now," she says. "Just look at it." We both stare at the once pure water, running so muddy now that our children can no longer swim in it. "The silt by the reserve will continue to build up until all we are left with are shallows and sandbars," she says. "Not to mention no more place upriver for us girls to get away to."

Darren and Matthew continue visiting us when they can, playing with the children and talking with us. At first, we don't trust them — we never fully do in those days of camping — but they become a regular enough sight, and try to learn everything they can about how the dam is going to change things in big ways for us. We rely on the river for everything from transportation to food to drinking water. Now it is going to end up in someone else's control, its volume and even its course changed by the flick of some stranger's fingers on a couple of buttons. We've been cheated out of any say by one of our own and by strangers who don't care.

By the eighth day, I can see our camp is losing its focus. Some have packed up and left, and the ones who remain grumble more and more about what good we can possibly be doing. I admit that the shine of an unexpected camp-out is beginning to dull for me too. The ground is hard at night and there is little shade during the days. Unlike our autumn and spring outings, there is no anticipation of the arrival of geese and the happy work they bring, the gossip and laughter while plucking and cleaning and smoking. The one positive thing that remains is that Remi has made a new friend in Darren, and actually speaks to him. After Remi's brief stint as reserve prophet when he was young, it was like his tongue had thickened; he grunted more than he spoke as he grew older. But sitting near him and Darren as they lounge by the river, I hear him say words like "construction" and "Darren" and "Abitibi" as clearly as if he was never born a frog child. And I am happy for it. If only I knew what I am exposing my boy to.

We shout out on the tenth day when Patrick pulls up in his freighter canoe with the news that he's gotten an injunction. Work stops. Even the crew looks happy. But not the foreman. He walks down to where Matthew and Darren sit by us, and fires them on the spot.

"Don't come back when work starts up again," he spits at them. Remi looks as scared as I've ever seen him, staring up at that man.

"Fuck you," Matthew shouts at him, standing up and pushing him. The foreman snaps his arm out and drops Matthew with a solid punch in the mouth.

"You want some too, nip?" he says to Darren. Darren just looks away. "Hanging out with goddamn Indian retards," the foreman mutters, walking away. "We'll be back and working soon enough," he shouts at us. Mary stands to follow him, but I hold her back.

"We won," I told her. "All they got done in ten days are those stupid mounds." I point to them and all our eyes follow. Darren helps Matthew up and they walk away without a word to Remi. Within hours we have broken camp and are on the river back to home.

That night word began trickling down to us that the foundations of the dam have been blown up. Some actually claimed they had heard the explosion, like distant thunder in the middle of the night. At first, talk was that the crew had done it on purpose, on the orders of the government. They weren't going to bother fighting a long battle with us in court. But then word spread that the explosion had actually been a horrible accident and that was when we learned that the foreman had been killed in it. We felt bad for him, for his family if he had any. But that did seem to put an end to any talk of a dam. The way I figured it, the manitous were protecting special land. They were the ones responsible for the explosion.

That summer's events were quickly becoming local legend when a month later Richard, the Equalizer, came knocking for Remi.

"You're joking," I said to Richard.

He shook his head sadly. "RCMP's got two men in custody. They name Remi as an accomplice."

That's when I started laughing, when Richard blushed. I called for Remi and he came to the door, looking guilty. When he saw Richard he began to wail, and that's when I knew.

At first, Remi was held on reserve by the band's police force, in a little cell underneath the station. They let us see him only after Patrick threatened them with words I'd never heard come out of his mouth before. With Richard sitting nearby, we talked to our son, but he had gone somewhere deep into his mind — somewhere neither of us had seen him go before, and a place neither of us could get to.

"It's going to be OK, boy," his father told him.

"I'll have you home with me soon," I said. But Remi just stared down at his stocking feet, drooling. Richard had taken his shoes and belt for fear he'd hang himself. That was the strangest thing to me. Did my son have any idea about such things?

We stayed as long as we could. Richard had to practically drag us out. Within a week, the OPP came and escorted Remi south by train to North Bay. Patrick and me, we followed, spent every penny we had on a hotel while we waited weeks for trial, and visited Remi every day.

I waited and worried, left with only little events and remembrances to try and piece it all together. There were dark places, shadows in all of this that I could only guess at. We got us a lawyer from Indian Services, a tiny little Crow woman from somewhere out west. Everyone who knew of her said there wasn't any better. Her name was Angela Blackbird. She finally began filling in some of the pieces for us.

"The accused are a Matthew Cross and a Darren Shin," she told us. We sat with Remi in a little meeting room in the institution he was being held at. Remi was still deep in his mind. "At first, these two tried to pin the whole thing on Remi here, but under questioning by police and the Crown attorney, one of them admitted that Remi only carried a box of explosives that was too heavy for them. This one, Darren Shin, said on record that Remi didn't even know what he was carrying and that he's innocent of wrongdoing."

Patrick and me, we looked at each other and smiled for the first time in a long while.

"So what about Remi?" Patrick asked. "Why isn't he free to go?"

"That's the catch," Blackbird said. I watched Patrick's smile fade. "The OPP are still investigating and recommended that the Crown press charges of complicity so Remi doesn't disappear. He's going to have to go to trial. The good news is, I got him his own trial so he's not tied in with those other two. They're both being charged with first-degree murder, on top of explosives and theft charges. I wouldn't want to be those two."

Remi's trial came first. It made the papers. "Mentally Handicapped Cree Faces Charges for Abitibi Dam Explosion."

Everyone showed up to support us — Mother, Mary, Shirley, Suzanne and their kids. Angela Blackbird fought like a warrior for us. Got Darren on the witness stand. Matthew refused, but Darren had already pleaded guilty to all of it, knew he was doomed. Angry as I was at him, I admired him for trying his best for Remi. The day Darren took the stand in court, handcuffed and with his feet chained, wearing an orange jumpsuit, was the first time since Remi's arrest that I saw Remi come out of himself a little. He stared at Darren, then waved to him.

"The accused had nothing to do with the planning, preparation or carrying out of the explosion on Abitibi River?" Angela asked Darren.

"Nothing," Darren answered.

"His only involvement was unwittingly carrying a box of explosives too heavy for the two of you, with no idea of the contents or of your purposes with those contents?"

"Correct," Darren answered.

Then it was the Crown's turn. "So why did your story change so much from statements at arrest as compared to a week later?"

"I couldn't live with myself for lying about Remi's involvement. I couldn't pin it on him when he was innocent," Darren answered. Every last person in the court knew he was damning himself by speaking those words.

"So what you're saying is that Remi had nothing to do with this, other than carrying a box, having no idea what it contained."

"Correct," Darren answered. "We befriended him, and tricked him into helping. He's got an environmentally induced mental handicap, for chrissakes! How hard could it be to fool him?" As if on cue, Remi waved to Darren again, and the court broke out into laughter.

In the end, it was the judge who was left with the decision. Angela was confident. So was Patrick. "It's clear to me that the accused was an unwitting accomplice in this act of terrorism and, may I add, murder," the judge said, his voice nasal. "But as small a role as he played, let us keep in mind the destruction to property and to human life. It leaves me to ask this question: where were the parents of this young, handicapped man that he could be befriended by admitted terrorists and, furthermore, made a pawn by them? I do not blame the child here. I place blame on the parents. With this in mind, I deem it necessary that Remi Chakasim be made a ward of the state until it can be proven beyond a reasonable doubt that his parents are fit for the duty of his complete welfare. The proper authorities will decide upon his new place of residence, as well as the terms for his release back to his parents' custody. Case closed." With that he dropped his hammer, and I watched Remi being escorted out of the court.

And that is what I'm left with. It has been two months now and Remi is in the North Bay Centre for the Mentally Challenged. I take the ten-hour train ride once a week and spend Saturdays with him. His father fights hard on the phone for his release.

Darren's and Matthew's trial was not much longer than Remi's. Darren pleaded guilty and got forty years, twenty-five for killing the foreman and fifteen for the explosives. Matthew pleaded not guilty even though the case was sealed shut against him, and got life with no chance of parole for his effort. There was no greater reason for what they did. No honourable plan to help us Cree fight the corporations and government. They simply hated the foreman so bad that they figured he'd lose his job if they blew up his work. Darren claimed in his trial that they didn't want to kill the foreman. It was just a severe case of wrong place at the wrong time. I believe him.

I received a letter from Darren the other day. He's in Kingston Pen and he's sorry for Remi. Darren wrote me that he hooked up with Indian inmates and is involved in their sweat lodges and ceremonies now. They took him as a brother, even though he told them he's Japanese. He's become a celebrity with some Indians for blowing up that dam.

All I can do is keep faith in Remi's release. No one's really talking to us. No one knows who's in charge, it seems, or what course to take in order to get him back to us. Remi just sank back into wherever that place is that he goes. Two weeks after he was sent away, I sat and talked to him. I held him in my arms and rocked him and hummed him some old songs I hummed for him as a baby. Suddenly he sat straight up and stared out the window and spoke. His voice sounded like someone else's I'd heard a long time ago.

"Our world will be covered with water," he said. "Repent now, sinners. Make plans and be saved."

I stared, frightened by my child. All I could do was hug him and cry.

NORTH
Home

LEGLESS JOE
VERSUS BLACK ROBE

No roads connect Sharpening Teeth to the rest of the world. But we got roads here on the reserve, thin and covered in dirt like my nephew Crow. Four streets that form a square. In my dream a motorcycle gang, a bunch of hairy bikers, ugly bastards, roars down First Street, makes a left on Wabun, roars down Wabun, makes a left on Takan Road, roars down Takan Road, makes a left on Maheegan Street, roars down Maheegan and ends up right back on First. They pass like clockwork, every three minutes or so, never able to get out of second gear, getting madder and madder. Bikers would get bored pretty fast on a reserve like this, I tell you. They'd tear this town up quick.

It used to be the reserve was so small it couldn't even fit a full-time drunk. But then the economy worsened and the government shrank Indian benefits and most of the tourists quit coming here in summer and my wife left me. It got so bad I was a sad country song. I started my own little gang of serious drinkers. They call us the Cold Duck Four.

Booze affects a body in all sorts of ways. You might not eat nothing because you save all your money for a bottle, but still you get a paunchy stomach and soft face. I do, anyways.

The other weird effect is that when I started drinking, I began growing black whiskers on my face, enough now for a scraggly little goatee and funny long patches on my cheeks. Before I was a drinker my face was smooth as a woman's ass. My theory is that Cold Duck wine is a ploy of the white man to get us Indians drinking and at the same time to get us looking more like them. It seems to be working. The bastards. But one thing that drinking hasn't affected is my dreams.

I've dreamed all my life. Most do. But me, I try to live by my dreams. To act in waking hours as I do in sleep. To believe what they tell me. I can't always act the way I do in my dreams, obviously. I'm not about to wrestle giant, beautiful women with great hunting abilities whose clothes tear off effortlessly. But I try to get meaning from the dreams, to trust them. That's why, when I dreamt my niece Linda was dead last night, I knew she really was when I woke this morning. She killed herself, I knew. So I walked to her mother's, my sister's, to find out how.

"She ate pills," is all my sister tells me with red eyes. My sister won't let me hug her. I know how bad I smell. Linda was all by herself at school in Timmins, and that's when she did it.

"Let me help you with the funeral," I say. There is a purpose for me in the sadness. I stand taller and hold my chest out in order to battle the sobbing that is building inside of me. "I'll drum with the singers for my niece." I was once the best. A powwow circuit legend. Lead drummer with Black Water Singers.

"Father Jimmy doesn't allow drumming," my sister says and then tells me to leave.

I leave and look for Father Jimmy. This funeral will be Indian with the Catholic. I think of my sad niece Linda who slept with boys so they'd like her or because she was too drunk to say no, who ate too much to smother her guilt. She was a pretty little kid whose laugh made my breath hitch in my throat, her laugh was so clean.

The priest is smoking cigarettes and drinking coffee at the Sky Ranch, staring at Elise the waitress, my relation, who he calls Pocahontas.

"My niece is dead and I want the Black Water Singers at her wedding," I tell him soon as I sit down across the table. The wide-eyed look of fear settles back quickly into his squinty eyes. I've always frightened Father Jimmy with my stinky, big body and long black hair.

"So if she's dead, why does she want to get married?" the priest asks me. He hasn't shaved in a while and his round face is speckled with sharp grey hairs. My tongue grows thick so that I'm worried I won't be able to breathe. I get up quickly and leave, half as big as when I walked in.

People on the reserve tell me I'm a wino. I am known as Legless Joe the Wino. So what if I got legs? What's in a name? Actually, I got my nickname back in my biker days, on a bad acid trip one night. I convinced myself and the rest of my buddies that my legs had melted off. We cried and wailed about the horrible accident for hours, until somebody muttered, "Poor Joe. Poor Legless Joe Cheechoo." Needless to say, that got somebody giggling, and before you know it we're all laughing so hard, a few of us threw up. The name stuck. Now it precedes me. That story was one of Linda's favourites.

Drinking isn't an easy career, considering the price of a bottle of Cold Duck and the three lousy bums I hang with always trying to steal sips off me. My girl Cindy, she's one of the gang. She loves me. I call her my fly girl. I heard that in one of those music videos before and immediately I thought of her because she's pesky and likes to get into shit. Henry's so white he's yellowy coloured like an old newspaper and he's always trying to get into Cindy. He came up clearing bush for the railway years ago and stayed. He liked the speed of life around here, of living on Indian time. Henry's got some mighty weepy cold sores, but that's only half the reason I don't like him sipping my Duck. You can't overlook he's a white man. A good white man, mind you. But haven't white men taken enough from us? Silent Sam, the fourth Cold Duck, his mind has been surrounded by a fog not unlike the kind you see on a river in early morning. This is due, I believe, to his over-drinking and is where all of us will be in a few years.

A lot of white people here on the reserve find it easier to blame my drinking on the fact I was buggered in residential school up in Fort Albany when I was a boy. I let them think this is the reason, if it makes their life any easier. But lots of Indians around here were, and most of them don't drink at all. A government commission travelled up here a few years ago to chase down allegations and I was one of the only ones who would speak to them. Made me high-profile. Father Jimmy said that being able to say out loud that I been buggered is part of healing. I told him it made me feel like buggering him. But that was a year ago when he first come up to take over the church from the crazy old priest who called us heathens and swore more than me and went berserk during mass one Sunday.

On this sad morning that Father Jimmy makes fun of me at the Sky Ranch, I leave and head back into the bush to our summer place on the river, away from people. The bad news is already travelling the reserve. Everybody will know by noon. My girlfriend, Cindy, is still sleeping. I can hear her snoring ten metres away from our blue tarp teepee. Bottles and cans are scattered all around, glittering in the sun. I sit down and stare at the river and think about my niece Linda when she was just a skinny little kid with feet too big for her, slapping around town in rain boots. I can see her round face looking up to me, framed by messy braids, her asking me for a quarter to get a Popsicle at the store. Hard as I try, I can't see her face as an adult. Something inside won't let me. I hum an old song to myself, and bang time on my lap. It is the Death Song, the Funeral Song, sung by Grandfathers long before they ever knew of white men or Cold Duck.

It is an Indian summer this year, but still the mornings are cold when I wake up, and soon it will be time to make winter plans. The last three years running I've mostly been able to do small things like steal food or break windows, so the band constables are forced to keep me in a warm cell and feed me three times a day. Last year all of the Cold Duck Four was in jail at the same time for a solid month, waiting for the Crown attorney and judge to fly up and condemn us.

We'd broken into the Meechim Store late at night and ate potato chips and white bread and drank pop until we threw up. Cindy stayed in the cell next to me and Henry and Silent Sam and I communicated with her by tapping a quarter on the wall. It would have been easier to shout back and forth, but tapping felt good and it was a nice break from her gravelly voice.

The Crown said time served was enough punishment and our lawyer agreed with him, so the next day we were forced by the cold wind to break into the Meechim Store again. We sat there all night, eating and getting bored, waiting for the band cops to show. Finally we fell asleep, and we weren't discovered until the store opened the next morning. That got us through the rest of the winter. But the judge talked a long time about the three-strikes policy and it makes me think this winter I should be more careful or I'll end up in a maximum security joint down south somewhere, for the winter and summer and next couple of winters and summers too.

When Cindy and Henry and Silent Sam wake up, I tell them about my niece. Cindy begins to cry and holds me to her, wetting the shoulder of my shirt. Linda was one of the few people in my family who still talked to me and Cindy. Henry and Silent Sam sit side by side and look out to the river, not sure what to say. Sam has been a part of my life so long that we are brothers. This is the first time in a long time that I've seen my words actually make it through the thick haze surrounding his brain. He's crying too when he turns around to look at me.

"We got to drum for her at her funeral," he says. I nod. Me and Sam used to ride together in a motorcycle gang in our youth. There were eleven of us, called the Apostles. Hard as we tried, we could never find that twelfth member. We agreed to be communistic about the whole thing — no general, no lieutenants, no hierarchy. We rode around the north in summertime, drinking a lot and doing acid, having religious visions and helping people out who were in trouble. Stranded motorists, old ladies with flat tires, lost tourists. We put the fear of God into all of them when we pulled up, and left them with the love of Jesus in their hearts when we pulled away.

We were into our own Indian Catholic thing, all of us long-haired like the Man and treating others as we liked to be treated. You never saw so many back rubs and good words and rounds of beer bought without complaint as in our motorcycle club. But our gig didn't last long. We were too nice. Nobody would take the reins. When I think back on those days now, I realize that I was trying to make sense out of the bad part of my youth — wanting to believe that we should love one another, but not in the way adults I trusted at residential school sometimes loved me. Linda adored those stories of my biker days. They always made her laugh hard.

By the afternoon we're at our picnic table drinking.

"My niece was a good one," I say. The other three nod solemn. "She didn't need to die." The other three nod again. "Her mother's heart is broken for good," I say. "It is a bad day for the Cheechoo family."

Father Jimmy walks out of the Meechim Store, pretending not to notice us. But then he turns around and walks straight to me.

"There'll be no drums or chanting at Linda's funeral," he says to me. "This is a Catholic mass." I turn my head away from him. I can feel the anger like a heat coming from him. He thinks I'm a devil, that we're all devils. "It is hard enough on her mother that she committed suicide. You know what the Church says about suicides," he whispers, his face close to mine. "For the sake of the living, don't even show up at the church, Joe Cheechoo." He turns and walks away quickly. Cindy makes a twisted face at his back and sticks her tongue out at him.

I look over to Silent Sam. "He smells like Father McKinley back in Fort Albany," I say. Sam just looks away. Sam has the same recurring dream. He told me once. The scrapes of Father McKinley's feet as he climbs the stairs to our dormitory room, my eyes wide with the fear he would pick me again that night.

It is night and I'm drunk by the time I decide to go to my sister's house to help her prepare for the wake and the funeral. When I walk in the door, the number of people standing and sitting in the house makes me very nervous. Linda's brothers stand around, their hair out of ponytails. They talk to one another and sway to some music only they can hear. They are drunk too, which surprises me. But Crow, my youngest nephew, Linda's little brother, is nowhere to be seen. He was sitting in the reserve jail last I heard, charged with one thing or another. Friends and neighbours stand everywhere, most choosing to ignore me, but I get dirty looks from some of the old ladies. The house is so crowded it is like the whole reserve is here. Someone mentions that Linda's funeral won't be for almost a whole week, time for faraway relatives to get to Sharpening Teeth. I hear someone else say that Linda's body is in a freezer down in Timmins, and that they will fly it up in a couple of days.

My grandfather, Linda's great-grandfather, stands in the kitchen by himself. He is an old, old man now who spends much of his time talking to stray dogs and to birds. He sees me and smiles kindly. I'm a little shocked. He is the first person in a long time to do so.

I make my way through the crowd and see my sister sitting on the couch with Father Jimmy. He is holding her hand. He stands up when he sees me.

"You're not welcome here right now," he says. "You gave up the right to your sister's house when you picked up the bottle." My sister won't look at me. Everyone knows that Father Jimmy's favourite drink is Scotch on the rocks. His face is red from it now.

"I'm here to talk to my sister, not to you," I tell him, trying to hold in the shouting that hisses up from my stomach and burns my throat.

"You're here to try and talk your sister into a past that is gone forever," Father Jimmy says.

"Talk to me, sister," I say. She doesn't look up. "Talk to me, sister." Everyone is quiet, looking down at their feet. My sister won't look at me. I turn and leave.

There is nothing in me for a while, maybe two or three days. My insides are a hot, black cave. I lie in the blue tarp teepee and refuse to talk or eat. I only accept the half-finished bottles of Cold Duck that Cindy brings. I can smell autumn in the air and I know the leaves will change their colour overnight very soon. Whenever my eyes close in this blue teepee and I fall into sleep, I dream my autumn dream. I am on the back of a huge snow goose high over the swampy muskeg. I can feel the power of this goose as it flaps its wings. Below us I see a hunter aim his shotgun. He fires and the snow goose begins to fall to earth like a spinning feather. I hold onto its neck and wait for the impact. I see my frightened face reflected in the snow goose's black eye.

By the third day I know what I must do. I call a meeting. "What we're going to do," I tell my little gang, "will put us away for the winter, probably longer. You don't have to do it, but I'm going to." They ask me what, so I tell them. Cindy and Silent Sam agree but Henry is scared.

"I won't join you in this one," he says. "What about the third strike?" He is afraid for a big white prison. "I left the south and I don't want to go back," he says. But me, I no longer care.

When I commit a crime, I hear music. It's music I heard in a spy movie once, slinky sounding, with lots of drums and pianos.

Me and Cindy and Sam try to bust the church basement window quietly. There is no moon tonight, and in two days when it begins coming back, all my relations will be here and the funeral will begin and end. The window doesn't want to give so I kick it as quietly as I can but it smashes, cracking, then tinkling onto the basement floor. The police station is next door and I'm surprised they don't hear it. It's a sign I'm doing right. The three of us slide in, clumsy but safe.

All the excitement gets Cindy going. Soon as Sam makes his way upstairs, she pulls me to her and starts whispering unchurchy thoughts in my ear. She knows this might be our last chance for a very long time. But this church basement brings back memories of another church basement long ago and my throat gets tight. I whisper, "Can't," and push my way upstairs.

Sam has already found the sacristy and the Halo Vino and we thank the Lord the bottle caps twist off. It's no Cold Duck but it does the trick and within an hour we're talking and laughing. We know this is the party of the season and soon it will be over so we go hard.

I'm pretty drunk when I put on Father Jimmy's vestments. I lead Cindy and Sam to the altar and say a few words. I get rolling into my sermon with a bottle in one hand and it's not long before they're rolling in the aisles and I'm shouting out that they're blast-femurs and devil's spunk and children of the corn. "In the name of your father," I say, "and the sun, and the holy mackerel, bend over, because this priest is going to drive."

The more they laugh and the more we drink and carry on, the more hard thinking I do. Maybe it's because we're drinking red wine and I'm not used to it, or maybe it's because I know this is my last night of freedom for a long time, but suddenly I realize that this collar and black robe and the gold chalice and the white Host are like a costume an actor uses in a movie to make himself fit the part. All my life I been told that these things are what gives a priest his power, that they're his medicine. But that's not it at all. What you got, good or bad, comes from inside. A simple realization, I admit, but it makes me start looking in a new light at what a long-ago priest did to me. He wasn't the Church. He was a bad man acting like he was good. As for Father Jimmy, all I can say for him, standing here looking down from where he normally stands, is that he really believes what he does and says is right.

Oh, drinking the Halo Vino and sermonizing to Cindy and Sam, I really did begin feeling the warmth of that righteous light. Maybe I wasn't ready to forgive the world for all its sins, but I got a glimpse into the understanding, the thinking behind forgiveness. There's these two nuns that live by Father Jimmy, who help him with his work and cook and clean for him besides. A good deal if ever I heard of one. Sister Jane, she can swear like a sailor, and Sister Marie is all fat and smiles. It used to be I'd sit long hours and chat with them, back before Father Jimmy came to the reserve. We'd sit on my picnic table by the Meechim Store and soak up the sun and talk. They're good women. I'm sad we don't see each other much anymore. But it was them who first talked to me about it being impossible to be perfect, to instead try to be like God wants us to be, which is always trying to be better. Suddenly I know how to end my sermon.

"Pass me another bottle, Cindy, and I will sermonize thee further," I say from the pulpit. Cindy struts up, trying to do a sexy wiggle, flashing me her saggy breasts after she hands me a fresh bottle. She goes to sit back down with Sam.

"There are many things us priests know," I begin. "There are many secrets of the world we possess, secrets like how to get into boy-sized pairs of underwear." Cindy and Sam hoot at that one. "We know things you don't know. We got a direct phone line to God." I take a gulp of wine. "I will keep this short so we can socialize after mass. As Jesus said, wherever two or three of you Indians gather in my name, get loaded. What I must tell you is that man makes mistakes. He is not perfect. Look at Father Jimmy. Look at you and me. We get drunk, we fall down. We do bad things, we've got to take the fall for doing them. In other words, man is fallible. But God, *Gitchi-Manitou*, the Great Spirit, now there's someone who is perfect, who knows everything, who makes no mistakes. Hey, way up in those clouds, he can't afford to fall, because it's a long way down to earth. So God's gotta keep his balance. In other words, God's pretty much infallible."

Cindy and Sam nod respectfully as I walk from the pulpit. "Drink to me and I'll drink to thee," I shout at the bottom of the altar, tipping my head and drinking as much of the red liquid as I can. I smash the bottle on the ground, and it feels as good as anything I've done in a long time. God knows I'm not dishonouring Him. Sam and Cindy and me head back to the sacristy to drink more and wait for the law.

But they don't come. We drink and shout and drink some more. Bottles lie everywhere. We've smelled the place up, so I open a window for air. Cindy nods off. In a rare mood he saves just for me, Sam sings me a Cree song he learned from his grandmother when he was little. His voice carries me up to somewhere soft and I lie back and let it hold me.

I dream a good dream, a strange one. There are many images, lots of dreams swirling around one another like the northern lights do at this time of year, just above your head so that you feel you can jump up and touch them. At one point there's me and Sam and Henry and Cindy and Linda and a half-dozen other Indians, including some of my old motorcycle gang members, sitting around a long wooden table with the Man

Himself with his long hair and robe. He's not saying who he is, but he's got nobody fooled. There's a halo on his head. There's no mistaking him. We're all about to eat. He picks up a big silver lid in the middle of the table and a Canada goose pops out and struts about the table, ruffling its feathers. The goose stops in front of Linda and honks and Linda stands up. I'm happy I can picture her face again. She climbs onto the table and begins to grow small, shrinking before our eyes. She climbs up on the goose's back and it flaps its wings and flies off as Linda looks back at us, smiling and waving.

We all feel good and Jesus mutters, "Goddamn, that was a big goose." Then he looks at me and says, "Legless Joe — can I call you Legless Joe? This is a pretty easy dream to read, I mean your niece flying off into the sky on the back of a goose. You don't need too much of a tricky mind to figure that one out. I know you are mad at me for some past wrongs done to you in my name, but let me tell you not to lie there sleeping any longer, because that Father Jimmy, he's a prick, and he'll make sure you go up the river for a long time. So in my name, get up, walk, be free. Hit the road before dawn."

Jesus turns his head to look up at the sky and Linda is still in the picture, on the goose's back, getting smaller and smaller, looking over her shoulder every once in a while, smiling shyly and waving. Then Jesus walks to his waiting helicopter and climbs in. The blades start turning in a *thump-thump-thump* and I wake up to the thumping of the sacristy window we opened for air last night banging in the wind. I get up quick and grab Father Jimmy's robe and begin wiping off all the bottles and doors and the altar, the spy music pounding in my head. I'm not too worried about fingerprints. Sometimes I think the police around here couldn't find the river if they had to. I wake up Sam and Cindy and scoot them downstairs and help push them through the basement window. I use a chair for a boost and the sun is just starting to break as we make our way to the school where we can get out of the cold for a while and drink a cup of coffee.

It's been two days and I haven't had a drink in that whole time. The elders tell me that alcohol and drumming are like a hard frost and a flower, or a cock and ice water. Father Jimmy knows I'm responsible for the break-in but can't prove it. Last night I found my grandfather and asked him to do a sweat lodge with me, to purify me. Then I sat by the river and drummed a long time.

All my relations are here and I walk into the church carrying my big drum in both arms and sit down at the back. Everyone is turning their heads and looking at me. Linda's casket is in the middle of the aisle, up front, by the same altar I preached at two nights ago. It arrived later the same morning we got safely out of the church. The whole reserve turned out at the airfield, and we watched as her casket was unloaded off the plane and we all followed the chief's big red pickup as it drove her slow from the runway to my sister's house. It was the most powerful, quiet thing I ever saw, that long line of people walking behind her. They had the official wake that evening, but I stayed away, sat on the river with my grandfather, drumming and thinking.

Father Jimmy enters from the sacristy followed by two altar boys. He blesses everyone and says some prayers and reads from scripture. When he's done that, he starts his sermon.

"All of you know by now the crime committed against this church the other night. Most of us have a good idea who's responsible." I can tell by the way Father Jimmy says this that he doesn't even realize I'm here. "This crime has put a further damper on our community. I came close to not being able to perform this funeral mass today, I was so upset." The whole congregation's eyes are looking at the floor. He doesn't even realize that he speaks to them like little children, I see.

"The Church has taken your hand and led you a long way," he continues. "But there are those among us who would take your other hand and pull you in the opposite direction. You get nowhere that way. You must decide on your path and stick to it. Do not become tempted by Satan, for he can only lead you to harm. Satan comes in all forms, in the bottle, in the drum, in the form of pre-marital sex, in drugs. Look for him, and be on guard against him." The congregation continues staring at the floor, everyone but me, it seems. I stare up at Father Jimmy.

"In her depression and drug- and alcohol-induced haze, Linda Cheechoo committed a mortal sin," Father Jimmy says. "She took the life God gave her and threw it back in His face. Without realizing what she was doing, she spat on Him. I tell you with a sad heart that this is precisely the behaviour that bars a person's admission into the Kingdom of Heaven."

I see my sister's head move, way up front in the first row. It turns to look at Father Jimmy.

"I thought long and hard about what to say to you today in this time of great sorrow. You all know me to speak my mind, and know that I believe in tough love. I offer you all a warning." Other heads rise up to look at Father Jimmy. My grandfather's, my nephews', my aunts' and uncles'. "What Linda has done is reprehensible." He says this word carefully. "It was an act of cowardice." More heads turn up to him. "Yes, I am a believer in tough love, and these are tough words and, if we are to believe scripture, Linda must now spend eternity in purgatory as payment for her sins." Everyone is now looking up at Father Jimmy. "If all of you take this as a hard-earned lesson, the hardest lesson you will ever learn, and live your lives according to the Bible, you can still enter heaven. Poor Linda Cheechoo will only be able to peer through the gates like a child outside an amusement park, desperately wanting to get in but having no admission ticket. You must live God's Law or suffer His consequences."

I lift my big drum up from the seat beside me and carry it to the centre of the aisle at the back of the church so that it is lined up with Linda on the other side. I kneel by it, lift my stick and bang the drum once, hard. It echoes in the quiet church. Father Jimmy looks back to me, his face turning red. He shouts, "There will be no blasphemy here, Joe Cheechoo!" but I cut him off with another hammer of the drum. It travels well in here, like a strong heart.

I bang again and then pick up a rhythm, the rhythm of the river. My funeral song. Father Jimmy rushes from the pulpit. In the aisle he is cut off by Linda's brothers and my uncles and my grandfather and some cousins as they make their way back to me.

They kneel around my drum in a circle just as I begin my best wail. It is pure and true and rises to the rafters and sends a shiver down my back. The others join in the drumming, picking up the beat with hands or shoes tugged off their feet. I constrict my throat more and the song sails higher, bringing others in the church to stand in a circle around us. My grandfather answers my wail and the others in the circle join us too, eyes closed and throats tight. We sing high and drum hard. We sing for Linda's *uchak*, her soul, our voices rising to pull it from her quiet body at the front of the church and carry it, protected by her relations, to its resting place.

Father Jimmy retreats to his pulpit, his face flushed, a look of fear in his eyes. He turns and goes back to the sacristy. The rhythm comes faster and I think hard of Linda, of her as a little girl running around wearing rain boots too big for her small feet. I think of her flower-patterned dress, of her red bike, of her drinking one night with me, of her laugh, the sadness that dulled her eyes the last time I saw her. I look up to see my sister, her mother, looking down at me. Her eyes are Linda's, a little of the spark returned.

GASOLINE

Crow swears he's been growing whiter over the last year that he's been huffing. Not white like a white person, but like a ghost or a vampire. Crow kind of likes that idea. He sways on the road, talking out loud to the ghosts, laughing spittle, snot running from his nose. He holds his arm in front of him, lines it up with the road, stares at what lies ahead. The streets of Sharpening Teeth look as long and skinny to Crow as his own arm. Especially at night with the few streetlights spaced far apart, brightening the pale dust and gravel like a thin scar running into the black. He stumbles and falls down, laughing at the scrape that starts to bead droplets of blood on his palm.

"I am sixteen today!" he shouts. "I am sixteen and today I am a man." He pulls the plastic shopping bag out of his pocket and places it over his nose and mouth, then hyperventilates. He thinks he must look like a bullfrog, white bag of throat expanding and collapsing. A mighty, mighty bullfrog, able to leap over cars and fences and bushes. He can leap so far he can fly.

Crow climbs up onto a car, stomping up the hood and onto the roof. Crow leaps and flies off, flaps his thin wings and takes flight for a moment. He lands in a bush and can feel its sharp branches sticking him. Rolling onto his back, he stares at the stars. He needs to find more gasoline.

When he closes his eyes, the stars remain, tattooed on the inside of his eyelids. He can feel the prick and needle heat burn on the insides of his lids, the heat burning brighter as his head begins to thump and shriek. It used to take longer before the crash. It's time to break into the tank of a car or snowmobile and resoak his rag.

The crunch of tires on gravel sends stones popping and ricocheting in his skull. Truck doors slam. Feet pound. Hands grab. Crow opens his eyes and his rigid body goes slack. Jack and Ron pull on his ears, slap his face.

"How you feeling, Crow?" Jack asks.

"You huffing again tonight, Tonto?" Ron asks.

Crow knows it's best to become a turtle with the police. He sinks into himself. If he says nothing they can't hit him as hard, charge him with more charges, threaten more punishment. Jack-ass and mo-Ron. Hands rifle his pockets, pull his secrets from him.

"What's this? Something you found for show-and-tell come Monday?" Ron asks. He's Mohawk from somewhere way down south. Not Cree at all.

"Or part of a Molotov cocktail in a plastic bag? You weren't thinking of firebombing the police station, were you?" Jack asks. He's Metis, looks white as the judge that flies up to Sharpening Teeth every month. Crow shrinks deeper into his jacket. "Let's take him in," Jack says. "Destruction of private property, for one. Look at the dents on the hood of that new Blazer. Trespass to boot."

"I hope he doesn't shit himself in lock-up again," Ron says. "I hate cleaning that up."

Crow sometimes wishes he remembered how to speak his language. Snatching phrases from old women and men walking by like he's pickpocketing them, he listens to the harsh syllables and light tongues that make Crow remember when he was a baby, a year old. His first memories, his great-grandfather talking to him about trapping brother beaver and drawing his shotgun on sister goose. Old man is crazy now. Talks to dogs. Crow steals change from his money jar whenever he goes over. Oldest man in the world. What a family he is from. As if the old man isn't bad enough, his uncle is Legless Joe, the town drunk. So drunk all the time he doesn't even notice he's got legs.

"Full name," mo-Ron asks Crow from across the metal desk. Crow slumps in his chair, tries to focus hard on the pain in his wrists from the handcuffs.

"Francis Cheechoo," Jack-ass answers for him. "Come on, Francis. Cooperate with us so we can get on with our lives."

"Age?" Ron asks. The harsh lights of the station burn Crow's eyes. His head aches fierce. "What are you? Fourteen? Fifteen?"

"I am sixteen today," Crow answers quickly.

"Jesus, Francis, you still look fourteen," Jack says. "You better quit the huffing and start eating proper. You're a skinny little bugger."

"Sixteen today, huh?" Ron butts in. "Well, I guess we got to charge you like an adult."

Crow's been in more fights than he can remember. He's got a knife scar on his neck from juvie hall in North Bay. More broken-bottle cuts than he can count on his arm. Had his leg broke in a fight once. Got it stomped on. Not his right leg. The other one. But it isn't called the wrong leg, either, although that's how he thinks of that side of his body. He can't remember what you call the other side. Crow forgets the simplest things now. It's not right, it's wrong.

He's been in lock-up for three days. When he's not huffing, Crow becomes Francis again. He doesn't know why. His mother hasn't come that he knows of, and neither has his mother's cousin, his Aunt Elise. Nothing to huff for three days. Nothing to do in the cell but tell the old drunks next door to fuck off and quit stinking up the place, or shout at them to speak English, goddammit, because Cree sounds like fucking Chinese. Francis is shaking all the time now, like it's cold in here, even though the few others who pass through complain of such heat in September.

"The geese don't know to fly south," one old drunk tells the other. "Suddenly it will be cold fast and then they'll be in trouble."

"Indian summer, eh?" the other one says. "That's what I think we should call this drunk tank, ha!" Both men laugh loud. Francis thinks they're stupid.

Aunt Elise shows up but doesn't have bail for him. Rules change at sixteen, she finds out. Bail is higher. Everybody knows Elise has no money. The bingo hall and Meechim Store have her money tied up.

The police let her talk to Francis. "Look at you," she says. "Ever sick-looking, you. You're going to end up just like your uncle. It runs in your blood. You want to be the second Legless Joe on this reserve?" Aunt Elise is nineteen and works sometimes at the Meechim Store and the Sky Ranch. She is the reserve beauty, and all his friends want to be with her. She spends money on girls' magazines and makeup.

A couple of days pass and Francis' stomach gets worse and

worse. He can't hold anything down. He shakes and shivers. The old men in the cell next door get released. One, then two new ones arrive. Francis realizes that one of them is the same old man.

"Hey, let's call this place Indian summer, ha!" he laughs.

Francis takes to walking up and down in his cell. It is six steps by six steps. At nighttime he dreams of taking a five-gallon red plastic container of the ultra-super unleaded gasoline that makes boats, cars, trucks and snowmachines run clean, raising it above his head and pouring it on himself. A shower of power. The pure burn of gasoline in his eyes and in his throat turns to fire. A cold blue fire that shimmers and splashes around Francis, altering him, burning him so hot he glows white, pale white like a ghost. Crow's arms stretching up higher until feathers made from that stuff that doesn't burn sprout from his arms, then his chest and shoulders, feathers sprouting on his ass, even, and on his legs. The feathers singe black and he lets out a mighty caw that swallows up the blue flame and Francis is Crow. Black Crow. Burnt by fire and slashed by knives and indestructible, flying up above Sharpening Teeth and across the river, free.

A week after Crow gets busted, Great-grandfather shows up and pays his bail. He buys Crow lunch at the Sky Ranch and laughs at nothing, like a crazy old bugger. Crow excuses himself as soon as he can, to look for gasoline.

Crow is with Jerry Meekis by the river a couple of days later when his Aunt Elise finds him. Crow is buzzing hard. Elise is crying. "Your sister Linda is dead," she says, looking down at him. "She OD'd on sleeping pills last night, down in Timmins." Crow looks up at his aunt, her head is framed by the sun. Her lips move but he doesn't get the message real well. Doesn't want it right now. Elise walks away, crying. Jerry stares at Crow. Crow picks up his plastic bag and takes deep breaths. Jerry doesn't take his eyes from him for a while.

Edwin Blueboy invites Crow over to his house that night. Crow knows that Edwin thinks Crow's cool because Crow told Miss Lanscomb to kiss his balls and was suspended from school for it and never went back. Edwin is three years younger. He informs Crow that four times now he has told different teachers to kiss his balls, but all he gets is months' worth of detentions. Mr. Hughes the gym teacher actually laughed when Edwin said, "Kiss my balls, Mr. Hughes."

After he stopped laughing, Mr. Hughes said in his Scottish accent, "I'll bite the wee buggers off, ya little bastard. Go to the vice-principal's office."

Crow is on Edwin's porch after dark, with all six hours of *The Stand* on videocassette and a two-and-a-half-gallon red plastic container filled with super unleaded. Over at Two Bays Tackle he slipped the three cassettes one at a time into his pants whenever Maggie the cashier wasn't looking. When he saw how easy that worked, he picked up the red plastic gas can from a pyramid of them in the middle of the store, walked out the door, walked up to the gas pump outside, filled his can with the high-grade, put the nozzle back, waved to Maggie as she chatted on the phone, then walked away. He really is becoming invisible.

"Where's your mom?" Crow asks.

"She's at your mom's house with everyone else. What happened to your sister?" Edwin asks, looking nervous. "Did she really kill herself?"

Crow ignores him and walks into Edwin's room. He rummages around and finds a white T-shirt.

"Don't use that," Edwin says, standing behind him. "That's my new shirt." Crow walks to the kitchen and pulls a Northern Store plastic bag from the cupboard. He opens the gas can and pours a good amount on the shirt, Edwin whining, then places the shirt in the bag. He hyper-breathes into this new bag until he falls flat on his back, like he's been hit in the forehead with a long board.

When he is feeling able, Crow goes through Edwin's four-room house, looking. Edwin follows, acting afraid and talking. Crow finds her stash of booze locked in a wooden box. He carries it to the kitchen and smashes the box apart with an electric can opener. Edwin tries to tell him no, but Crow gets Edwin to shut up with a mouthful, then another, of rye. In an hour, Edwin is so drunk he throws up in his little sister's room. Claire is eleven and Louise is nine. They peer into the kitchen from the hallway at Crow and their brother sitting at the table.

"You're a pussy," Crow says to Edwin. "You never even taken a little sniff in your life." Crow holds his bag out to Edwin. Edwin shakes his head. Crow places the bag over his nose and mouth to prove he's bad to the bone, and breathes in and out quickly. He hears little popping sounds in his head now whenever he huffs, hundreds of little bubbles, like bubble bath popping inside his ears. Edwin's sisters stand there in the doorway in their nightgowns, watching with big eyes. Edwin keeps sipping on the rye bottle, making a gagging noise in his throat each time.

"Here, try it," Crow says to the girls, holding out the bag. "This is the same stuff that makes cars run, boats float and people fly." He laughs hysterically at his words. Edwin's sisters duck away quickly into the hallway. But then the oldest one,

Claire, walks into the kitchen and over to Crow, her hand stretched out to the bag.

"Claire!" her sister hisses from the doorway. Edwin is so drunk all he can do is laugh hysterically.

"Let me try it if it's so good," Claire says. Crow sees his sister Linda in her eyes, hears her voice in Claire's.

"You're at home safe with Mom right now," Crow says. "You can't have any."

"Gimme, Crow!" she says, holding out her hand to his hand clutching the bag.

"Only if you put my movie on," Crow says. Claire darts off to the living room and digs through the pile of videos until she finds it. She slides it into the VCR and *The Crow* pops up on the screen. Brandon Lee, son of Bruce, dodges bullets, bleeding, living on although they shoot him and stab him. Crow is drawn to the pure sounds of violence on the flickering walls. Claire sits cross-legged in front of the screen, transfixed on the men shooting guns and Brandon Lee's pale ghost face.

"That is me," Crow says. "I am Crow. I am invincible."

"He is Crow," Edwin says from behind, drawn too to the sounds and shadows. "This is Crow, the invincible, invisible man. Stabbed one hundred times and still alive!" Edwin begins to giggle uncontrollably. Claire doesn't seem to hear her brother, her mouth half open, eyes fixed on the screen, unblinking. Something pops loud in Crow's head.

"Look at me, Linda!" Crow screams at her. "Look here at me!" He runs to the TV, picks it up and smashes it onto the floor. Claire screams and jumps up, runs away. Edwin begins laughing harder and falls down. Crow wants to stop, but he can't. He grabs pictures from the walls and hurls them, runs to the kitchen and rips cupboards open, smashes the cups and bowls and plates. He runs back to the living room and upends the couch, throws the coffee table against the wall. He runs to the window and pulls the curtains down, then grabs a chair and hurls it against the glass, the window shattering. "I am Crow, Linda!" he screams. "I am invisible, not you!" Then he remembers his can of gasoline.

He walks around with it, sloshing floors and walls until the little house stinks with the fumes. He reaches into his pocket and pulls out his lighter, flicks it and touches off the gasoline. The blue flame runs quickly away, the blue licking the orange carpet and yellow walls, the blue licks disappearing into the walls and blowing out smoke. The smoke gathers quickly on the ceiling, then drops down onto the rest of the house like a choking fog. Claire and Louise scream and run for the door, but the blue licks pop up in front of them, turning to an angry black and red on the front door. Crow runs to the girls, his eyes stinging, and grabs one under each arm. He blindly stumbles over the mess he's made, tripping over the giggling Edwin. Crow drags the girls to where the now black smoke runs out of the house. He lifts and pushes each girl through the window and onto the lawn.

His eyes are useless now. The house roars yellow and red and black. He can't breathe, crawling on his stomach, his hands groping for Edwin. "Edwin!" he screams in a cough. There is the roaring sound of big things cracking open, wooden walls going up. Crow is scared. A little boy. He gives up to the smoke, thinks of black scorched wings and dead Cree boys, burnt and oozing. He slips into a nap, barely feeling Edwin's hands pulling at his feet, Edwin laughing and choking, the shouts of Edwin's sisters on the lawn.

Crow was lucky, the doctor says. He is lying in a bed in the little hospital beside the church. He's having a hard time breathing. There is oxygen and a mask beside his bed to help him when he needs it. Jack-ass the cop is posted at his door until he's well enough to fly out to Cochrane for court. "There's no getting out of this one with easy time," Jack tells him. "No more juvie hall for you. You entered the big time."

Crow's mother comes to visit, and his Aunt Elise and uncles and cousins he hasn't seen in a long time. They've all gathered for Linda's funeral. "This is not what I needed at a time like this, Francis," his mother tells him, her eyes red and puffy. "They're going to take you away." His mother cries some more. Crow wants to cry but can't. His mother talks to the doctor about Crow's huffing and the doctor starts giving him medication that makes him feel light-headed, maybe a little better. But he sucked up so much smoke he still can't stand up. He thinks of his sister Linda, of when they were little kids out at the goose camp. He misses her. Her laugh. Her eyes.

A couple of days later, Crow hears the commotion outside. The plane with his sister's body has landed at the airport and everyone on reserve has gone out to meet it. All Crow can do is look from his window on the second floor at all the people walking around below. Then the chief's red pickup passes by with Linda's casket in the back. Crow tries to call out and coughs up black soot and blood.

That night he wakes to the sound of a drum and Indian singing on the river. He wants badly to be where the sound is coming from. It is music he can imagine Brandon Lee as the Crow listening to. It matches the beat of his heart under his hospital gown. The medication makes him fall back asleep.

On the day of his sister's funeral, the doctor refuses to give the family permission to bring Crow to the church. "He's too weak," the doctor says. "He suffered severe smoke inhalation to the point he's permanently damaged his lungs. Not to mention all the damage he'd already inflicted with gas sniffing."

Crow stares out the window at the church spire. He hears the drumming again, but this time he's sure it is not a dream. He hears one voice, Indian singing, then many. The song is coming from the church.

Tears come to Francis' eyes. He feels a little relief, is able to sit up in his bed now. He taps his hand on his thigh in time.

GOD'S CHILDREN

SEPTEMBER 1

I've been here a year, and a lesser man would have been driven mad or been driven away by now. These people are obstinate, stubborn creatures for the most part, who smile and nod at me when I offer advice and then do just the opposite. I never asked to be sent to this parish. The middle of Northern Ontario is worlds away from my beloved Toronto. Today, despite the warm spell, is, after all, the harbinger of autumn, which means that the snows and arctic winds are not far behind. Perhaps this is the reason for my blue mood.

Father Wilkes, God watch over the mad old bastard's soul, did more damage on this reserve and drove more Cree from the Church than a plague of locusts could have. Over the last year, Sisters Jane and Marie have filled me in on his behaviour, how it became more and more bizarre, how he turned mass into rude and scatological monologues, how he railed against everyone. As Sister Jane put it, "He'd say a whole lot of fuck, shit, piss, heathen and devil worshipper in his homilies." I was taken aback by the language, I must admit.

In his defence, it isn't hard to see how one can go mad in such an isolated community. Satan comes in many forms here — in the sweat lodges, in the bottle, in the Cree drumming and dancing. Although I consider myself a modern man, it isn't difficult for me to slip into pre-Vatican II mode, sensing the devil's work all around, feeling the need to fortify myself against it. Although Sisters Marie and Jane sometimes offer decent conversation, it isn't enough. I need to find another outlet for this malaise that builds inside me.

SEPTEMBER 3

I discovered another of Father Wilkes' mad ramblings this morning, this one scribbled in black felt-tip marker in the strangest of places. My dresser drawer was sticking, so I removed my clothes and took the drawer from the dresser. On the bottom of it I found this note: "The Indians don't take me seriously. I can hear them laughing at me from as much as a half kilometre away." Clearly, he'd lost his senses by this point.

In the first month or so, I found his notes everywhere. One of my favourites is "These nuns are trying to poison me with their blueberry pies and farts." Why he had it taped on the back of the television remains a mystery. Another one, scribbled in the coat closet by the mud-room, reads, "Indians purposely created the canoe to be a giant replica of a woman's holy place. I know now why they sit in them and laugh and point fingers at me." One that was a little spookier read, "The flies, no matter what I do, return to this house. I'm hearing voices of the damned most nights when I close my eyes."

His most lucid scribbling was a full note taped in the cupboard, which I would never have found had I not been cleaning so thoroughly that day. "The old man who talks to dogs called me over this morning. I was surprised, for we rarely even wave to one another. I was even more surprised when he spoke English to me. He called me Black Robe and told me this: 'You think us Indians are children with little hearts, and your heart is big. Listen careful, Black Robe, for I want to help you understand these people. Their hearts are bigger than you know, and they know more about things than you guess.' Then he walked away, with a mangy, toothless dog following and growling behind him."

I wasn't sure what to make of that particular note. I know who the old man is that he speaks of, and the note was the most sane of any of his writing. But the words of the old man echoed in my head for a long time.

SEPTEMBER 4

I ran into the wino Legless Joe Cheechoo and his gang of miscreants again today. If there is someone who embodies all of the poorest qualities of the Cree more than this one, I have not met him. They were sitting in their usual spot on the picnic table by the Meechim Store, Joe and that ugly tart Cindy groping one another in plain view of whoever wandered by. When he saw me, he dared offer me a drink from his bottle of cheap wine. "Good day, Father," he said to me. "Sit down and have a swig." My declining seemed to egg him on more. "Oh, there's going to be some loving tonight, Father," he continued, kissing Cindy full on the mouth. "This one, she's a warm one. Oh yeah, Dad," he said. I simply walked away. I had no other choice.

I wanted to help him. Back when I first arrived here, he expressed to me that he'd been abused by a priest in his youth. I told him that I'd pray for him, and that expressing this was the first step on the road to healing. What I thought were kind words seemed to anger him more. It was my first taste of befuddlement when trying to understand these people, in trying to relate to them so I can begin the process of leading them back into the fold.

At dinner tonight I again broached the topic of Father Wilkes and his actions in his last months on the reserve that seemed to so alienate the people here.

"It wasn't his actions, only," Sister Jane said. "We never had the majority of the reserve coming to church at all." I don't believe her. She seems to have a chip on her shoulder. Maybe she's been here too long.

When I first arrived here to Sharpening Teeth and I'd had my first encounter with Joe Cheechoo and his disreputable bunch, I made the mistake of telling Sisters Jane and Marie about it at the dinner table that night. None of us was talking. I'd already learned that Sister Jane had a dirty mouth. Sister Marie is the shortest, fattest woman I've ever seen. She has these horrible, supposedly uncontrollable gas attacks that leave me gasping for air. But I told them of the hulking, long-haired Indian sitting on a picnic table by the Meechim Store. I told the sisters of how he'd waved me over and introduced himself as Legless Joe and blurted right out, as if I'd known him forever, that a priest in his youth had sodomized him. "I didn't know what to say," I told the sisters at the dinner table that long-ago night. "He offers me a sip from his wine bottle. I turn around and tell him that the only wine I drink is on Sunday during mass. I can tell he's a scoundrel, and I don't really believe his talk.

"Anyway, the older one with them, who has only a few teeth, asks, 'How do you manage to keep it hidden from the congregation?' I'm not sure if he's trying to pull my leg so, as earnestly as I can, I explain to him that my sipping the wine is not something to be hidden but to be shared, that it is a

celebration of the Eucharist, that it represents Jesus' blood."
I remember looking at the sisters at this point. Sister Marie
listened intently, her big eyes opened wide. Sister Jane sat
with her hands folded in front of her mouth, staring at me
as if looking for the opportunity to catch me in a mistake. I
continued telling them my story.

"They all look at me oddly for a moment and then this
Legless Joe character pipes up, 'So you're one of them watcha-
callits? One of them vampires or something?' They all laughed
at that one, laughed at me. I realized I was wasting my time
with them, so I stood up, wished them a good day and walked
away. Later that day, when I saw them again, they looked at
me and held their hands over their necks." It was a simple story
I told to the sisters, one meant to be entertaining as well as
educational about one of my first days on this reserve. But
Sister Jane made it into something very different, and right
then was when I realized that she was a troublemaker, that she
was far too liberal.

"Well, you damn well better believe that Joe Cheechoo
was a victim of sexual abuse up in Fort Albany. The government formally charged a number of the sick bastards who were
responsible, including a priest. If you want my opinion, Father
James, what the people here need is someone who listens to
them, who tries to understand that they're not of our white
culture — not someone who walks away."

Sister Marie looked horrified at the attack on me. But I
took it in stride. I'd already researched these two nuns, and I
knew Sister Jane was of an order that didn't look down on nuns
smoking cigarettes and using foul language. These nuns were
well known for living in the inner cities and trying to convert
drug addicts and prostitutes with education and handouts. That

was all fine and good, but I was of the other school, the more conservative of the Jesuits who'd witnessed these lax policies for over a decade and had watched as the Church lost its grasp on its people. What both the converted and unconverted needed was a dose of reality, of what Sister Jane would call tough love. Obey God's Law or pay the consequences of an eternity of suffering. What the world needs — what this reserve needs — is a dose of simplicity, of someone telling them what is right and what is wrong, not being told that their godless actions are fine and dandy. Sister Jane and I are diametrically opposed. As for Sister Marie, well, she's a bit of a simpleton.

All this stirring of memory has left me a touch frazzled. I look forward to my glass of Scotch tonight, my one indulgence. Keeping it hidden from the sisters is wrong, I know, but all I need is to hand ammunition to Sister Jane, to have it known on the reserve that I imbibe the occasional drink. I've even gone so far as to work it so that I receive my supply directly from Toronto, on the mail plane.

SEPTEMBER 7

It was warm today, on my daily walk. Hot, actually. The sun beating down on my head and neck was a wonderful mood elevator. I will try to enjoy these last days of summer, these days that are truly becoming an Indian summer, to their fullest.

I decided to treat myself to a soft drink and so I walked into the Meechim Store. That pretty, young Indian woman, Elise Cheechoo, was at the counter, talking to a friend. I hovered close to them, pretending to decide on a choice of potato chips, in order to see what they were talking about. As it turns out, Elise's young nephew, Francis, whom most of the young people around here refer to as Crow, had been arrested and was languishing in the reserve lock-up for one petty crime or another. He is one of a number of youngsters on the reserve who've reportedly been involved in the behaviour of sniffing gasoline in order to get high. I'd read about this practice in remote northern communities while preparing to move up here. Another sign that these people are wandering aimlessly and need the Church for guidance. I made a mental note to try to fit this development into my homily on Sunday.

I've been having troubling dreams lately. After each one I pray to You for them to stop. They involve myself and that young girl Elise. They are the first erotic dreams I can remember since my teenage years. She truly is a striking-looking woman, long black hair and the noted high native cheekbones. She is slim and well-groomed. But it is her eyes and her smile that get to me. The combination is at once innocent and provocative beyond explanation. She always greets me with a shy "Hello," and I become like a chattering schoolboy in her presence. Sometimes it's almost as if she knows that I dream lewd dreams about her, which leaves me red-faced and departing her store quickly. To make matters worse, she's now working at the Sky Ranch Restaurant as well, and I catch myself admiring her figure when I stop by for a cup of coffee. I've taken to calling her Pocahontas on account of her beauty, which sometimes makes her smile. I pray to You for a little advice. Self-flagellation is too extreme, I think.

Elise's family is an interesting and large one. As with many Cree families, it is nearly impossible to keep track of full brothers and sisters, half-brothers and half-sisters, aunts, uncles and grandparents. Virtually everyone on reserve seems to be a cousin or distant relation of some sort. Elise's cousin Mary Cheechoo is one of the regular flock at mass on Sunday.

That number remains at around eighty to one hundred. On a reserve with a population of close to eight hundred, that is a pitiful number, especially considering that most were at one time or another baptized. Mary's brother, coincidentally, is the infamous Legless Joe. Whether or not he is a half-brother, or even possibly a stepbrother, I am not sure. Mary has a daughter, Linda, who is off down south in Timmins studying at college. She seems to be a success story on reserve. Linda has a number of brothers, Crow among them. Some of the brothers still trap furs for much of the year, with their uncles. As sometimes happens in large families, it works out that Elise is Crow and Linda's aunt, although she is not much older than them, maybe a couple of years older than Linda. I've tried to work out the family lines in my head and on paper, but it still mystifies me.

Who I assume is the patriarch — the Old Man, I call him, for I've never learned his name — is Mary's grandfather. Quick calculations put his age at right around a hundred, which is astounding, considering his physical condition. He walks the reserve daily, followed by at least a few stray dogs, one among them the ugliest beast I've ever laid eyes on. His mental health is sadly not up to his physical state. He's known to everyone as Old Cheechoo who talks to the dogs. I saw him as well today, taking advantage of the beautiful weather. He was walking slowly down Maheegan Street. Normally he doesn't seem to notice me, but today he greeted me, saying, "*Wachay.*" I answered him with a "hello."

Twice now I've caught him standing and puffing, shaking his fist at a large crow on the wire above his head, speaking to it in his strange-sounding Cree dialect. Obviously, he doesn't reserve his talking for dogs. Once I watched as he tried to hit a crow on a wire above him with a stone, but it arced feebly and the crow cawed raucously, as if laughing. That wretched mutt that sometimes accompanies him followed him today. Its mouth appears stuck in a horrible snarl, exposing its red and bleeding gums and a few black teeth. It apparently has the mange or some other ailment, much of its raw skin exposed through matted, dandruff-flecked fur. This mutt yelps constantly at the old man, and the old man will talk to it as he walks. I only wish I knew what he was saying. Although I am not positive, it seems obvious that this is the same old man Father Wilkes wrote about in the note I found, the one in which the old man talked about the size of hearts and of the Cree as children. They are children. Your children.

SEPTEMBER 9

Turnout for Sunday mass today was the worst I've seen since I arrived. Fifty souls at best, spread throughout the pews so that their number actually looked smaller. In my homily I discussed how our youth become more and more dispossessed and how they need the Church for guidance. It was not a fire-and-brimstone sermon, I'll be the first to admit it, but I actually caught Sister Marie yawning and Sister Jane picking at her nails. I wish for the fire of my youth back, sometimes, for the times I could take the plainest subject and become Your voice with it.

I've been perusing my copy of the *Jesuit Relations* for the first time in many years. The writings of Brébeuf and LeJeune are stimulating and intense. Their bravery in travelling into the Canadian wilderness and converting the Huron, and their eventual martyrdom at the hands of the Iroquois three-and-a-half centuries ago, was what gave me strength to pursue this path. I hate to say it, but 350 years, and so little progress has been made with the Ontario Indian. That fact saddens me.

An epiphany of sorts today. I am lonely. Sister Jane and I only argue when we talk. Sister Marie is not what you'd call a deep thinker. Speaking of her, I am convinced that her gas attacks at the dinner table are on purpose, that she is trying to draw attention to herself. I had to actually get up and leave the table tonight, she was so explosive. Perhaps Sister Jane is not the only one up here too long.

About my epiphany. Not only have I realized that I am lonely but, with my forty-fifth birthday approaching, perhaps I am having some sort of mid-life crisis. This very conveniently explains my lustful infatuation with Elise Cheechoo, as well as my general malaise. I find myself turning to my Scotch more nights than I ever used to, but can I be blamed? We all need ways to vent, a little escape. A drink right now sounds like just the thing. I'll have to remember tomorrow to order another case.

SEPTEMBER 10

Some very sad news arrived this morning. I received a call very early informing me of the death of one of the band members. Mary Cheechoo's daughter Linda, who was away to college, apparently took her own life yesterday. It seems out of the blue, as I'm sure most of these tragedies seem. I went first thing and spoke to Mary at her home. It was the least I could do. She has been a loyal churchgoer since my arrival. Linda apparently took a large number of sleeping pills washed down with a bottle of vodka. A sadly stereotypical way to commit a mortal sin. From what I could gather, Linda was not doing well at school there. I can imagine. There is no way the schools on reserve can prepare young adults for college in the bigger world. I've sat in on classes in the grade school and high school, talked to the teachers. They teach the children spoken Cree and Cree syllabic writing when the children cannot even speak English properly. Linda had gained weight and had not been calling her mother much, both signs of depression.

There seems to be much tragedy in the Cheechoo family. Mary's husband drowned out on the river two years ago. There is young Crow, who seems headed for certain trouble. And of course there's Legless Joe. Apparently, Mary's husband was somewhat of a traditionalist. He drummed and sang in a group called the Black Water Singers (with Legless Joe, of all people!) and kept a sweat lodge in their backyard. Mary told me that she wanted his spirit there at Linda's funeral mass. I was shocked. Here I was, thinking she was a solid Catholic, but she doesn't even realize that she asks for pagan ritual to be included in one of the holiest of Catholic masses. I very carefully and sternly explained to her the inherent problems with this. She remained quiet, but I think she understood.

Walking home from her house, I realized suddenly that I had been presented with the perfect opportunity to turn tragedy into something positive. Here was a chance to galvanize the reserve, to give the people a necessary focus, to bring everyone together. It was time to gather the scattered flock from the bars, the traplines and sweat lodges, to shepherd them back into the fold of my small church. You work in mysterious ways, and I was afforded a brief glimpse into Your workings.

Later this morning I had a run-in with Legless Joe. I'm sitting in the Sky Ranch, having a cup of coffee and admiring Elise's work habits, when he rolls in menacingly and sits down at my table. At first I was a little concerned for my person. He is a big man, well over six feet and two hundred pounds, with long, black, unkempt hair and a little scruffy goatee that makes him look quite frightening. Apparently he was in some sort of motorcycle gang in his youth. One that tried to convey Christian ethics. How bizarre! Sister Jane talks about it as if it were the greatest thing she'd ever heard of.

"My niece is dead," he blurts out to me. "I want to drum at her wedding." I must admit that catches me off guard. I begin to laugh.

"If she's dead," I ask, "why does she want you drumming at her wedding?" He gets this funny, flustered look on his face. Apparently he has no answer to that. Alcohol abuse can do horrible things to a person, and Joe Cheechoo must learn that. He gets up and leaves.

I'll be damned if there will be any heathen worship practised in my church.

This evening I went back to Mary Cheechoo's house in order to console the family. I knew there were going to be quite a few people there, but I wasn't prepared for the large turnout. Far more people than come to church were crowded inside the house and outside on the porch and lawn. I was quite touched and surprised by the solidarity these people were showing. Although it is quite rare that I do it, I had buoyed myself before this impromptu wake with a little Scotch. Some people, mainly the younger ones, had obviously been drinking, and Mary tried to keep those outside as best she could.

I sat beside her on her couch, holding her hand for the evening, speaking encouraging words. Many, many people came up to her and either said a few words in Cree, looking down at their feet, or just took her hand in theirs for a moment and said nothing at all. The old man showed up and he and Mary spoke for a long time in their language, the old man nodding to me once in a while. I don't think they even realized that what they were doing was rude. I made sure after he was finished, in case he too was trying to pressure Mary into heathen funeral practices, to explain once again to her exactly what the Catholic funeral mass dictates.

Getting Linda's body back to the reserve and the funeral itself are both being handled in a typically Indian fashion, which is to say slowly. The family will fly it up in a couple of days on a charter flight and won't hold the funeral until all her relatives arrive a few days after that. I've got the work week to prepare a sermon. It will be difficult considering that this was a suicide, and the Church's view of such.

As if I were being tested at the wake by Satan himself, in walks Legless Joe, straight up to Mary, blurting that he will drum at Linda's funeral. I scolded him and squeezed Mary's hand hard, trying to give her the strength to deny this man. Thankfully she would not answer him, would not even look at him. If only he knew the pain he were causing. If only he knew.

SEPTEMBER 12

Tragedy upon tragedy. On the very night of the wake, Mary's youngest son, Crow, apparently set a friend's house on fire, nearly killing three youngsters as well as himself. I did not find this out until yesterday morning. The house was still smoking, a charred pile of wood, at noon yesterday. By all accounts, this was no accident. Crow — or Francis, as his mother calls him (Crow must be his Indian name) — poured gasoline throughout the house and set it on fire. There is some question as to whether he too was trying to kill himself. His friend dragged him out just in time, but he suffered severe smoke inhalation and is in the tiny reserve hospital until he is well enough to be flown south for trial and incarceration. These people are so ill-equipped to deal with things.

I've been working on my homily for the mass. It is important, possibly the most important of my life. On my next report to the archdiocese, I want to be able to say that attendance is up and the Cree people of Sharpening Teeth Reserve are making great progress in their pursuit of Jesus' teachings. Tonight at the dinner table, in my excitement with my new mission, I was foolish enough to bring it up with Sister Jane and Sister Marie that this was going to be a very special sermon, and I tried to make light of the fact that it was a difficult chore trying to keep old pagan ways from slipping in through the church doors.

"Well, Father Jimmy," Sister Jane immediately piped up, "the best way to drive the rest of our congregation out is to browbeat them about the spirituality of their fathers and grandfathers, to go on about how it's so wrong."

"Well, it isn't Catholic doctrine. It is animism," I answered, "and that's akin to worshipping false gods."

"Do you want to know what I think is the trouble with the youth around here?" Sister Jane asked, changing tack. Before I had a chance to answer, she continued. "They've been born into a situation that would be impossible for most any young person to rise above. Half this reserve doesn't have running water in their homes! And us on the eve of a new goddamn millennium!" I'd heard Sister Jane's rhetoric before. I was here to teach these people God's message. The rest of it — the economic improvement, the education, the social advancement — would follow. But that was impossible to explain to Sister Jane, so I listened politely. "They've been given reserves and a measly handout each month and told that if they leave the reserve, the government will take even that little bit of money away. Don't forget, Father Jimmy, that not so long ago this was a self-sufficient people. The young people around here are struggling between what once was and what's to come, between everything that defines them as a people and how we want them to become."

I raised my hand to cut her off. "Sister Jane," I spoke up. "That is all fine and good. But you seem to be losing your way. You're not seeing the forest for the trees. Our mission is simple. We must shine God's light upon a people who live in darkness. If their language dies, if their old ways are abandoned, if they accept the ways of the dominant culture, then this is God's will. I've read nowhere in the Bible that it is all right for me to allow an influence that I deem pagan at the funeral of a young and, may I add, baptized woman."

Sister Jane gave a huff, stood up and left the dinner table. Sister Marie, so quiet that I'd forgotten she was present, got up as quickly as her body would allow, her eyes wide with concern, and waddled after Sister Jane, no doubt to console her.

SEPTEMBER 13

I witnessed quite an extraordinary event today. As I waited with Mary Cheechoo for Linda's body to arrive in the little charter plane, people began showing up. Some walked, some who had cars drove, others pulled up on ATVs. By the time the plane landed I would estimate that pretty much all of the reserve had gathered, waiting by the portable that serves as the airport terminal, the people spilling out onto the road leading up to the airport. The chief himself pulled up in his big red pickup truck beside the plane when it taxied, and Mary left me to meet him. Her sons and brothers helped to carefully lift the casket from the belly of the plane, and eight of them placed it into the bed of the chief's truck, all the people watching quietly.

The chief walked Mary to the passenger side and helped her in. If they made these arrangements earlier, I was not made aware. I hadn't heard a word around town of this congregation. The truck then pulled away from the dirt airfield and slowly drove the road leading back to the reserve, towards Mary's house. People fell in line behind the truck, so quietly that I could hear its tires crunching gravel, until there was the whole reserve in a procession behind it, walking one of their own back to her home. I still don't know if this was a planned event or an impromptu gathering. I expect a full church in a couple of days.

SEPTEMBER 14

They say that bad luck strikes in threes. To my horror, when I opened the doors to the church this morning and walked into the sacristy, I discovered that my sanctuary had been robbed and vandalized. My vestments lay scattered about. The perpetrators had opened and drunk a case of communion wine, some bottles had been smashed, drawers had been looted and, downstairs in the basement, where they'd apparently gained entry, a window had been kicked in. The worst thing, though, was finding that a partially filled bottle of wine had been smashed in front of the altar. Whoever had done this, and I had a very good idea who, had absolutely no respect or regard for my most sacred beliefs, and that was what stung me the most. Before calling the police, I actually wept for a short time.

"It was Legless Joe Cheechoo and his gang," I told the band constables as soon as they arrived.

"How do you know this, Father?" the one named Ron asked me.

"Who else?" I asked.

"We need evidence to make an arrest," he answered.

I told him to find the evidence, to dust for fingerprints, to do whatever was necessary to bring Legless Joe to justice. He explained that their hands were already full, with one officer assigned to Francis Cheechoo's room twenty-four hours, but that they would do a thorough investigation as soon as they were able.

I was stunned. I was angry. The thought of these strangers arriving unwelcome and unwanted, and fouling my church, was so upsetting that for a short time I contemplated whether or not I'd be in shape to go through with a funeral mass the day after tomorrow. After much soul-searching I realized that I had to do it. There was no choice. The more I turned it over in my mind today, the more I've been galvanized by the fact that I have been sent here for a reason, and that that reason will begin to make itself clear tomorrow, when I am offered the chance to make real headway in bringing my children back to the fold.

SEPTEMBER 16

Why, Lord, have You forsaken me? I am Your faithful servant. I try to serve You well. Are You angry with me because I drink? Don't You know that You created imperfect beings? In front of my eyes I watched my congregation rebel and, dear Lord, there is nothing more painful for Your faithful servant than that.

Oh! Maybe You are angry with me for lusting in my heart and in my mind! But, dear Lord, I never lusted with my loins.

Is that not worth something? I came here to help these people, to shine the light of Your love upon them. Now they are cast out like sand cast to the wind.

Did You watch from above as I explained to the congregation today Your very own message? That suicide is a mortal sin? That they are a people being pulled in two directions? That they must accept Your word or face a less than happy eternity? That Linda Cheechoo made the wrong decision and that, when a wrong decision is made, there are unfortunate consequences, purgatory first and foremost among them? Oh, Lord! I could very well have preached what so many of Your servants have preached — that the taking of one's life is a mortal sin punished not by purgatory but by hell. I was trying to be easy on them! Is that where I went wrong?

Were You watching, Lord, when that damned Joe Cheechoo carried his drum into Your church and beat it? After I'd already lost my lambs, watched them stare up at me with anger because they weren't prepared to hear my homily that Linda Cheechoo's act was not acceptable in Your eyes? Did you see how, when I shouted out for that devil to stop his drumming, the others rose in his defence, preventing me from throttling him? How they actually joined him in that pagan worship, their voices like the voices of devils? Did You witness all of them — the Old Man, Mary Cheechoo, the brothers and uncles and aunts of Linda Cheechoo, the relations and friends, even Sister Jane — join the congregation around that drum? And in Your own house!

Forgive me, Lord, that I am angry with You right now. You know me better than I know myself, and so surely You know that in a few days or weeks or months, when I have had a chance to dwell in this pain, I will again be ready to preach Your word. It is in my darkest hour that I look to You to give me strength. Give me guidance. I ask You this one thing, a man holding on for his life. Tell me they are Your children.

OLD
MAN

I lose my days, me. Maybe it's that *Weesageechak* takes them. My great-granddaughter is dead, I know that much. Little Linda Cheechoo. Black eyes like my Minnie's. It's their story I need to tell.

Weesageechak, he was out bothering me again today. He was in the form of a dog again. Bit me in the ass when I wasn't looking. When he wasn't looking I gave him my boot in the mouth. We're even for now. I know that it was just a week or two ago that we all walked Linda home. It isn't so bad, not remembering everything. As long as I remember the good things. Walking her home was a good thing on a bad day. I stood watching the plane come in. I watched it touch the earth, slide its wheels on the gravel like a goose slides its landing feet onto water. Then I watched some nephews and grandsons lift the casket from the belly of that goose and into the back of a pickup truck. The whole reserve watched with me. We walked slow behind that truck, walked Linda all the way to her home.

The sonofabitch *Weesageechak* followed too. He'd shape-shifted into the form of a one-toothed mutt with dried shit hanging from the fur below his tail. He darted out in front of the pickup, made it hit the brakes hard. The casket slid a little off-centre. *Weesageechak* started yapping at it crazy, like the mange rotted his brain. He stopped when he saw me and pulled back his lips so I could see his one tooth and bleeding gums.

Me, my fingers are all bent now and my eyes get foggy in the morning, and at night too. That trickster *Weesageechak* likes to bother me, likes to remind me that life is a lot of laughing, even if that laughing is all at me. Sometimes he's a crow in the trees watching me with his black pebble eyes, cawing at me with his silly laugh when I stop on the road to catch my breath. Mostly he's a dog, one in particular. Ugliest dog in the world. Sometimes he's a wind and puffs up his cheeks and blows a cold breeze down my back that makes my hands shake and spill hot coffee onto my lap. I'm so old now that he is my only friend left. All the others dead. I'm not sure how old I am, me. My granddaughter, Mary, Linda's mother, says I'm a hundred. That sounds like a good age. Nice and round for a skinny old man.

Lots of family. So many I don't know all my great-grandsons and granddaughters. But I knew Linda. She looked after me. I told her stories in exchange. Gave her her first pair of rain boots that she wore all through childhood.

I had my nephew Remi drive me over to Mary's to visit with her family. This was before they were able to fly Linda's body home, I think. I look out the car window and think of my old life. I had lots of children. Thirteen. Twelve are still alive. My wife is dead a long time. We were happy living in the bush. Daytimes spent trapping and hunting. Nights telling stories and making babies. I'll see her again soon.

When I lived in the forest, everyone knew me as the man who could heal sicknesses. My wife and me would collect roots and plants, keep certain parts from different animals, dry them out and crush them up. Cured lots of people. Nobody knows that about me anymore. I protected family and friends. My daughter Minnie, my oldest, she was the only one I could not protect. When the government told me one day that they would take my children to teach them, that's the day I began losing my power. It's the day I gave up living in the bush to be close to my children. I'd still go out, take my children when they were not in school. But that wasn't too often. The less I went out in the bush, the more the sonofabitch *Weesageechak* came to visit me. He loves it when someone catches me talking to him. People think I'm a crazy old man talking to dogs and crows. That's OK. Maybe, if they live long enough, he will come to visit them too.

When Remi drove me to Mary's house, it was before Linda came home on the plane, before we walked her casket home. It was the night after Linda took her life. Mary told me her body would be home in a day or two. It's the small things that confuse me now. I can't keep order of all the events. Linda was down south in a school. Linda took her life. I went to her mother's house the next day. Lots of people there. Linda came in on a plane three days later and we walked her body home. The funeral a few days after that. I think that is how it went. Me, I try to remember these things so I can tell the story proper. I think it's *Weesageechak* taking my memory and shaking it up before he gives it back to me. I'll have to scold him when I see him.

At my granddaughter Mary's house, lots of people. Much of the reserve, all of Linda's friends. But Linda wasn't there. Mary reminded me that they couldn't get her body home for a day or two. So I pictured Linda in my head instead. I could still see the little girl I took out to the muskeg in autumn for the hunt, the girl I called Little Goose, the same name I called my own daughter Minnie years before that. Linda was one of the last of my relations still wanting to learn the old ways. So I taught her. She was just like Minnie.

Mary started crying, so I reminded her of the pet goose I used to have when she was a little girl and my daughter was still alive. It was a good goose. I'd canoe up to the marshes that I knew would be busy with birds ready to fly away for the winter and my goose would swim behind me. All the other hunters figured I had some magic they didn't know about, and some were jealous enough they threatened to eat my bird.

I told this story and from wherever he was hiding, *Weesageechak* blew hot air into my stomach and I made a loud fart. I grinned and this made Mary laugh a little through her tears. I told her the rest of my story, of how I would get out decoys and when the geese swung low to investigate, I'd send my pet bird out to swim around and draw them in the rest of the way.

Some little boys hid behind the TV listening so I took out my pretend shotgun and tracked the geese. The boys' heads followed along the arc of mine and when my head was just slightly ahead of the geese I said, "BANG BANG!" loud enough to make the little boys jump, and everyone who listened to my story tracked the geese falling like feathered V's to the earth where they splashed in the marsh outside Linda's window.

The hunting moon rose above Linda's house, as big and orange as anyone had seen it. It would be a good night to drum and sing a mourning song but I didn't know if anyone knew how to anymore.

Some of Linda's brothers got into the booze and took their long hair out of their ponytails and they grew louder. Their mother told them to go outside and the boys told her Linda was their sister they grew up with and played with and fought with and she would want them to tip a drink in her honour. Linda's father is no longer here. Drowned a few summers ago. It was dark now and the crowd was bigger. They spilled out the front and back doors and everyone talked and some cried and some laughed for the sake of Linda.

Before Mary left me I told her the story of my daughter Minnie, my Little Goose — how, many years ago, when my hair was still black and thick, I brought her and my pet bird to autumn camp and left them there for the day while I checked the traplines. It's a story everyone has heard a hundred times from a hundred mouths, but it was good right then for Linda's mother to know that another knew her suffering.

"When I returned, my Minnie was gone," I told her, holding my hands out and weighing empty air. Hours later I noticed that my bird was gone too. Both of them, gone without a trace. When the Mounties came out days later they said she was dead and drowned in the swollen river. Some older ones on the reserve still tell their grandchildren when they stray too far from home that the *windigos*, the forest cannibals, got her. My wife's heart cracked from the weight of our Little Goose being gone.

I let Mary go by telling her I had to get some fresh air. Outside I could feel *Weesageechak*'s eyes staring at me, but I couldn't locate him in the crowd of people talking and gesturing and wiping eyes. I made my way over to Linda's friends. They were the closest to her of anyone gathered there. I could tell by the way they'd separated themselves from the others, how they talked quietly and had shut themselves off. I found a seat on a snow machine waiting for winter and listened to them.

"She was a fucking bitch," one of the girls said. She had short hair, and a black leather jacket on. The other two girls and the two boys with them nodded angry, puffing on cigarettes.

A second girl said, "Only a bitch doesn't call when she's feeling down like that."

"Especially when the last thing she says to you before she leaves is that she loves you like a sister," the first one said.

The two boys in the group stayed quiet, let the young women say what they needed to.

"If she was a sister the bitch would have called one of us," the first girl said. "Stupid slut." The boys just nodded and looked at their shoes, smoking their cigarettes quickly.

"I'd call you first if I was going to pull some shit like that, wouldn't I, Minnie?" the second girl said, nodding to a silent third girl standing closest to the boys. "I wouldn't go pull no shit like Linda," she said in her sing-song way of talking. Her words made the first, tough girl begin to cry. The others didn't know what to do.

I looked up at the third girl, Minnie, and it was my Minnie I saw in the darkness. She looked over at me and her eyes were black pebbles. She was still young and beautiful after all these years. She was upset that Linda took her own life. Minnie so desperately wanted to keep hers. One of the boys reached out and hugged the tough girl. If I went to hug Minnie, I thought, she would disappear. A dog on a leash yapped somewhere behind the group. I saw that Minnie had permed her hair just like Linda.

I know just what *Weesageechak* was trying to get me to do. He was taunting me to cry and shout to this girl who was my daughter's ghost. He wanted me to make an old fool man of myself. Sometimes he's as easy to read as a north wind carrying snow clouds. His jokes have turned cruel lately. The dog that'd been yapping began to howl and pull on his leash. I recognized the voice. One of the boys in Minnie's group walked over and swatted it on the nose. This gave me an idea.

Standing up, I walked over to my young Minnie's group. It felt like I was young and drunk on rye for the first time. *Weesageechak* couldn't believe my nerve. He barked when I came near. The young ones looked at everyone's shoes but mine when I said *wachay* to them.

"Linda was a good girl," I said. "She should have stayed with us longer." Her friends didn't say anything, just stared at the ground. "I don't know why she took her life," I said. "I don't know if anyone knows." The dog strained on his leash and whined, on the verge of a howl. I forced myself not to look at my daughter. "Linda should have stayed to experience what all of us older ones have experienced. I want all of you to stay here a long time and see all of the things I have seen," I told them.

I reached out to feel each one's warmth. Minnie shivered when I touched her last. She was cold in her T-shirt. "I'm sorry I left you to check my lines," I told her. Words I waited sixty years to speak. "All I want now is for you to still be here." The dog lurched at his chain, howling, and Minnie jumped. My hand was left shaking in the cold air.

"I'm cold," she said. "'Scuse me, Grandpa, I'm going to get a smoke and a coffee inside." The others mumbled and left with her. I sat down by the dog.

"I said what I needed to," I told him. He whined and licked my hand. "You are a sonofabitch," I said, and he howled. I unlatched him from his leash and he trotted off. I looked up at the big moon and laughed.

Inside, I saw the priest sitting with Mary now. Before he came to this reserve there was another black robe who treated us like we were little children. He could not see the size of our hearts and, because he didn't understand us, believed they were small. I remember him. I actually told him one time that he didn't know us, that he did not know how big our hearts were. That made him angry. I watched this one get angry at my grandson Joseph because he drinks and wanted Linda's funeral to be Indian. I watched as this priest told Mary not to talk to her own brother, and I watched as Joseph left Mary's house. This priest thought he had no heart at all. This priest is no better than the other. I went over and told Mary to remember the old ways with the new. I told her that we are a people with a heart strong as a drumbeat. I said this in our language because this belongs to us. Poor Mary. I could see she felt pulled in two.

After that night I didn't see *Weesageechak* for a couple of days. I'd gotten him good at that wake by doing what he didn't expect me to. It is a good feeling to trick the trickster.

Seeing my grandson Joseph again made me start thinking about drumming and singing. He was once the best singer I had ever heard. He looked like my father and had his size. But Joseph lost his path somewhere along the way. That he wanted to drum at his niece's funeral was a good thing too, on a bad day. *Gitchi-Manitou* makes it so that there is always some reason for the death of a relation. In Linda's death I was able to say what I needed to say to my Minnie, and my grandson saw hope.

Joseph came to me after the wake and asked me to go to the sweat lodge with him. We got some rocks hot on the fire so they glowed red. Then we brought them in the lodge and closed the flaps up tight and sat naked together, praying and singing, pouring water on the stones so that the heat burned our lungs and all of the bad poured out of our bodies. After, I teased him that I got drunk on his fumes in there, that he'd lost all the weight of his liquor. He smiled and looked happier than I'd ever seen him. I was happy too that in our loss, good things began to come.

That night I sat by the river and listened to him drum again. I let the sound of his voice carry me up above the river and onto a cloud where I dreamed I was with Linda and she told me that she was OK and that she was sad for what she had done and how she had hurt her mother. I held her hand and we smiled at one another. Before she left me in my dream, Linda told me that the drumming and singing were a good thing to hear again, that the drumming was our heart, our little heart growing big, that the singing was the children not born yet, talking to the Grandfathers who were gone. It was our way of surviving through everything we had to survive. Linda had grown wise since crossing over to that place where I visited her.

As I stood outside the church before her funeral, *Weesageechak* showed up in his ugliest-dog-in-the-world costume, but he kept a distance, worried I had another trick up my sleeve. I waved to him and he barked. An old nun I'd known for many years came up to me and we talked a short while. I said to her, "Hello, Sister Jane," and she said, "Hello, Mr. Cheechoo," and we talked of Linda when she was a little girl, and how she always wore her rain boots, rain or shine. That nun and me, we had a good laugh together. She asked me to sit with her during the mass.

When that priest began telling us that Linda could not go to heaven because she committed suicide, Sister Jane began to shake. But I wasn't angry. I knew Linda was already there. I watched my granddaughter Mary raise her head to look at this priest, and then I watched all my relations who had come from many different places raise their heads too. We all raised our heads up as if we were one big person, growing bigger by the minute.

And then it came. A single drumbeat from the back of the church, travelling through it the way I once saw lightning travel through water. And then it came again, then again. The priest, he didn't like that. He shouted and began to walk towards Joseph and his beating drum in the back of the church, but by the time he got to Linda's casket we had already stood as one, blocking him from going farther. All of us who knew how circled the drum and beat it with him, using our hands, our shoes, our palms. We lifted our heads up and tightened our voices and sang a song for Linda and for her mother. For all of us. I looked to my granddaughter Mary, her dark eyes Linda's, Minnie's. I looked to my grandson Joseph and he looked to me. I looked around me at all my relations around this drum, and to Sister Jane, who'd come to join us. We all stood in a circle and lifted up our voices to Linda and to *Gitchi-Manitou*, to God. And I began to feel something good that I'd not felt in a long time.

ACKNOWLEDGEMENTS

As always, my son Jacob, I'd walk a continent for you.

My northern friends: William Tozer and family, the best and craziest bush pilots and guides in Northern Ontario. The world, for that matter. Remi and Rachel Chakasim, you've inspired me with your quiet strength and wisdom. Judy Wabano of Peawanuck, thanks for your translations and friendship. Shane Enosse of Moosonee, Linda Smith, née Goodwin of Kashechewan, Stephen Spence of Fort Albany, all artists of incredible talent. Ed Metatawabin and the Metatawabin clan, you were inspirations long before you knew me. *Meegwetch* to all.

My southern friends: Rick Barton, you've pushed me to succeed. Joanna Leake and Jim Knudsen, patient teachers extraordinaire. My trinity of trouble and eternal drinking posse, Joe Longo, Jen Kuchta, and Mike Mahoney. Jay Poggi and John Lawrence, epitomes of New Orleans art and music in human bodies.

My family: Mayer Hoffer, you are a blood brother for saving my life. David Gifford, prestigidateur with a paint brush. My four sisters, Mary, Veronica, Julia, Suzanne, my three brothers, Bruce, Francis, Raymond, and my three half-sisters, Angela, Theresa, and Claire, it would take pages and years to thank you enough. Mom, how'd you do it? I love you. Amanda, the best editor and trapeze artist I've ever known.